TEETH OF THE JUNGLE

PART 2

THE PRICE OF INDEPENDENCE

PETER SZABO

Teeth of the Jungle: Part 1 – The Price of Independence
Copyright © Tycoonitos, 2024
All rights reserved.

Tycoonitos
Peter Szabo
peter@tycoonitos.com

This is a work of fiction. Names, characters, places, and events are either the product of the author's imagination or used fictitiously. Any resemblance to actual persons, living or dead, events, or locales is purely coincidental.

ISBN: 978-1-7637959-0-7
First Edition: December, 2024
Website: tycoonitos.com

TO MY READERS

Dear Readers,

Welcome to the world of *Teeth of the Jungle*. This series is more than a survival story - it's a metaphorical journey that mirrors the challenges and complexities of modern life. The Jungle is not just a physical space; it represents the struggles we all face, simplified and amplified to reveal important lessons.

As you read, think of the Jungle as a stage where ambition, resilience, and human behaviour come alive. The characters' battles with storms and wildlife symbolize life's unpredictability, while the Voivokis' society reflects the systems we navigate. Bill's manipulation of the kids through debt is a stark reminder of how power and greed can ensnare the unsuspecting, urging us to stay aware and take responsibility for our choices.

The challenges faced by the characters are designed to entertain but also to provoke thought about business, relationships, and personal growth. Their upbringing, their decisions and consequences invite reflection on your own journey and how to navigate life's complexities with wisdom and integrity.

I encourage you to read with curiosity and an open mind. The characters' struggles are universal, reminding us all of the courage and strategy needed to face our own "Jungles." Whether you're here for the story, the lessons, or both, I hope this series inspires you to take charge of your journey. Thank you for joining me - I'm excited to see how *Teeth of the Jungle* resonates with you.

Warm regards,
Peter Szabo

CHAPTER 0

"When we first laid eyes on Bill's village, we thought our hardships in the Jungle had finally come to an end," one of the survivors continued her speech, her voice tinged with lingering disbelief. "After the terrible accident, we longed to find a community and hoped for much-needed assistance. It never crossed our minds that entering the village could lead to being trapped. We were filled with euphoria, like fresh high school graduates who think the hardest part of life is behind them - no more study hours, assignments, tests, or begging for pocket money.

Our school in the Jungle was not unlike the one we know in the City, but the stakes were far higher. Our failed assignments meant hunger, our tests were often life-threatening. We received no pocket money, and our parents were absent, unable to guide us. Our classroom had no boundaries and our teachers were often the relentless forces of nature, the vicious wildlife, and most importantly, the people we met along the way. Instead of algebra, history, or science, we learned the harsh realities of life in the Jungle and the ways of the Voivokis, the people who call this unforgiving place home.

Fortunately though, our ever-mysterious friend Vaipor would occasionally appear, reinvigorating our spirits just when we needed it most.

As we approached the village, we clung to the hope that soon we would return to our safe and comfortable lives in the City. But when we learned of our true fate, those hopes crumbled, much like the disillusionment of high school graduates who suddenly realise they're facing decades of work just to support themselves and their loved ones.

It was a devastating moment. We were not prepared to spend the rest of our lives in the Jungle, working for Bill. Despite the meagre value of the Lapes we earned selling Mapa seeds at the markets, and the taxes we had to pay to the Voivokis' government - the Vilais - the freedom to carve out our own paths seemed infinitely more desirable than a lifetime of servitude, working off debts we hadn't even chosen.

But here's an important realisation: when I talk about our unfortunate - or perhaps necessary - experience in Bill's village, many people in the City fail to see that they are, in many ways, living in a similar 'village' themselves. Their homes may be far from the dangers of a literal Jungle, and they likely don't think of themselves as Voivokis, but they shoulder the same burdens as Maria, Rose and the others there.

If you find yourself working to cover your bills and loan repayments, you're not so different from the Voivokis, or from us back then – a group of 14-year-olds trapped in Bill's village, robbed of our freedom."

CHAPTER 1

The guards paraded their latest catch - a wiry boy thrashing and screaming - as they dragged him by the feet towards Bill's house. The boy's desperation was palpable, his cries cutting through the humid air like jagged glass. Bill stood waiting on the porch, a cruel grin stretching across his face.

"Didn't I tell you?" he sneered, his voice dripping with menace. "Nobody leaves without my permission."

With a calculated swing of his boot, Bill struck the boy's thighs, the sharp impact sending a sickening thud into the heavy silence. The boy gasped in agony, his slender frame curling in on itself, his strength rendered useless beneath the guards' unyielding grip. Villagers glanced away, wincing as his anguished cries echoed through the village.

"Lock him up," Bill snapped, waving the guards off. They hauled the boy, now limp and trembling, towards a hut at the edge of the village. His screams trailed behind them, long after he had disappeared from view.

Manu and the others arrived just as the guards tossed him into his confinement.

"It's Asim," Imogen gasped, her face pale. Her voice wavered as she clutched Leila's arm.

Manu frowned but didn't flinch.

"This isn't the first time his temper's gotten him into trouble," he said evenly. "He really needs to learn to control it."

Roger stiffened, his eyes darting to Manu.

"That's cold, even for you," he muttered, unable to hide his unease.

"We can't just stand here and do nothing!" Imogen cried, her voice climbing. "We have to help him!"

Manu turned to face her, his expression hard.

"And what do you suggest? March into Bill's house and demand he let Asim go? Get ourselves thrown into that hut too?" His voice was measured but edged with steel. "Think about Maria. She's been here nearly her whole life because she didn't know when to stop fighting. I'm not going to end up like her."

Leila stepped forward, her voice steady despite the fear in her eyes.

"I want to go home too, Manu. But leaving Asim behind isn't right."

"We're barely surviving as it is," Manu replied. "How could we help anyone else? We can't save everyone." His tone softened slightly, but his resolve remained firm. "I have to talk to Bill before he locks up for the night."

Without waiting for a reply, Manu turned and strode towards Bill's house. The others stood in silence, the boy's fading cries haunting the air.

Roger crossed his arms, glancing at Imogen and Leila.

"He's not wrong," he said reluctantly. "It's like being broke - you can't give what you don't have. If we're trapped ourselves, how can we help Asim?"

But even as he spoke, his chest tightened, the logic doing little to quiet the knot of unease in his gut.

Bill, ever cautious, rarely entertained visitors alone, but Manu's persistent knocking left him with no choice. He opened the door, scowling.

"What is it now?" he barked, his irritation plain.

Manu stepped forward, his voice calm and deliberate. "We'd like to sleep outside tonight."

Bill arched an eyebrow, his lips curling into a sneer.

"Only animals sleep outside, with the rain and the millions of creepy-crawlies. You're not a dog, are you?"

"No," Manu replied, his tone unwavering.

"Then why would you want to?"

"We don't have 30 Lapes each to sleep in your huts," Manu said simply.

Bill's eyes narrowed, his gaze raking over the boy before him. For a moment, the air hung heavy between them, the faint sounds of the village fading into the background.

"I've already told you, I'll just add it to your balance. You can pay it off when you have enough."

Manu stood his ground, repeating his request: they wanted to sleep outside to save the 30 Lapes per night. Bill's scowl deepened, but with a reluctant grunt, he finally conceded.

"Fine, but if I catch any of you sneaking into one of my huts, you'll be charged double. Understand?"

Manu nodded, his face calm and unreadable. Without another word, he turned and walked back to the group.

When the others heard what he'd done - that he hadn't even mentioned Asim, instead negotiating for them all to give up the relative comfort of the huts - anger rippled through the group like a rising tide. Shock quickly followed.

"How could he be so cold?" whispered Sina, her voice tight with disbelief.

"What's wrong with him?" Mai muttered, shaking her head.

Manu met their stares with an unflinching gaze.

"If you think begging Bill will save Asim, go ahead," he said flatly. "I'd rather get some proper sleep tonight so I can stay sharp tomorrow. Who's coming with me to find a place to sleep?"

His words hung in the air like a challenge, cutting through the tension and leaving the group momentarily stunned. The suggestion that he valued sleep over their friend's suffering felt almost surreal. For a moment, no one responded, their emotions caught between anger and confusion.

Seeing their hesitation, Manu added:

"If you want to stay in the huts, better let Bill know now. Otherwise, he'll charge you double."

The silence shattered when Olivia crossed her arms and declared:

"I'm done with sleeping outside."

She turned sharply and strode towards Bill's office. Susan followed without hesitation, and Mai, Sina, and Leila trailed close behind.

Joe lingered, glancing between the girls and the boys.

"Guess I'm sticking with you two," he mumbled, motioning towards Manu and Roger.

When the girls emerged from Bill's office moments later, the door slamming behind them, Imogen was still frozen, torn between her options. Manu's unwavering expression and the thought of double charges finally tipped the scales. With a resigned sigh, she muttered:

"Fine. I'll stay with you guys."

The two groups exchanged brief, uneasy goodnights before parting ways.

"This way," Joe said suddenly, surprising everyone as he took the lead. Manu and Roger exchanged a look but followed without comment.

Joe led them through the plantation, weaving between rows of yam until they reached a small, makeshift shelter. Hammocks hung neatly beneath the simple roof - likely a resting spot for plantation workers seeking refuge from the midday sun or torrential downpours.

Roger's face broke into a grin.

"How the heck did you find this place?"

Joe shrugged, his expression nonchalant but tinged with pride.

"I dunno. I guess I developed certain skills while playing video games."

Manu raised an eyebrow, sceptical.

"Are you seriously telling me those ridiculous shooting games actually taught you something useful?"

Joe grinned.

"Yeah, well, in those 'ridiculous' games, you only get a few seconds to scan your surroundings before everything blows up."

Roger snorted.

"So, what - you're treating the Jungle like some kind of real-life game?"

"Maybe," Joe shot back with a laugh. "You guys can thank me later when we're all still alive."

Roger chuckled, shaking his head. "Alright, I'll give you that one, Joe."

Manu allowed himself the smallest of smiles as they climbed into the hammocks. Joe's good-natured response to the ribbing earned him some respect, and the group settled in for the night, their earlier tension softened, if only slightly, by the unexpected discovery.

After a week of sleeping on uneven branches, layered with a thin mat, the swaying hammocks felt like pure luxury. Their tired bodies sank into the gentle embrace of the fibre, the rhythmic rocking lulling them into a rare moment of peace. Above them, the sturdy roof offered shelter from the rain, while the hammocks kept the Jungle's crawling inhabitants at bay. It was a cocoon of tranquillity they hadn't experienced in what felt like forever.

For a few blissful hours, it seemed as though they'd found a pocket of serenity in their chaotic lives. But the illusion shattered with the abrupt pounding of a village drum echoing through the air. The sound tore through their slumber, a harsh and unwelcome reminder of their reality.

Imogen groaned, rubbing her eyes as she glanced at her watch. Her voice was thick with sleep as she muttered:

"We still have two hours to walk back to the village, grab breakfast, and make it to the factory. Why do they have to wake us up this early?"

Manu's laughter broke the groggy silence, startling her.

"What's so funny?" she asked, her cheeks warming in irritation.

He shook his head, a faint smile lingering as he replied:

"Just the irony. We finally find a bit of comfort, and the drumming ruins it. It's like this place doesn't want us to forget who's really in charge."

His gaze drifted towards the distant silhouette of Bill's village. The humour in his voice faded, replaced by a quiet bitterness.

"But I'll tell you one thing - I'm not eating at Bill's restaurant. I won't give him another chance to tighten his grip on me."

Roger sighed, running a hand through his messy hair.

"Manu, we're already his slaves. What's the alternative? We don't have time to start a fire, bake bread, and make it back by 9 a.m."

Manu's eyes swept the plantation around them.

"We're surrounded by food. Fruits, vegetables - we don't need Bill's scraps. We just need to help ourselves."

Imogen stiffened, her brow furrowing in concern.

"But what if someone catches us?" she whispered. "You saw what happened to Asim."

Roger nodded, his face grim.

"She's right. Bill wouldn't hesitate to throw us in that jail of his. It's not worth it."

Three pairs of eyes were fixed on Manu. There was concern in their expressions, but also hope - hope that he could somehow provide an answer, a way out. Manu felt the weight of their expectations pressing on him like a physical force. He hated feeling powerless, hated the way Bill's oppressive control cornered them at every turn. His mind churned, desperate to reclaim some sense of agency, some shred of freedom, but he knew better than to act on impulse alone.

"You guys go ahead," he said finally, his tone calm but resolute. "Have breakfast with the others. I need to figure something out."

Roger studied him for a moment before nodding. He trusted Manu's judgment, confident his friend wouldn't do anything reckless.

"He just needs space to think," Roger thought, leading Joe and Imogen back towards the village.

When they arrived at the restaurant, the atmosphere was almost cheerful - a stark contrast to the weight they carried. The others were gathered around a table, laughing and savouring their meals. Sandwiches, cakes, and steaming cups of hot chocolate filled the table, but the sight only deepened Roger's unease. Every bite and sip came with a cost, each indulgence tightening Bill's financial noose.

"Guys, come over here!" Olivia called, her voice bright with excitement. "They've got hot chocolate on special today!"

Roger's gaze flicked to the menu board, where the words Hot Chocolate - 3 Lapes were scrawled in bold letters. Their entire group had just 5 Lapes to their names - barely enough to cover two cups even with the so-called discount. But Olivia's enthusiasm was unrelenting, her focus entirely on the fleeting pleasure of the moment.

Roger sighed inwardly. Despite her young age, Olivia had clearly inherited her mother's habit of chasing instant gratification without thought for the consequences. The weight of their debt meant nothing to her, not when there was a chance to indulge. As the others debated what to order, Roger found himself wondering how much longer they could continue like this - bound by Bill's rules, inching deeper into a trap they could all see but couldn't escape.

Regrettably, Olivia wasn't the only one lured by Bill's cunning incentives. The tantalizing aroma of food and hot chocolate was too seductive for the group to resist. They indulged with relish, savouring each bite and sip as though it were their last meal. In their hunger and exhaustion, the fleeting joy of a good meal blinded them to the looming consequences of their choices.

Their brief respite, a rare indulgence in an otherwise harsh existence, was abruptly shattered when Bill strode in, his sharp voice cutting through their momentary peace.

"Training starts shortly," he barked, his presence as oppressive as the debt hanging over their heads. The kids scrambled to finish what was left of their meal, hurriedly making their way to the factory, where the reality of their situation awaited.

Maria was already there, her movements brisk and focused as she prepared for the day. The weight of responsibility bore heavily on her. With yesterday's quota unmet, failure today was not an option she could afford. She glanced at the kids as they entered, her expression a mix of sympathy and resolve.

Before the workday began, Rose appeared, her usual bright demeanour replaced by an air of sorrow. Her eyes were red and swollen, her voice trembling as she spoke.

"I came to say sorry," she began, barely able to meet their gazes. "I've been trapped here for 46 years. My only way out is to meet my daily sales targets. I promise to do everything I can to help you so we can all regain our freedom. Please, believe me."

Tears welled in her eyes as she bowed her head, her regret intense. With that, she turned and left, leaving the kids in a storm of conflicting emotions. Rose's apology sounded sincere, her anguish undeniable, but her confession of being trapped for nearly half a century made her words feel hollow. How could they trust someone who hadn't managed to escape in all that time? Worse still, the warnings she withheld the previous day might have spared them from their current plight.

The kids stood there, grappling with the uneasy mix of hope and mistrust. Was Rose truly an ally now, or was she just another pawn in Bill's game?

A sudden burst of hurried footsteps broke their contemplation. Turning, they saw Manu sprinting towards them, arriving just as Bill's drumming signalled the start of the workday.

"You made it!" Leila exclaimed, throwing her arms around him. "Are you alright?"

Manu grinned, though the tension beneath his expression was unmistakable.

"Of course, I'm fine," he said, catching his breath. "I found some guards cooking over a fire. I baked bread for everyone, and they shared their meals with me. They even agreed to let me join them again tonight. Oh, and I asked about Asim - he's alive, but he's in bad shape. He's quite sore from the beating and will be sent to the Kilisi in a few weeks unless someone pays Bill 20,000 Lapes to bail him out."

"Twenty thousand?" Sina's voice quivered with disbelief. "Why can't he just work off the debt?"

"Because Bill's making an example of him," Manu replied grimly.

"What do you mean?" Imogen asked, her face paling.

"He's using Asim to scare everyone," Roger explained, his tone grave. "It's a warning - if anyone tries to escape, they'll suffer the same fate."

The weight of their words sank in like a heavy stone, the gravity of their predicament chilling them to the core. The oppressive reality of their debt to Bill now felt suffocating. Twenty thousand Lapes might as well have been a million. Asim's plight wasn't just his own - it was a grim reflection of the trap they were all ensnared in.

For the first time, the kids truly understood the depth of the Jungle's teeth. The fight for their freedom wasn't just against Bill - it was against the crushing system that kept them all bound, and every step forward felt like two steps deeper into the quicksand.

The thought of Asim being sent to the Kilisi was unbearable. Vaipor's descriptions of the place painted it as a merciless prison, designed to strip its victims of hope and humanity. While Asim wasn't particularly close to them, the idea of losing him forever gnawed at their hearts. If they ever made it back to the City, how would they face his parents? What words could possibly explain such a fate?

The crushing realization that their own escalating debt might be the reason Asim would end up in the Kilisi filled them with an overwhelming sense of guilt and helplessness. The tangled web of their predicament became clearer with each passing moment: their struggle was not theirs alone but a shared burden that linked them all to the same grim outcome.

Maria tried her best to soothe their anxiety, her voice soft and motherly, but it was clear she carried her own heavy load. By midday, her usually composed demeanour was beginning to crack. The strain on her shoulders mirrored the same daunting truth she had faced the day before: Bill's impossible quotas loomed larger than ever.

"You see," Maria began, her voice tinged with exhaustion, "Bill always sets my targets so high that meeting them without a single mistake or disruption is nearly impossible. And now, with the responsibility of training all of you… well, these next four weeks feel too much." She sighed, her tone apologetic as she added, "I'm sorry if I've been short-tempered. The stress is just… overwhelming."

Manu, quiet until now, studied her with furrowed brows, his mind already turning over possible solutions.

"Maria, what happens if you exceed your target? Do you earn any extra Lapes?"

Maria's expression darkened with frustration.

"If I consistently exceed my target, Bill just raises it higher. There's no reward, no relief. If it were easy for any of us to meet our quotas, no one would owe him anything, and he'd lose his workers. This whole system is rigged to trap us in endless struggle."

Manu pressed further, his tone calm but probing.

"How come you're the only one making clothes and shoes?"

"For a long time, Bill could barely sell what I made. There wasn't a need for more workers. But then, a few seasons ago, he struck deals with traders. Now, they buy everything I produce, and the demand has skyrocketed. The pressure to work faster has never been greater." She sighed again, her voice laced with bitterness. "And now, with all of you here, he must think he's hit the jackpot."

The steady beat of the drumming cut through their conversation, signalling the arrival of lunchtime. Its rhythm, once eagerly anticipated, had become a monotonous reminder of their servitude. Just days ago, the drumming had marked the excitement of the market - a break in routine, a glimmer of freedom. Now, it was a sound they associated with obligation, reinforcing the mechanical routine they had fallen into so quickly.

"Maria," Manu said, his voice gentle but resolute, "I know my bread isn't a fancy meal from the restaurant, but I want to help you reach your target today. If we work through lunch and eat the bread I baked this morning, you could save time and money."

Maria smiled at his thoughtful offer, her expression softening.

"Thank you, Manu. That's very kind of you. But I think I'll still head to the restaurant. A proper meal and a moment away from all of this… it's the only thing keeping me going right now."

Manu was bewildered by Maria's choice. To him, skipping a decent meal and a short break seemed like trivial sacrifices compared to the urgency of escaping Bill's grasp. Yet his youthful optimism couldn't fathom the slow erosion of will-power that comes with years of toil. The burden of survival, Maria knew, didn't just weigh on the body - it dulled the spirit. For her, each day was a tightrope walk between rest and relentless effort, and sometimes, the promise of immediate comfort tipped the balance.

As she walked away, Manu stood motionless, grappling with a mixture of confusion and disappointment. Sacrifice was second nature to him; he firmly believed in the power of delayed gratification, in the idea that every hardship endured now would pay off later. But Maria's weariness, shaped by 46 years of this life, eluded his understanding. He couldn't reconcile her reluctance to seize every possible advantage with the burning determination he carried within himself. With a heavy heart, he turned to leave, his thoughts preoccupied as he made his way to meet his new friends, the guards.

"Lightning!" Manu called out as he neared the fireplace where they had shared breakfast that morning.

"I can't leave my post. Come here!" Lightning's voice rang out from a nearby watchtower.

Lightning was a wiry, sharp-eyed Voivoki who had served Bill for over 12 years. His nickname stemmed from his astonishing speed, a skill that had seen him survive countless encounters in the Jungle. Despite their age gap, Manu and Lightning had quickly developed a bond. Manu's curiosity drove him to dig for insights about the Voivokis and Bill's tightly controlled village, but Lightning had little knowledge - or perhaps little interest - in the deeper workings of the system. Instead, he regaled Manu with vivid tales of his encounters with the Jungle's wild creatures, his stories punctuated by bursts of laughter.

When it was time for Manu to return to the factory, Lightning insisted on paying for the bread he made.

"I can't take your money," Manu said, shaking his head. "You need it as much as I do. Bill may have assigned us different roles, but we're both trapped here, aren't we? We're on the same side."

Lightning blinked, startled by the boy's words. Before he could respond, Manu grinned, nodded, and took off running back to the factory, leaving the guard standing there in stunned silence.

"What have you been up to this time?" Maria asked with a faint smile as Manu burst into the factory, his shirt drenched in sweat from running through the humid midday heat.

"Just lunch with a friend," Manu replied between gulps of air, brushing stray hair from his face.

Maria's smile lingered, but her gaze softened. She could see through his casual words. There was something about Manu - a fire, a determination - that reminded her so much of Rica, her old friend. Rica had been the same: bold, unrelenting, and fiercely resourceful, never letting anything stand between her and freedom. And though Manu's resolve stirred hope in Maria, it also unsettled her. She knew the weight of the mountain he was trying to climb.

Manu, for his part, was already living on the edge of frugality. Refusing to spend on accommodations, eating only the bread he baked, and cutting every nonessential cost, he was trying to claw his way towards freedom. Yet Maria knew these sacrifices could only take him so far. At some point, cutting back isn't enough - the only way forward is to earn more, to outwit the system itself.

As Maria reflected on her past and Rica's journey, a bittersweet warmth filled her chest. The memory of their shared dreams and relentless optimism made her ache for Manu's future. And so, that afternoon, she resolved to do more than watch from the sidelines. She began to share practical ideas, business strategies she had learned during her years of survival. Her voice carried a newfound energy as she spoke, and the kids around her leaned in, their eyes bright with hope and inspiration.

Manu, however, couldn't shake the question that haunted him: How could someone with so many great ideas remain stuck at Bill's factory for 46 years? It hovered on the edge of his thoughts, tempting him to voice it aloud. But he held back, not wanting to expose Maria's vulnerabilities in front of the others. He understood the fine line between curiosity and insensitivity, and he chose to tread carefully. Instead, he resolved to wait, hoping for the right moment to speak with her alone. He wanted to better understand her struggles, to learn from her missteps, and to help the group avoid the traps that had kept her bound for so long.

This cautious approach was something Manu had learned from Rich just days earlier. Rich had emphasized the value of studying both the triumphs and failures of others, urging Manu to see every experience as a lesson. It wasn't enough to admire success; one had to dissect mistakes as well.

As the workday neared its end, Maria's animated talk about her endless stream of ideas was interrupted by the deep, rhythmic thrum of drums. The beat, lively and insistent, seemed to vibrate through the air, filling the factory with an almost magnetic energy. It was unlike the drums they'd heard earlier - this rhythm was alive, a joyful invitation.

"Who-hoo!" Maria exclaimed, her face lighting up. "The full moon dance festival is tonight! You have to go. It's the best thing about this place!"

For a woman worn by decades of hardship, her sudden burst of excitement was almost startling. She leapt to her feet with the agility of someone half her age, her eyes sparkling with delight.

"It's only 20 Lapes!" she said, grinning as she looked at the kids, daring them to resist the call of the drums.

Her enthusiasm was infectious. The others, swept up in her energy, sprang to their feet, their exhaustion momentarily forgotten. But Manu remained seated on the bamboo floor, his hands methodically weaving raw materials, his focus unbroken.

"Shouldn't we help Maria reach her target first?" Manu asked, his voice tinged with quiet disbelief. How could she abandon her goals so easily?

Maria smiled gently, but there was a wistfulness behind it.

"Oh, Manu, if all you do is focus on targets, you'll never really live."

As if to emphasize her point, she swayed lightly to the music, letting the rhythm guide her movements. The carefree smile on her face was a stark contrast to the woman weighed down by years of struggle.

"Come on, Manu," she urged. "This party doesn't happen often. You'll have a blast. And who knows? You might even make some new friends."

But Manu wasn't swayed. It wasn't the heart-to-heart he had hoped for, but her actions spoke volumes. In that moment, she taught him a lesson more powerful than words: the mindset of the unsuccessful. Like so many others, Maria sought refuge in fleeting pleasures - a special meal, a lively festival - to escape her daily grind. But what she failed to see was how these small indulgences compounded over time, creating an insurmountable barrier between her and the freedom she so desperately craved.

"I'll skip it this time," Manu said quietly, his tone steady. "I don't have 20 Lapes."

Leila, trying to persuade him, chimed in:

"We can always pay for it later, once we pass our test."

"I know that," Manu replied. "But for me, freedom will be far more rewarding than a few hours of fun."

The others hesitated, his words giving them pause. But the pull of the festival - the music, the promise of a reprieve from the harshness of their lives - was too strong. Even Roger, his closest friend, chose to go. For a brief moment, Manu didn't know what to do. Was his unwavering focus worth jeopardizing the bond they'd shared for years? But the fire inside him burned brighter than the allure of camaraderie. The thought of breaking free from Bill's grip, of reclaiming his life, was worth the sacrifice.

With quiet resolve, Manu wished them all a good time and set off on his own. As the sound of laughter and music faded behind him, he sought out Lightning.

"Lightning," Manu called out, approaching the wiry Voivoki cautiously, "can I ask you a big favour?"

Lightning stiffened, caught off guard by the request. What could Manu possibly want from him? The only thing that crossed his mind was that Manu might be asking him to help him escape, but that was a risk Lightning wasn't willing to take – not when it could mean ending up in the Kilisi.

"What is it?" he asked, his tone uncharacteristically cold. "You know I can't let you leave this place."

"Relax, Lightning," Manu said, sensing his unease. "I know it would be too risky for you to help me escape, and I'd never ask that of you. I just need permission to go and collect some Mapa seeds."

"Mapa seeds?" Lightning scoffed, the tension easing slightly. "Only the lowest of the low bother with Mapa seeds anymore. Why would you want to do that?"

"Those Mapa seeds may come handy one day," Manu replied, trying to downplay the importance.

Lightning's expression hardened.

"Sorry, my friend, but I can't take that risk," he said firmly. "You seem like a good bloke, but I've only met you. I can't put my life on the line for someone I barely know. There was another guard once – he trusted someone too much and ended up in the Kilisi when that Voi betrayed him and ran."

Manu tried to convince him, appealing to whatever trust they had built in such a short time, but it was no use. Lightning's fear of betrayal outweighed any bond they had formed. Disappointed, Manu nodded, understanding the guard's hesitation, even if it stung.

After dinner, Manu cautiously approached the hammocks, the soft glow of the evening stars guiding his steps. One hammock swayed gently in the breeze, an unsettling sight that made him pause. He hadn't expected his friends to return from the party so soon. His mind raced with possibilities – was it a plantation worker seeking refuge from the noise, or perhaps an intruder from the wilderness? Determined to reclaim their campsite, he stepped forward, his nerves on edge, and called out:

"Is anyone there?"

"Just me, enjoying the evening breeze," came Vaipor's calm reply.

Manu exhaled in relief and quickly closed the distance between them.

"How do you like this place?" asked Vaipor.

Ever since meeting Vaipor, Manu had been eager to get closer to him, hoping for personal guidance. With the other kids irresponsibly partying on credit extended by Bill, tonight had finally given him that chance. The fear that had gripped him moments before was replaced by a surge of excitement. He eagerly began recounting his experiences at Bill's village, detailing Asim's capture and the grim likelihood of him being sent to the Kilisi. His frustration with Bill's ruthless and unfair treatment poured out, his voice tinged with bitterness.

"Essentially, we're all slaves to him," Manu said, his resolve hardening. "I can't wait to be free again."

"What makes you think that you're slaves?" Vaipor asked.

Manu's eyes burned with conviction.

"Well, it's quite obvious. No one is allowed to leave, and the wages are so low that we can't even make a dent in our debts. Maria is a perfect example – she's been trapped here for 46 years. Every time she manages to consistently meet her quota, Bill just raises it higher, ensuring she falls short on some days. By paying her only half of her wage on those days, it feels like taking five steps forward, and one step back."

Vaipor listened intently, his expression thoughtful.

"Has anyone ever managed to break out of this trap?"

"Yes, there was a Voi, named Rica," Manu replied, a mix of hope and scepticism in his voice. "She worked tirelessly and eventually paid off her debt."

Vaipor raised an eyebrow.

"Did she have some kind of superpower or privileges?"

Manu shook his head.

"No, nothing like that."

Vaipor leaned in, his voice steady but carrying an undercurrent of bitter truth.

"Most of the Voivokis have the desire to regain their freedom, yet they often succumb to temptations and lack the necessary determination and discipline to achieve their goals. Without these three D's - desire, determination, and discipline - they will never reach their goals. It's much easier to complain than to put in the effort."

He paused, letting the weight of his words settle.

"You and the others are no longer on your own in this vicious Jungle. You no longer have to worry about wildlife, poisonous plants, building shelter every night, or sleep hungry. You're part of a community now, surrounded by Voivokis with interesting stories and frequent entertainment. However, it's important to acknowledge that all these remarkable benefits come at the cost of your personal freedom."

Vaipor's word struck a chord with Manu, stirring memories of his father. His dad had often dreamed of an isolated life, living off the land, far from the complexities of modern life. He thought it would offer him an escape from the frustrations of bills, taxes and the burdens of everyday grind of the City. Manu could hear echoes of that idealism in Vaipor's speech.

"It's easy for everyone to fall into a routine – working all day and spending what little they have on essentials and entertainment," continued Vaipor. "But how many Voivokis do you see hassling before and after their shifts?"

"I haven't been here long enough to see, but I highly doubt many are working tonight after the party."

"That's exactly what I am talking about," Vaipor said, his tone sharp. "Most Voivokis don't realise that attending these parties does them harm in two ways. First, they spend 20 Lapes on admission, and then they likely splurge on food and drinks. Second, they miss out on earning extra Lapes they could have made working. It's a double blow to their chances of breaking free."

"I tried to convince Maria twice today to work extra to meet her quota," Manu said, frustrated. "I also wanted to collect Mapa seeds, but Lightning wouldn't let me leave. He said, he couldn't take the risk, even for a few hours."

"If you were in his position, would you risk spending the rest of your life in a Kilisi?" Vaipor asked.

"If I knew I could trust the person asking, I would consider it," Manu replied.

"It's a dangerous gamble," Vaipor said firmly. "Never trust someone so completely that your entire future could be jeopardised if things go wrong. Always weigh the risks against the rewards and ensure they align with what you're willing to accept.

Think about your situation with Lightning. If you were exceptionally generous and give him half of the Mapa seeds you collect, say 60 out of 120, that's about 6 Lapes. As a guard, he probably earns over 200 Lapes a day. The risk of his job versus the 6 Lapes you offer isn't a fair trade."

Manu's shoulders slumped, his gaze fixed on the ground.

"I understand that," he said quietly. "But if I can't collect Mapa seeds, how am I ever going to have enough Lapes to regain my freedom?"

"If you surround yourself with individuals who don't share your aspirations, they will only drag you down," Vaipor said. "How many of your friends suggested finding ways to earn more Lapes instead of going to the dance festival?"

"None of them," Manu admitted. "They all wanted me to join them."

"Surround yourself with high achievers, and they will push you to levels you never thought you could reach."

Manu glanced up, curiosity piqued.

"Are you saying I shouldn't stay friends with the other kids and the guards?"

Vaipor shook his head.

"No, it's good to be friends with many, but consider this: Lightning has been a guard for 12 years, right?"

"Yeah."

"Unless you want to have the same stagnant quality of life, he can't help you achieve your goals. It's not about his job; success isn't tied to one's occupation. There could be other workers, guards or otherwise, who are on the brink of breaking free. They might offer the insights you need.

Ultimately, you'll learn from everyone, but not every lesson will advance you. You have 24 hours each day to shape your path, and it's up to you to choose which individuals and activities propel you forward.

You must choose your circle of friends wisely and listen to your subconscious to discover innovative ways to create real value. Once you grasp this principle and act on it, the floodgate of Lapes will open."

Vaipor stepped closer to Manu and gently placed his hand on Manu's bowed head.

"You have everything given to reach your goals, but you must maintain your focus and remember the three D's."

Manu sat quietly in his hammock, his mind adrift. He barely noticed the stillness around him, or the storm clouds that gradually eclipsed the star's faint glow. He was lost in a haze of thoughts. Below him, tiny streams of water snaked through the earth, glistening faintly in the moonlight. As he stared, something extraordinary happened. The streams shimmered, growing wider and faster until they morphed into a dazzling river. Sparkling objects cascaded from an unseen height, tumbling like a radiant waterfall. The sunlight danced on the surface, scattering shards of brilliance in every direction.

Manu's eyes widened as the sight drew him in, his heart pounding with wonder. He reached out, his fingers brushing the glimmering treasures, but the moment they touched, the objects dissolved into golden mist, leaving a faint, ethereal glow on his hands.

"Manu!" a voice broke through the spell, startling him. The river, the waterfall, the glittering mountain - all vanished in an instant, leaving behind the modest streams below his hammock.

"Manu!" the voice called again.

Blinking, he looked up to find Roger and Joe standing nearby.

"We thought you'd be asleep by now," Roger said, a note of concern in his voice.

"I think I nodded off for a moment," Manu murmured, leaning back into the hammock, reluctant to let go of the dream.

꙰ ꙰ ꙰

The following day unfolded like the one before, a routine that had quickly entrenched itself in their lives: wake at 7 a.m., breakfast at the restaurant, and work from 9 a.m. to 5 p.m., broken only by a short midday pause.

"Where's Imogen?" Manu asked when Roger opened his eyes.

"She moved in with Leila," Roger replied. "After hearing everyone rave about sleeping without mosquito bites or getting drenched in the rain, she couldn't resist."

"Are you coming to breakfast?" Joe asked.

"No, I still have some flour," Manu replied, his mind elsewhere.

Vaipor's words from the previous night still echoed in his thoughts: Choose your circle of friends wisely and listen to your subconscious; that's where you'll find creative ways to generate real value. Eager to delve deeper into their meaning, Manu chose to skip breakfast and wandered off in search of solitude.

He climbed to a vantage point overlooking the valley, struck by its breathtaking beauty. If not for Bill's suffocating grip on their lives, the place could have been a sanctuary. The warm breeze rustled the verdant canopy, carrying the sweet scent of tropical flowers. The symphony of chirping birds and buzzing insects mingled with the distant chatter of monkeys, creating a melody that felt alive with possibility.

Manu settled on a smooth rock, letting Vaipor's advice replay in his mind. He closed his eyes, trying to connect with his subconscious, but the effort felt abstract, almost elusive. As he sat in quiet reflection, fragments of ideas began to surface - some vague, others vivid.

With no pen or paper at hand, Manu relied on memory, mentally sorting through each thought. Some ideas were discarded as impractical, but others sparked a glimmer of hope. Gradually, the images became sharper, and the pieces of a plan started to take shape.

Before long, his excitement grew uncontrollable. Leaping to his feet, Manu hurried towards the factory where the others were gathering for their training. His energy was infectious, drawing curious stares as he approached.

"What happened to you?" Imogen asked with a bright smile, pausing in her work to look at him. "You seem... different."

CHAPTER 2

With the help of the kids, Maria finally met her daily target, a relief after falling short for two consecutive days. It was no small feat, especially given the time she had spent training her new colleagues. The kids cheered for her accomplishment, their excitement genuine, but for Maria, it was just another hollow victory. For 46 long years, her life had been an unchanging cycle: meeting quotas, struggling to stay afloat, and enduring Bill's suffocating control. Each day bled into the next, a monotonous loop of toil and exhaustion, leaving her emotionally numb.

After delivering the finished products to Bill's office, Manu gathered the others in the factory. Instead of rushing to dinner like usual, he proposed something different. His voice carried a spark of determination as he addressed them.

"Why don't we stay back a little longer?" he suggested. "We need to start taking actions to break free from this place."

At first, his suggestion stirred curiosity. The idea of finding a way out felt like a faint glimmer of hope in their bleak reality. But that hope was fleeting.

"I can't. I'm meeting my new friends for dinner," Susan said, already heading for the exit.

"Same here," Olivia added, following close behind.

One by one, the others found excuses. Roger was the last to leave, offering a tired shrug before walking out.

Manu stood alone, disappointment washing over him. He understood their weariness - after all, their days were gruelling - but their unwillingness to push beyond the daily grind stung. Breaking free would demand more than just meeting quotas; it would require extraordinary effort and sacrifice. Yet none of them seemed willing to take that step.

Working in the dim factory, the humming of insects was his only company. He weaved clothes under the weak glow of torchlight, but as night fell, so did his enthusiasm. The realization hit him like a weight - every move he made only served Bill's interests. Working harder wasn't the answer. A new plan was needed.

Driven by a sudden impulse, he abandoned his work and headed to Bill's office. He had no idea what he would say or why he even felt compelled to go. All he knew was that something deep within urged him forward.

❋ ❋ ❋

Meanwhile, at the restaurant, Susan and Olivia revelled in the company of their new friends, Jane and Jess. They avoided the other kids entirely, fully immersed in their new social circle. Jane and Jess had arrived at Bill's village after hearing about the festival, eager to experience it firsthand. Their polished demeanour and effortless generosity hinted at their affluent backgrounds. They treated everyone to drinks and snacks, luxuries that set them apart. Unlike the rest of the group, they stayed in Bill's exclusive Guest House, a privilege reserved for the wealthy.

For Susan and Olivia, who had grown up in comfort, it was natural to gravitate towards the pair. The previous night, they had quickly bonded with the visitors, sharing laughs and swapping stories. The allure of the affluent Voivoki lifestyle captivated them.

"I'm an influencer with over 300,000 online friends," Susan declared proudly, savouring the attention. "Companies are always sending me products to promote. It's pretty fun!"

"Three hundred thousand?" Jess repeated, wide-eyed. "I don't think I've even seen that many Voivokis in my life!"

Susan leaned in, relishing the moment.

"I've only met a few of them in person. Most of them are online. We connect through my social media channels. They send me friend requests, and if I want to, I accept it."

Jane and Jess exchanged bewildered glances. To them, words like "internet" and "social media" were unfamiliar concepts from another world. Susan and Olivia wished their gadgets hadn't been rendered useless the moment they'd leapt off the bus. With working devices, they could have dazzled their new friends with photos, videos, and undeniable proof of their glamorous lives.

Not wanting to lose their captivated audience, Olivia too launched into a vivid tale of the luxurious wellness centres and exclusive beauty salons she frequented with her mother. With each detail, she unconsciously embellished, striving to match Susan's aura of success.

Their subtle competition, weaving stories of affluence and status, might have been entertaining to some. But to others, it came across as desperate posturing, an attempt to cling to an identity they could no longer embody.

"If someone could free us," Olivia said, her voice softening, "we'd love to show you the City one day." Her words carried an unmistakable undertone, a plea for help veiled in casual conversation.

Like many Voivokis, Jane and Jess had heard whispers of the City, a mysterious place that existed only in rumours and fantasies. Meeting people who claimed to be from there was exciting. Though sceptical, Susan and Olivia's stories intrigued them. They couldn't help but wonder - was the City real, and if so, what was it truly like?

"We'll come back with more Lapes," Jane offered, her tone surprisingly earnest. "Maybe we can help pay off your debt. Then you can take us to this 'City' of yours."

Her words landed like a spark in the hearts of Susan and Olivia, igniting something they hadn't felt in a long time: hope. For a moment, their bleak reality was softened by the prospect of salvation, however distant or uncertain it might be.

Excitement bubbled beneath the surface, but so did impatience. In the City, they'd never needed to wait - instant gratification had been their norm. Now, with no choice but to wait and see if Jane and Jess's promise would materialize, they were forced to confront an unfamiliar reality.

"I wish you had a system like ours," Susan said wistfully. "No one carries Lapes in the City. We use phones or watches to pay - or even just a fingerprint or eye scan."

Her words, so far removed from the Voivoki world, sounded utterly fantastical. Jane and Jess burst into laughter.

"Alright, enough with the fairy tales!" Jane said, rising to leave. "We've got to head out early tomorrow."

As Jane and Jess disappeared behind the gates of Bill's Guest House, Susan and Olivia were left sitting under the dim evening light. In their new friends' company, they had felt the intoxicating pull of freedom and the faint echo of their old lives in the City. But as the gates shut, the illusion crumbled, leaving them grounded once again in the harshness of their reality.

※ ※ ※

The following morning, as the humid air carried the chirping of birds, Manu sat up in his hammock, his expression unusually bright. Nearby, Joe and Roger were still groggy, their eyes half-closed.

"I made a deal with Bill last night," Manu announced, a proud grin spreading across his face.

"Yeah, what kind of deal?" Roger asked, his tone half-curious, half-sceptical. After all, no one willingly approached Bill unless they absolutely had to. Fear of him was universal in the village.

Manu leaned back slightly, his grin widening.

"I've been thinking about Maria's life - and all of ours, really. About how Bill keeps us stuck here. So I went to him and suggested something different."

He paused for effect, earning curious looks from his half-awake audience.

"I told him he should pay us per product we make instead of a flat daily rate. At first, he rejected it, of course. But I pointed out how easy his current system is to exploit. Voivokis slack off because they know they'll get the same pay no matter what. I told him he'd make more money with a performance-based system."

Joe looked confused, so Manu took a moment to explain further.

"Bill sets these ridiculously high daily targets," Manu said. "If we miss even one, we get paid only 50%. And if we hit the target consistently, he just raises it, making sure we'll eventually fail. He knows it'll make him pay less. It kills motivation. Even if we could produce more, we wouldn't, because there's no incentive. I told him, though, that if he paid us per item we make, everyone would have a reason to work more efficiently. We could all win."

"Wow! That's brilliant!" Roger exclaimed, his eyes wide with admiration. "How did you come up with that?"

Manu turned to Joe with a grin.

"Joe actually had some great ideas yesterday," he said, giving him a nod. "He suggested we split into smaller groups and focus on specific tasks, rather than trying to master everything all at once."

Joe blinked in disbelief. To hear one of the sharpest minds in the group give him credit for such a game-changing idea was like winning a small battle. If this plan worked, it wouldn't just improve productivity - it could revolutionize how Bill ran his operations. With happier, more motivated workers, everyone, even Bill, would stand to benefit. Word would spread throughout the Jungle, and skilled Voivokis might start lining up to work voluntarily, eager for a fair system rather than being trapped in oppression. Bill wouldn't need to force anyone to work anymore - he could hire the best and drive greater success for everyone involved.

"Most of the others didn't buy into Joe's suggestion yesterday, but that's fine," Manu continued. "They don't need to be part of our success. Are you two in?"

Without hesitation, Joe and Roger both nodded, eager to join in.

"But it's not all good news," Manu added. "Bill won't let us skip the four-week training or the test. He said we have to finish the whole course and pass the test first."

"What course?" Roger scoffed, clearly not impressed.

"I know, but if you think about it, it's no different from our system in the City," Manu sighed. "I don't agree with it either, but even in the City, we have to study for years to get certificates, regardless of how much we know."

"I get that, but it's still ridiculous," Roger grumbled. "He knows we could pass the test in a couple of days. Why force us to 'study' for four weeks? Maybe we should swap with the Guest House keepers. Their training only lasts three days."

"Three days versus four weeks!" Manu exclaimed. "That's a huge difference. But I'm guessing they don't make as much as Maria when she hits her target."

"They do," Roger replied. "But their shifts are 12 hours long. From what they've said, the job's so boring, they'd gladly trade places with anyone."

"Hold on! Let's run some numbers," Joe interrupted, grabbing a piece of paper and starting to scribble down calculations. "If their training costs the same as ours, they're paying 3 times 79 Lapes, which totals 237. Compared to our 1580 Lapes. That's a massive difference! But their job is dull, and they work 12-hour shifts, so their hourly rate is just 15 Lapes, while ours is 22.5. I wouldn't want to spend 12 hours standing around for the same pay as a factory worker. No wonder they want to swap."

"You're right, Joe," Roger said, pausing as he considered the figures. "I take my suggestion back. Swapping with them based on cheaper training fees doesn't make sense. And neither option seems to help us pay off our debt to Bill and get out of here."

"I disagree," Manu said, leaning back, his gaze flickering between the two boys. He was lost in thought, weighing the options carefully. His silence was deliberate - a tactic he often used to ensure his ideas were fully formed before speaking.

"We have 24 hours in a day, and we certainly don't need 12 hours just for eating, sleeping, and getting to work," Manu continued. "So, working 12-hour shifts is manageable. They get the same pay we were promised, which is a plus. You also mentioned they're bored because they don't have many guests, so they have plenty of idle time. They could easily occupy themselves with other activities."

"Yes, but they can't leave the Guest House," Roger countered. "They have to keep up appearances, constantly cleaning and staying ready for guests at a moment's notice."

Manu raised an eyebrow.

"Do you really think they're wiping everything down as efficiently as possible?" he asked. "I bet they're dragging out their tasks just to pass the time. If we worked at the Guest House and kept making clothes and shoes for Bill, we could double our earnings compared to the other workers. Look at Maria and the rest of the so-called 'slaves'. They're not slaves. They're just victims of their own laziness. Maria even admitted she chose to enjoy life rather than put in the hard work to earn her freedom, unlike Rica."

Manu's eyes were steady, his gaze unwavering as he spoke.

"Bill might have made life tough for all of us, but these Voivokis are also trapping themselves in their work. Their lack of ambition and low efficiency come from the mindset of working just to get by, not to break free."

He paused, letting his words settle.

"Have you ever noticed how some restaurant attendants in the City clear tables in a flash, while others seem to hate their jobs? It's not just about the job - it's about how you approach it."

"Yeah, but what does that have to do with us swapping with the Guest House keepers?" Roger asked, still puzzled.

Manu leaned forward, his tone sharp.

"Think about it. The efficient attendants are the ones who get noticed and rise through the ranks. The sluggish ones? They stay stuck. If there's an opening for a leadership role or an entrepreneurial opportunity, it won't go to the lazy ones. Business owners seek people with a strong work ethic, those who can deliver."

He paused, carefully gauging Joe and Roger's reactions. He needed to make sure they were following him.

"We can be those efficient ones. By excelling at keeping the Guest House spotless, we set ourselves apart. Then, we can use any free time to make clothes and shoes. That way, we'd not only get more done, but we'd also carve out time for what really matters in the long run - our bigger goal."

Roger, who had known Manu for years, always admired his natural leadership and entrepreneurial flair. But this time, Manu's words struck him deeper than ever before. He marvelled at how someone so young could grasp business dynamics so effectively.

'Perhaps it's true that desperation brings out the best in us," Roger thought, his respect for Manu growing.

He believed Manu's promise - he wouldn't stay in Bill's village forever. But the others? They probably dismissed it as a frustrated outburst from a kid who couldn't see past his current situation. They didn't know Manu the way Roger did.

Joe, eager to contribute and stay in the loop, quickly did the math in his head. If they could double their income, he realised, they could pay off their debts in just six days, even if they slept in a hut and Manu ate all his meals at the restaurant. The plan was starting to take shape.

The thought of regaining their freedom in just a week filled them with an intoxicating sense of euphoria. It was as if the weight of the world had been lifted, replaced by a rush of hope and exhilaration. The mere idea of escaping the suffocating grip of debt and Bill's village ignited a fire within them.

"We have to keep our plan under wraps," Manu said, his voice unwavering. "Got it?"

The others nodded, but Manu's eyes hardened, sensing the other two didn't take him seriously enough. He pressed them again, his tone sharper.

"Our freedom hinges on this. Do you understand?"

Roger let out a light chuckle.

"Yeah, yeah, we got it, Manu."

Manu exhaled, still unsatisfied.

"Alright, here's the breakdown. Roger, you'll arrange the meeting with the Guest House keepers. Once we have their word, I'll speak to Bill for his endorsement. After that, we'll probably have to face Bill's office, where he'll outline the job swap conditions. The four-week training period might make the Guest House keepers hesitate, so I'll push for a better deal with Bill. Any questions?"

The boys exchanged looks, the plan settling in.

"I assume Roger's going with you to the Guest House?" Joe asked, his brow furrowing.

Manu gazed out towards the valley, lost in thought for a moment before turning back to Joe.

"No," he said, his voice firm. "I'll be the outsider - managing the supply of raw materials. Once I pass the test, I'll handle submitting the products to Bill."

"Damn it!" Joe swore, frustration leaking into his tone. "I forgot about the four-week training. So much for leaving in six days…"

"Four weeks is still better than being stuck here for 46 years like Maria," Manu reminded them, his voice steady but carrying the weight of the reality they faced. "Oh, and one more thing: you'll have to handle the talks with Bill, since I won't be officially involved."

Roger and Joe exchanged uneasy glances. The idea of negotiating with Bill, especially for Joe - who had a hard time talking to anyone his age, let alone someone as imposing as Bill - felt overwhelming. But after a few long moments, they nodded reluctantly. There was no other option.

"What about the guard at the gate of the Guest House?" Roger asked, a frown knitting his brow. "We can't have him blowing our secret."

Joe grinned, clearly proud of himself.

"Don't worry. I made friends with him. He's really intrigued by my video games. At first, he didn't believe me, but when I showed him my broken tablet - what he calls a 'magic box' – his doubt softened. He said if he ever gets out of Bill's village, he's going to search the path to the City to find a 'magic box' for himself."

"That's great, but just because he's excited about your stories doesn't mean he'll keep quiet," Manu said, filled with scepticism. "We'll need to talk to him, make sure he's on our side. And if it comes down to it, we'll offer him your tablet in exchange for his silence."

Joe's chest tightened at the suggestion. He had only gotten the tablet a few months ago, and even though it was broken, it contained photos, videos - memories that seemed almost sacred now. The thought of giving it up for their freedom hit him hard, but deep inside he knew it was a small price he might have to pay.

"I know it's a sacrifice," Manu continued, watching Joe carefully, "but if we're going to get out, we might not have any other choice. We'll see how he reacts, and if he's not willing to play along, we'll come up with something else."

Joe swallowed, the sting still raw.

"Yeah. I get it," he said.

Manu paused for a moment, considering other options.

"Maybe we won't even need to bribe him. Bill only said we have to pass the test to submit the products - he never said who has to make them. The biggest question is whether Bill will let us take the raw materials out of the factory. We'll figure it out."

The three boys, buzzing with excitement and energy, were ready to take on the day. Manu, especially, was eager for a break from his usual plain bread meals soon. With his yam flour nearly gone, he knew that soon, he'd have no choice but to eat at Bill's restaurant anyway - further deepening his debt. Though there were rumours of a market opening in the valley, his restricted movement and inability to gather Mapa seeds made purchasing more flour impossible.

As they left their campsite, Roger was surprised to see Manu heading in a different direction.

"Aren't you coming with us?" he asked. "I thought you'd be eating proper food with us from now on."

"I will, soon enough," Manu laughed. "But let's not count our chickens before they hatch. Besides, we haven't sealed the deal yet. And I want to keep building rapport with the guards - it might come in handy one day. You guys go ahead and enjoy your breakfast."

Like many successful entrepreneurs with a keen sense of people, Manu understood the power of networking. Vaipor had stressed how success is often shaped by the company one keeps, so from that morning on, Manu began to carefully evaluate everyone around him. The guards, despite their lack of ambition to improve their lives, were still valuable to him. He saw their potential for future alliances, and unlike the other kids, he didn't limit his interactions to his peers.

When they gathered for their morning session at the factory, Manu could hardly contain his excitement as he announced his ground breaking agreement with Bill:

"Bill agreed to pay us based on performance instead of his quota system. 125 Lapes for clothes, 212 for shoes. If anyone wants to switch, let him know by the end of today. But once you choose, it's final - no changes after that."

Maria barely hesitated. She blamed her age, using it as a shield to avoid the unknown. The thought of giving up her familiar routine felt like stepping into quicksand. She feared the slow creep of exhaustion that might force her to work longer hours just to scrape together the same wage. Alone for so long, the concept of teamwork and the potential for increased efficiency through mutual assistance didn't occur to her.

Olivia and Susan, however, clung to the quota system for reasons far deeper than practicality. Their pride, bruised and tender, fuelled their decision. They held themselves in high regard, and Bill's action of making them work for free, at least for the first four weeks, deeply wounded their egos. They felt insulted, their worth stripped away. No amount of Lapes could wash away the sting of those first unpaid weeks. So, they shut the door on Bill, holding tight to the fragile promises of freedom whispered by their new friends.

Instead of working like the others, they spent their days chatting, their idle behaviour a growing source of tension. The rest of the group, frustrated by their detachment, warned them again and again: even if their friends came through, they should still learn the craft in case their friends fail to return.

The other girls recognised Manu's faith in the pay-per-product system as rational, even though they couldn't fully grasp the nuances. They stood by him, willing to believe in his vision, trusting that the boys' perspective held some promise of a better future.

As the day wound down, Imogen took the opportunity to claim a rare moment of 'me-time', something she hadn't had in nearly two weeks. The constant presence of others had become overwhelming for her, considering that she usually spent most of her free time in solitude, expressing her thoughts and feelings through drawings and other creative activities. Thankfully, her notebook had endured the rain remarkably well, and now that she wasn't on the move every day, she could thoroughly dry it in the sun. Although the pages were wrinkled and stiff, they were still usable for her artwork. Her pencils had also survived the trials and tribulations, securely stored in the front pocket of her backpack.

She scanned the area for a quiet spot, eager to take in the breathtaking view of the village. Like most of the other kids, she found the valley captivating - the tiny village nestled amidst sprawling plantations, a peaceful sight that offered a fleeting sense of tranquillity. In an attempt to momentarily escape the suffocating thought of being trapped here indefinitely, she turned to her passion: drawing. The sunset over the valley, with its vibrant hues painting the sky, should have been the perfect muse.

But just as the calm of the evening began to settle in, a guard came charging towards her, his face contorted with agitation.

"I can't believe I can't even have a moment to myself in this place," she thought, frustration bubbling to the surface. *"Not even a minute."*

Her gaze sharpened as she watched the guard approach, her confusion mixing with irritation. She hadn't done anything wrong - at least, not that she knew of - but the look on his face suggested he didn't share that belief.

"You're outside of Bill's property," the guard snapped. "I'll have to tie your hands and take you to Bill."

For a brief, terrifying moment, Imogen felt her breath catch, a sharp pain seizing her chest. Her face drained of colour, and her limbs trembled, betraying her rising panic. Though her eyes remained fixed on the village below, her mind was overtaken by images of Kilisi - malnourished Voivokis with deep cuts, bruises, missing teeth, and ragged, unkempt hair.

In her mind's eye, she saw someone, hands bound, being dragged by their hair, their body limp and helpless. Others were tied to trees or to each other, their backs forced together in misery. Behind bars, a sea of desperate faces clawed for scraps of bread, their hunger savage, like a pack of ravenous hyenas.

Panic clamped down on her chest, making it harder to breathe, harder to stand. Never in her life had she imagined a day would come when she would be thrown into a prison of her own.

"Get up!" the guard barked, his command dragging her back to the present.

CHAPTER 3

That evening, the chef's skill and creativity seemed to have reached new heights. The aroma drifting from the restaurant was an irresistible invitation to indulge. The air was thick with the appetizing scent of tender, smoky grilled snake, its rich, savoury fragrance mingling with the earthy notes of exotic Jungle herbs. Paired with perfectly baked yam, the dish held the promise of captivating taste buds far beyond the confines of the village.

Sina's stomach growled in anticipation, the hunger in her belly urging her to join her friends in the long, winding queue. Her mind was already anticipating the first bite, but when she noticed that Imogen wasn't there, mingling with the rest, worry washed over her.

"Where's Imogen?" she asked, anxiously glancing around.

"I thought she'd be here with you," Leila replied, sharing Sina's concern.

The idea of Imogen missing such a delicious feast was unthinkable. As the seconds ticked by, a gnawing unease began to settle in. What if something had happened to her? Imogen, with her striking beauty, was undeniably a prime target for ill-minded Voivokis. Fear crept into their thoughts.

"We have to find her," Roger said, his tone urgent. "Sina, go get Manu. He's with the guards. We'll search everywhere else."

Sina nodded quickly, swallowing the lump in her throat, and without another word, she sprinted towards the incline, her feet pounding against the earth.

Meanwhile, Roger, Joe, Leila, and Mai scattered in different directions, their calls for Imogen echoing through the growing dusk. Each footstep seemed to intensify the looming sense of urgency, as the light of the day waned.

Unaware of the frenzy unfolding below, Manu was preparing his modest dinner with the two guards, Lightning and Muscalo. The trio shared a moment of quiet camaraderie as they worked, the crackling of the fire the only sound breaking the silence. Manu was busy rolling dough on a small timber slab, his mind focused on the task at hand. Between motions, he casually remarked:

"I'm running out of flour and nuts in the next couple of days. I don't have enough Lapes to restock."

Lightning, always the more talkative of the two, grinned, his eyes lighting up with a spark of enthusiasm.

"Kid, your bread is so good, I'd pay for your ingredients just to keep you making it."

Manu raised an eyebrow, a small smile tugging at his lips.

"Really?" he asked.

"Absolutely," Lightning replied, his grin widening. "I'd even pay extra for your special bread if it means keeping it coming. Trust me, you've got something good here."

Manu knew that if his plan with Joe and Roger succeeds, he'd soon find himself enjoying far more appetizing meals at the restaurant, diminishing Lightning's generous offer. But he was also mindful of the possibility that their efforts could fail, in which case, he would continue to subsist on his plain bread for the foreseeable future.

He kept his gratitude in check and politely thanked Lightning for the offer.

Their light-hearted conversation suddenly stalled when a series of sharp, staccato whistles sprung the guards to their feet, their faces tense with urgency.

"What's going on?" Manu asked, his eyes narrowing.

"One of the guards caught someone trying to escape," Muscalo said, his voice thick with excitement. "We've got to go and help."

Manu's stomach twisted in a knot. The guards were the very ones who held everyone captive, standing as a barrier between them and freedom. Yet, despite his resentment, he understood the gravity of their duty. If they failed in their roles, the consequences could be severe - life-threatening, even. Despite the inner conflict, the rush of adrenaline stirred something within him. As the guards bolted, Manu didn't hesitate. He shot to his feet and followed, eager to witness the drama unfolding ahead.

Meanwhile, in the village, Mai had just bumped into Susan and Olivia, hoping they'd seen Imogen. But the cold, dismissive sneers they exchanged told Mai everything she needed to know. The two girls, aloof and self-centred, didn't care about Imogen - or anyone else, for that matter. To them, they were already above the rest, untouchable in their arrogance. It was as if the dangers of the Jungle and the looming threats of captivity were nothing more than distant, irrelevant notions.

With a heavy sigh, Mai hurried away, continuing her search of Imogen.

"Do you even care about that guinea pig and her airy-fairy friend?" Olivia asked, dripping with snobbishness.

The two girls broke into laughter, their high-pitched giggles carrying an air of superiority, completely oblivious to the danger their arrogance invited.

By the time Sina returned to the village centre, the encroaching darkness had nearly consumed the landscape, leaving everything cloaked in shadow. Gasping for breath after her frantic running, she barely managed to sidestep Roger as he appeared in her path. She quickly relayed her fruitless search for Manu, her frustration palpable.

Roger, ever the strategist, didn't miss a beat.

"Manu's probably already at the campsite," he said. "I'll go and check."

Without another word, he turned and vanished into the night, leaving Sina behind, uncertain of what to do next. However, no sooner had Roger disappeared than a familiar voice floated towards her from the restaurant, soft and inviting on the evening breeze.

"Imogen!" Sina gasped, a rush of relief flooding her chest.

Imogen, with a wide grin plastered on her face, waved from a bench, as though nothing were amiss.

"Where have you been?" Sina asked. "We've been looking everywhere for you!"

Before Imogen could even respond, she added:

"We need to let the others know you're safe."

Once the group had gathered around at the restaurant, Imogen wasted no time in recounting everything that had happened, her voice tinged with a mix of incredulity and relief.

"I apparently strayed outside the boundary, so one of the guards tied me up and called for backup," she began, her grin turning remorseful. "They wanted to haul me off to Bill. Honestly, it was kind of ironic - the guard was twice my size, yet he called for help like I was a threat. At that point, I really thought they might lock me up, just like they did with Asim."

Imogen paused, the gravity of the moment settling over her as she continued.

"Shortly after, the other two guards showed up, and then Manu arrived. He asked what was going on, and the guard accused me of trying to escape - a complete lie, since I'd been sitting on a rock, drawing. I set him straight, but the guard wouldn't back down. He stuck to his story, insisting I was trying to flee."

A flicker of frustration crossed Imogen's face as she remembered the scene.

"Then Manu asked him if he seriously thought I'd have the guts to run off alone. The guard looked completely embarrassed but wouldn't admit his stupidity. Instead, he insisted I be taken to Bill.

Manu turned to his friends, asking them to vouch for me. Of course, the guards backed each other up. But Manu didn't give up. He offered them a bribe - my drawings. At first, they laughed, but then Manu showed them the sketch I'd done on the bus. The look on their faces... they'd never seen anything like it. They were hooked. One of them even asked me to draw something special for him tomorrow."

Imogen leaned back, a satisfied smile spreading across her face.

"So, here I am. Free as Bill's paid slaves can be."

Imogen's harrowing account of her encounter with the guard served as a stark reminder of Bill's oppressive grip on their lives — an ever-present danger they all faced.

As the adrenaline slowly dissipated, hunger began to take its place, and the group's focus shifted to more immediate comforts. The unsettling experience with the guards was pushed aside, and they sought solace in a hearty dinner, finding small pleasures in the face of their harsh reality.

Their quiet indulgence came to a halt when Manu showed up unexpectedly, lighting up their faces.

"We heard how you saved Imogen," Sina said, brimming with gratitude. "You're really good at handling tough situations."

Manu's face flushed with a mix of embarrassment and modesty.

"Thanks," he mumbled softly.

Noticing his reaction, Roger couldn't resist teasing him further.

"You're so awesome, Manu!"

Manu laughed awkwardly, his cheeks burning.

"Alright, alright!" he said, waving off the attention. "That's enough!"

The group burst into laughter, savouring the moment of levity.

"Are you joining us for dinner?" Sina asked, curious about Manu's unexpected appearance at the restaurant.

He shook his head.

"No, I have plans with the boys."

Manu settled at their table, waiting patiently for Roger and Joe to finish their meals. The plan was to speak with the Guest House keepers, but despite the village's small size, the keepers were nowhere to be found that night. Disappointed, they accepted that their highly anticipated conversation would have to wait until the next day.

❋ ❋ ❋

The following morning, as usual, everyone rose with the first light filtering through the dense Jungle canopy. The kids had long since adapted to the early hours, their bodies attuned to the rhythm of the Jungle. In contrast to their former lives in the City, where leaving behind soft mattresses and warm pillows was an agonizing daily struggle, the chill of the morning air, the ceaseless hum of insects, and the firm bamboo floors of their huts now acted as a natural alarm. There was no hesitation, no lingering under covers; the day began the moment they awoke.

Imogen, having received the guard's permission, made her way back to the rock she had claimed as her own - a spot that provided a sweeping, breathtaking view of the valley below. As she settled onto the cool stone, she briefly closed her eyes, allowing herself to slip into a quiet, creative trance. In her mind's eye, a vivid world took shape, each stroke of imagination coming to life as she meticulously crafted the next masterpiece. The dawn seemed to melt away as she poured herself into her art, and by the time the sun was high enough to break through the canopy, three impressive pieces lay completed before her. A sense of pride warmed her; they were her best yet.

She made her way to where Manu sat having breakfast with the guards. With a nod of appreciation, she thanked them for their leniency the night before, handing them the drawings with careful hands.

"Keep them shielded from the sun and rain," she advised, her tone earnest. "Exposure will ruin them quickly."

With that, she departed, joining her usual group at the restaurant, where the day continued to unfold.

After breakfast, the factory session dragged on for the boys. Time seemed to stretch endlessly, each minute heavier than the last. Itching to set their plan into motion, their thoughts wandered to the Guest House keepers, hoping they will be available to chat after work. The endless ticking of the clock became a test of patience. Then, the midday drumming echoed through the village, its rhythmic pulse a welcome disruption to the monotony. It was as sweet as the sound of a school bell signalling the start of summer break. Though the afternoon still lay ahead, the drumming carried a promise - each beat marking a step closer to the change they so desperately needed.

As the factory emptied for lunch, Manu pulled Imogen aside, his expression unusually serious.

"Can you keep secrets?" he asked quietly.

Imogen blinked, puzzled by the question. Her mind raced. Was Manu thinking about escaping the village? The thought sent a chill down her spine. Losing him - her anchor in this chaos - was unthinkable. Despite her usual confidence in keeping secrets, the weight of this one unsettled her.

"Yeah," she replied.

Manu glanced around before leaning in, lowering his voice.

"Do you remember what happened with your elephant drawing?"

Imogen frowned, her confusion deepening.

"Of course. But that was nothing - just a coincidence."

"No," Manu said firmly, his gaze locking onto hers. "It meant something."

His intensity made her stomach flutter uncomfortably. She shifted under the weight of his stare, unable to decipher his thoughts.

"What's this about?" she asked.

"We're stuck here," Manu explained. "I need you to try something for us - something different. I want you to visualise and draw a path. Maybe it'll help us find our way out."

Imogen's heart skipped.

"You think I can… draw us a way out of here? I can't do that. I don't have supernatural powers."

"Actually, you might," Manu insisted, his voice steady. "Back on the bus, when you drew the elephant. That wasn't random, Imogen. You have a gift - you just need to trust it."

Imogen let out a soft, incredulous laugh. She was skilled at letting her subconscious guide her art, but this? Drawing the future? It sounded impossible.

"I can try," she said hesitantly. "But… why keep this secret?"

Manu exhaled, his shoulders relaxing slightly.

"I don't want the others to ridicule us - or distract you. This is important. We need to find a way home."

Imogen studied him, realizing his concern wasn't for himself. Like her father, Manu wanted to shield her from mockery, especially from Olivia and Susan, whose sharp words could cut deeper than any blade.

Her father's voice echoed in her mind, a memory so vivid it felt like he was standing beside her:

"The power of words surpasses that of any weapon. Be mindful of what you share and with whom. Words can wound just as easily as they can heal - choose yours carefully."

The memory of his advice brought a lump to her throat. She hadn't seen him in what felt like a lifetime, and the ache of missing him suddenly overwhelmed her.

Manu noticed the tears welling in her eyes.

"Are you alright?" he asked.

Imogen covered her face, her voice trembling as she tried to compose herself.

"I miss my dad. I miss my family. I miss my h - "

Her voice broke, and she let the sobs escape. Without hesitation, Manu pulled her into his arms, holding her tightly.

"We'll find our way," he said softly. "I promise. You're not alone in this."

His presence quickly grounded her. She gently pulled back, wiped her cheeks with the back of her hand, and offered him a watery but tender smile.

"I'm alright. Thank you."

Manu smiled back warmly, then added:

"We'll get out of here. I promise. Oh, and by the way, the guards loved your artwork - absolutely loved it. They even want more. I told them you could draw all kinds of things, but not for free. This is business, after all."

Imogen's eyebrows shot up, caught off guard.

"You said that?"

"Of course," Manu replied with a casual shrug. "They asked how much your drawings cost, so I told them I'd check with the artist and get back to them."

Imogen felt a mix of emotions - a flicker of pride followed quickly by unease. While it was thrilling to hear her work was appreciated, the thought of charging for it, of turning her art into a transaction, made her stomach twist.

"My drawings aren't that great," she muttered, nervously twisting her fingers. "There are way better artists out there, and honestly, I'm not comfortable running a business."

Manu stood silently, his smile soft but knowing, waiting for her to run out of excuses.

"What if they don't like what I make next?" Imogen blurted, the words spilling out in a rush. "Or what if they refuse to pay? I wouldn't even know what to charge. And who's going to buy my drawings anyway?"

Manu couldn't hold back anymore. He burst into laughter, the sound warm and infectious.

"Imogen," he said, still grinning, "I'm trying to help you earn some extra Lapes doing something you love and are amazing at. Don't you want to break free from this place?"

She hesitated, chewing on her lip.

"Yeah, but…"

"But?" Manu tilted his head, waiting.

Imogen struggled to find the words. Creating art was her passion, her sanctuary. The idea of putting a price tag on it felt wrong - alien. Like many artists, she was her own worst critic, convinced her work wasn't good enough to be worth money.

Finally, she let out a small sigh.

"What if you handle the selling, and we split the profit?"

Manu's grin widened instantly.

"Deal."

He extended his hand, and she took it, his firm handshake sealing the agreement.

"Now," he said with a wink, "all you need to do is keep being brilliant. I'll take care of the rest."

Manu had a knack for spotting value where others saw none - a talent that hinted at the makings of a great salesperson. He'd seen enough of Imogen's drawings to appreciate the effort and creativity she poured into each one. Confident in her talent, he asked her to create two pieces for Lightning and Muscalo, promising to get good prices for them.

"Do you have many blank pages left in your notebook?" he asked thoughtfully. "Paper's not exactly something we can find lying around here."

"About twenty," Imogen replied.

"We'll need to ask the others if they're willing to hand over their notebooks. But don't tell them why - they might change their minds if they find out what you're using them for."

"I don't mind paying for them," Imogen said. "Our dollars are worth less here than the leaves we use for toilet paper."

Manu grinned at her bluntness.

"Save your money - it'll come in handy soon," he said, his tone carrying a glimmer of hope.

Without hesitation, Imogen set about gathering unused notebooks from her peers. By the end of their lunch break, she had collected a small stack.

At the end of their workday, she waited patiently outside the factory for Manu, eager to update him.

"Most of them couldn't believe they'd bothered hauling their soaked notebooks all this time," she said, smiling. "They asked why I wanted them, so I just told the truth - that I'll run out of paper if I keep drawing."

"Perfect!" Manu said with a wide grin. "My mum always used to say, 'One person's trash is another person's treasure.' That's never been truer. These sheets are worth a mini fortune now. No one else has paper here, so your drawings are about to become priceless. How many pages do you think you have in total?"

"Each notebook has about 120 pages," Imogen said, though she wasn't sure why that detail mattered.

"Wow! That means you've got over 840 pages!" Manu's eyes gleamed with excitement. "We should stash these away. If we create a sense of scarcity, the value of your drawings will skyrocket."

"Scarcity? What kind of city?" Imogen asked, confused.

Manu chuckled. "Not a city - scarcity. It means shortage. Like those supersport cars they only make a handful of, so they're rare and exclusive. Because of that, manufacturers can charge a fortune. We'll do the same. Only five drawings for sale at a time."

"But I can easily make ten or twenty drawings a day," Imogen said proudly, missing his point.

"It's not about how fast you can draw," Manu explained, his tone patient. "It's about making each one valuable. If there are fewer available, the Voivokis will want them more - and we can charge more."

"So, we start tomorrow?" Imogen asked.

"Are you busy?" Manu replied with a playful smile.

"No," she said, her voice tinged with a hint of sadness. "It's not like there's much to do for fun around here."

"Then why procrastinate? Why not start today? Remember, I've probably already got two buyers lined up."

Manu offered a fist bump and joined Roger and Joe, who were impatiently waiting for him a stone's throw away to talk to the Guest House keepers.

Imogen stood still, staring after him with a puzzled expression.

"Procrastinate?" she murmured to herself. "What does that even mean?"

Shaking her head with a small smile, she headed towards the restaurant, her mind buzzing with a mix of curiosity and excitement.

Near the Guest House, Roger called the keepers over.

"I've been thinking about how much you hate your job," he began, his tone casual but direct. "We feel the same about ours. Would you be open to swapping?"

The keepers blinked in surprise, exchanging glances. For years, they had maintained the Guest House to perfection. But with low occupancy, most of their days were spent in monotony, waiting for something - anything - to break the routine. The idea of a change sparked their interest, at least until Joe brought up the training.

"Four weeks? Are you serious?" one of the keepers asked, his smile faltering, enthusiasm fading.

Joe had unintentionally struck a nerve. Oblivious to the reaction, he pressed on.

"Yeah, and - "

Before he could say another word, Manu cut him off.

"Well, that might not even be the case."

Inside, Manu was fuming, itching to tape Joe's mouth shut. But he knew he had to stay composed to avoid losing the keepers' interest entirely. Forcing a calm tone, he continued:

"You've been here a long time. Maybe Bill will make an exception. We can't predict what he'll say. Best to just talk to him and see what he thinks. No harm in asking, right?"

The keepers hesitated. Though senior in age, they feared Bill just like the kids. The allure of the new job lost its shine. Sensing their unease, Manu offered to speak to him and get back to them with his response.

As soon as the darkness of the night concealed the boys from view, Manu spun around and grabbed Joe's arm, nearly yanking him off balance. Joe froze, his eyes meeting Manu's, wide with alarm.

"What were you thinking?" Manu hissed, his voice low and sharp. "You almost killed the deal by saying too much! If they knew for sure they wouldn't get paid for four weeks and had to cover the course fee themselves, they'd have shut us down on the spot."

Joe's face turned red. He opened his mouth to respond but quickly shut it, knowing there was no defence. He wasn't used to high-stakes conversations - years spent gaming had left him adept at strategy but clueless about delicate social manoeuvres.

"Next time," Manu continued, his tone like ice, "you keep quiet and leave the talking to Roger and me. Got it?"

Joe nodded quickly, mumbling an apology. But he didn't fully grasp the weight of his mistake, even as guilt gnawed at him.

Manu turned to Roger, who had been silent during the exchange. "You need to talk to Bill right away," Manu said firmly. "We can't count on the keepers staying quiet about this for long. If word gets out, we could lose this opportunity."

Roger nodded, his jaw tight.

"I'll take care of it."

With that, Manu stormed off, his thoughts a whirlwind of contingency plans and frustration.

✿ ✿ ✿

At the restaurant, Leila stood in line, patiently waiting for her meal. She glanced over and noticed Sina walking away, a dish in hand, instead of joining the others at the table.

"Where are you going?" Leila called out, curiosity tinged with concern.

"I'm going to share my dinner with Sika," Sina explained, casually.

"Sika?" Leila asked.

"Yeah, one of the old Vois," Sina replied. Her voice was steady, but there was heaviness in her tone. "She's older than Maria and unwell. She can barely work a couple of hours a day, hardly enough to pay her expenses. Bill wants to get rid of her."

"What?" Leila's voice rose in shock. "Where's she supposed to go if he kicks her out?"

"I don't know," Sina replied. "She can't survive in the Jungle on her own. I just… I have to help her."

"But what can you do?" Leila asked, her concern growing.

"I don't know yet," Sina said, swallowing hard. "In my culture, we look after our elders, no matter the sacrifice. The least I can do is share my dinner with her. She can only afford one meal a day with what little she has left. Once I pass my test, maybe I can do more. If she loses her hut, I might have to pay for it. I just… I can't stand by and watch her suffer. She reminds me of my grandmother."

Her voice trembled, and she blinked back tears, determined not to let her emotions take over. Before anyone could say more, she turned and carried her meal towards the outskirts of the village, where Sika's hut stood weathered and isolated.

The small structure leaned precariously, its roof patched with large leaves. Most villagers avoided Sika, leaving her to fade into obscurity, forgotten and ignored.

Sina's heart ached as she walked. In her culture, it was unthinkable to let an elder fend for themselves. The younger generation cared for the older, no matter the cost. But Sika had no family or close friends to turn to. She had grown up in a community, similar to Sina's, believing that when her time came, she'd be cared for just as she'd cared for others. She had never worried about saving for old age, trusting the cycle of support would continue.

But Bill's village was no place for such assumptions. Here, mistakes like hers - failing to save, trusting in the kindness of others - came back to haunt you. Now, with her health declining, Sika was trapped in a cruel reality, her past generosity rendered meaningless.

As Sina approached the hut, a chill ran down her spine. Bill was there. She could hear his distinct voice.

She froze, her breath catching in her throat. He stood just inside the doorway, his imposing figure casting a shadow across the dim interior. Was this it? Was he here to evict Sika?

Her stomach churned as she watched him step out, his expression cold and indifferent. Without a word, he crossed the dirt road towards another hut, his nose in the air as if the very ground he walked on was beneath him.

Sina's heart sank further. Is he targeting another elder? How many more will he throw out?

She wiped away a stray tear and squared her shoulders. Whatever Bill was doing, she couldn't let fear stop her now.

"Good evening, Sika," Sina said softly as she stepped inside, forcing a smile despite the anxiety twisting inside her. "I brought you dinner."

Sika looked up, startled but grateful.

"Oh dear, you shouldn't have," she said, her voice frail but warm. "When I was your age, I spent so much of my time helping others. And look at me now - an unwanted member of society, with nothing but the clothes on my back. I don't want you to end up like me."

Her words hit Sina like a blow, but she kept her expression gentle.

"You won't end up alone," she whispered to herself as much as to Sika. "Not while I'm here."

Suppressing her emotions with action, Sina quickly divided her meal and handed Sika half. They ate in silence, savouring each bite. Though still far from full, the persistent hunger in their stomachs subsided.

"I saw Bill visiting you earlier," Sina said, concerned. "What did he want?"

Sika's expression darkened, her frail hands trembling as she set down her makeshift leaf plate.

"He gave me four weeks to find another job," she said, her voice heavy with sorrow. "He claims he can't afford to keep paying me, even though my wages are low, barely covering my rent and a bit of breakfast. He offered to forgive my debt if I leave… but where would I go? I can't survive in the wilderness anymore. My only hope is that I'll find an opportunity with a merchant at the market he's opening here soon."

Sina's chest tightened.

"And if you can't find another job?"

Sika's sad smile was answer enough, tearing up Sina's eyes. Sika, frail and vulnerable, reminded her so much of her grandmother. The thought of this elderly, abandoned and helpless, facing such a cruel fate filled Sina with a crushing helplessness.

"Don't worry about the worst, my dear," Sika said gently, sensing Sina's pain. "Something will work out. I am hopeful and optimistic."

In an attempt to lift the mood, Sika began recounting tales of her carefree childhood - stories of laughter, warm homes, and simpler times. For a moment, the weight in Sina's heart lifted, replaced by the comforting warmth of Sika's memories. But as the tales ended, the grim reality crept back in.

Sina thanked Sika for the stories and excused herself, stepping out into the cool evening air. She wandered aimlessly, her thoughts racing, until she came to a fallen tree at the edge of the village. Sitting down, she stared into the dark Jungle, the distant sounds of nocturnal creatures blending with the faint hum of village chatter.

Her deepening thoughts were broken by a familiar voice.

"You seem quite troubled," Vaipor said softly, stepping out of the shadows and taking a seat beside her. "Is it about Sika?"

Sina looked up, forcing a weak smile.

"It is," she admitted.

Vaipor nodded knowingly.

"Unfortunately, her situation isn't unique."

Sina shook her head.

"I thought so. How many are like her - alone, vulnerable to illness, hunger, or worse?"

"There are many," Vaipor said gravely. "Here in Bill's village, there's one other elder – Broko - who's just as helpless. But outside of this village, among the Voivokis… the problem is far bigger."

"That's horrible!" Sina exclaimed, her voice shaking with anger. "Why don't the other Voivokis do something about it?"

Vaipor sighed.

"Some try, but there are too many in need, and resources are scarce. Your desire to help Sika is noble, Sina. But you must understand something - while your heart is large, your means are small. You can't save everyone, and trying to might destroy you."

"I don't care," Sina said, filled with defiance. "I can't just stand by and let her be thrown out like that! She has nowhere to go, no way to survive. She wouldn't last a day in the wild on her own."

Vaipor's expression softened, though his gaze remained steady.

"I know you feel that way now, but you're forgetting something important. You're trapped here too. You have no family nearby, no income yet, and even when you pass your test, your wages will barely sustain you. If you give everything you have to help others, what will you have left for yourself? And don't assume someone with a heart like yours will be there to save you when you're in her position."

Sina clenched her fists, her frustration bubbling over.

"So what? I'm supposed to do nothing? Watch her get thrown out, knowing she'll die alone in the Jungle?"

Her voice cracked.

"I didn't say that you shouldn't help the unfortunate, but consider this: what about Maria?" Vaipor replied. "She's getting old too, and her debts are suffocating her. One day, she'll be in the same position as Sika. And, like I said, it's not just them – there are many aging Voivokis here. It's an endless cycle, Sina. The circle of life. Some can't support themselves because of illness, old age, poor decisions, or trauma that altered their lives. Others may consume substances that take away their ability to think clearly. There will always be someone needing care."

"I get that," Sina said, her voice heavy. "But how can I simply ignore the fact that my friend is in desperate need and will probably die if no one helps her?"

"And what about your own family?" Vaipor countered. "Your grandma, your parents, uncles, aunties – maybe even your siblings or cousins? They probably miss you and need your help too. But first, you need to help yourself: you're trapped here, and it may take a long time to regain your freedom. If you start helping others, you could be stuck here forever and never see your family again. Your compassion for others, as noble as it is, could become your curse if it leads to your own downfall."

Vaipor's mention of her family struck a deep chord in Sina's heart.

"It's not fair," she said, her voice shaking. "Why did I end up here, torn apart from everyone I love? Even if we somehow regain our freedom, there's no guarantee we would make it home safely - we don't even know the way. And you..." her voice tightened. "You seem to know everything, but besides talking when it suits you, you don't actually help anyone."

"Sina!" Vaipor's voice cut through her frustration. "Don't let your emotions take control. You must focus on yourself and what's best for you. Life is a training ground, a series of challenges that teach you something new and help you grow. You have to consider what you can control and adjust your thoughts and actions accordingly. Yes, you have a sweet, caring heart, but you also need to protect yourself. If you don't, your kindness will be exploited, and you'll end up suffering even more."

"So what am I supposed to do now?" Sina asked, her frustration simmering. "Am I just supposed to abandon Sika and let nature consume her?"

"What about Broko?" Vaipor replied calmly. "Are you going to ignore him? How is that fair?"

Sina opened her mouth to protest but stopped, her thoughts tangled. Vaipor waited, letting the silence stretch before continuing with a curious analogy.

"Think about the monkeys of this Jungle," he said. "They forage daily, moving through the trees to find food. But, the elders and injured can't keep up. If you were their leader, how would you ensure they're fed?"

Sina hesitated, unsure. "I'd bring food back to them," she said finally.

Vaipor leaned forward, his gaze steady.

"And if you have to travel far to find that food? Who would protect your troop in your absence?"

Sina frowned.

"I'd take the troop with me."

Vaipor tilted his head.

"So you'd risk everyone's lives just to feed the elders? What if you're attacked along the way? Let's say you make it back to the elders - hungry yourself from the journey. Now you've fed them, but the rest of the troop is starving. When you return to where you found the food, it's nearly gone. So you have to travel even farther. What happens then?"

Sina's brows furrowed as the implications sank in.

"I see your point," she said with a quiet resignation. "At some point, I'd have to leave them behind… but how could I abandon another human being like that?"

"That's the challenge," Vaipor said gently. "You can't save everyone, Sina, but you can still make a difference without losing yourself in the process. Use your creativity. Think of a solution to ensure Sika will be cared for when you continue your journey. Once you have an idea, turn it into a plan - break it down into steps and work on it every day. Build something sustainable, not just for her, but for anyone in her position."

He rose to his feet and placed a hand lightly on her head. His touch was brief but carried a sense of reassurance.

"You have an extraordinary, loving heart," he continued, "but love alone isn't enough here. Stay alert, and your subconscious will show you the way if you let it."

"But how?" Sina asked, her mind churning.

Vaipor offered no answer. He was already walking away, his figure disappearing into the shadows of the trees. His words lingered in the air, like the faint echo of a distant call.

Sina sat motionless, caught between the warmth of his presence and the cold uncertainty of her situation. The conversation had been heavy, each question she posed met with a challenging truth or a cryptic reply. And yet, Vaipor's parting words carried a strange weight, resonating deeper than she expected.

"Your subconscious will show you the way."

The phrase looped in her mind, a quiet chant, a whisper she couldn't fully grasp but couldn't ignore.

"What does that even mean?" she muttered aloud, rising to her feet and pacing back and forth. Her frustration grew as she struggled to decipher the cryptic message. Was Vaipor referring to some hidden knowledge within her, a strength she hadn't tapped into yet? Or was it something else, something she hadn't considered?

For a moment, Sina's thoughts strayed to the concept of black magic. Was that what Vaipor meant? Something forbidden, shrouded in mystery, something she barely understood? Her parents had always warned her about the dangers of such dark forces, weaving cautionary tales of those who had been consumed by their temptations. But no. Sina quickly dismissed the thought. Vaipor wasn't like that. He wouldn't steer her towards something harmful, no matter how desperate her situation seemed.

She sighed, sinking onto the same fallen tree she had perched on earlier. Her fingers absentmindedly traced the grooves of the bark, as if seeking answers in its texture.

"Use your creativity," she recalled him saying. The corner of her lips curled into a faint, wry smile. Creativity? What did that have to do with survival? She wasn't an artist; she couldn't paint masterpieces or craft intricate designs. Drawing a straight line was challenge enough.

But maybe Vaipor wasn't speaking of creativity in the traditional sense. Perhaps he meant ingenuity, the ability to think differently and find solutions in unexpected places. Her mind shifted, considering the possibility. Could she find a way to help Sika, not by making something beautiful, but by crafting something practical - a plan, a strategy? The thought made more sense the longer she mulled it over.

Her heart stirred with a quiet resolve. She didn't have all the answers, not yet, but maybe that was okay. The path wasn't clear, but Vaipor's words echoed in her mind:

"Your sub-conscious will show you the way."

Ideas began to form in the edges of her thoughts. Could she find someone in the village to help care for Sika in her absence? Perhaps there were others who could share the burden. Resources were scarce, and everyone here faced their own struggles, but there had to be a way. She would start exploring tomorrow.

For now, she allowed herself to savour the fleeting calm. She didn't notice the storm clouds gathering above, concealed by the dark sky, until the first cold droplets hit her skin. The rain came suddenly, a downpour soaking her to the bone.

Sina ran through the village, her wet clothes heavy and clinging to her as the rain poured down. But even as she raced for shelter, her mind churned with questions and half-formed solutions. Vaipor had left her with more ambiguity than clarity, but perhaps that was the point.

When she finally reached her hut, she found Mai waiting at the entrance, eyes wide with concern.

"Where have you been?" Mai asked.

"I had dinner with Sika," Sina said, breathless. "Afterwards, I wanted some me-time. Vaipor showed up while I was sitting on a log. He said some… very interesting things."

They settled on the smooth bamboo floor, huddling together as the rain drummed against the roof. Sina recounted her conversation with Vaipor, and they both tried to unravel the meaning behind his cryptic words.

"I wish I could have an encounter with him too," Mai said wistfully. "I'd ask him straight up to take us home. He seems to know everything, so why doesn't he just show us the way?"

"Trust me, I asked him the same thing," Sina replied, a faint smile tugging at her lips.

"And?" Mai asked.

"No chance. He just went on and on about life being a training ground, making us stronger," Sina replied, shaking her head.

They sat in contemplative silence, the rhythmic patter of rain and the distant croak of frogs creating a strange sense of comfort.

However, just as they began to lose themselves in the peaceful sounds of the night, Bill's harsh voice broke the stillness.

"What do you want again?"

The comfort shattered, leaving Sina and Mai tense. They exchanged a glance, the weight of the moment settling over them like the storm clouds above.

CHAPTER 4

"I should check on them," thought Manu, pacing restlessly besides his hammock.

During dinner with Lightning and Muscalo, he had fully expected Joe and Roger to turn up, grinning ear to ear – a clear sign that their conversation with Bill had gone well. But the boys were nowhere to be seen.

After the modest meal with the guards, he had followed the trail back from their outpost – a simple setup of a fireplace and a shelter – convinced the boys would meet him at the hammocks to share the good news, safely out of the guards' earshot. Yet, when he arrived, there was no sign of them. Anxiety gnawed at him, making him wonder if something had gone wrong. Grabbing an umbrella, he decided to head to the restaurant.

As he crossed the plantation, the low, steady murmur of the workers grew louder, the distinct voices becoming clearer. Then, a familiar sound reached his ears.

"That's Roger's voice," Manu realised, surprised.

He had expected to meet him at the hammocks, but there he was, mingling with others, seemingly at ease. As Manu approached, Roger's laughter died, his smile faltering.

"How did it go?" Manu asked, his voice serious.

Roger's face grew red.

"We haven't spoken to him yet," he admitted, looking down, clearly embarrassed.

Manu turned away, taking a deep breath to steady himself, biting back the frustration threatening to spill out.

"What are you waiting for?" he asked, his tone sharp with disappointment. "The longer you procrastinate, the harder it'll be to find the courage."

Manu's father wasn't wealthy, but he had a sharp mind for business. One lesson he'd drilled into his son was simple but powerful: procrastination is a barrier to success.

"Excuses will keep you from reaching your goals," his dad often said. "Get comfortable with being uncomfortable. That's the path forward."

From a young age, Manu embraced that philosophy. When something needed to be done, he did it. When a conversation had to be had, he had it. Excuses were something Manu couldn't tolerate - not in himself, and especially not in others. So when Roger and Joe hesitated to approach Bill, Manu didn't give them the luxury of indecision. He pushed them, relentless, until they were left with no choice but to face the daunting task.

They approached Bill's office, the door ajar, light spilling into the open. Roger hesitated, hand raised to knock, but just as quickly, Joe buckled under the pressure and took a few steps back.

Before Roger could even react, Bill's irritated voice cut through the moment.

"What do you want again?"

The door swung open, and there Bill stood, his annoyance evident.

Seeing Joe frozen in place, Manu didn't wait. He stepped forward, pulling Roger with him, and went straight to the point.

"We want to swap with the two Guest House keepers," Manu stated firmly, leaving no room for ambiguity.

Bill raised an eyebrow, settling back into his chair behind his desk. His sceptical gaze lingered on them, sizing them up.

"Why would you want to do that? You should be grateful for the factory position I gave you. Once you pass your test, you'll be earning far more than you would as a keeper. Why give that up for a job with less pay?"

Roger shifted uneasily, but answered without hesitation.

"It's tough being stuck in one spot all day. We'd rather be doing something more active."

Bill leaned back, his fingers joined as he considered the proposal. The boys braced themselves for the next twist.

"Then why not join my guard squad? One of them's leaving next week. I need someone reliable, someone I can trust," Bill offered casually, but his eyes studied them, measuring their reactions.

The offer hit like a bolt from the blue. The boys exchanged startled glances, processing the new possibility. Becoming guards was a major step, one that brought new opportunities - and new challenges. Would they be allowed to gather Mapa seeds in their spare time, or would they be under constant surveillance? What about the dangers of the wild, or the new responsibilities of catching escapees?

Their thoughts flashed to Asim. Would they be forced to track down people trying to escape Bill's clutches, a task that weighed on their consciences?

Roger nodded subtly, signalling to Manu to take the lead, but Manu wasn't ready. He needed time to weigh the consequences.

"That sounds interesting," Manu said slowly, his voice measured, "but we'd like to think it over first. Can we get back to you tomorrow?"

Bill's expression softened, as if relieved by the non-committal response.

"That's fine," he said. "Come see me tomorrow."

Aware of how difficult it is to find reliable workers, Bill seemed happy by the possibility of an 'in-house' replacement, bringing him some peace of mind.

"What about the Guest House swap?" Manu asked, stirring the conversation back to their original request.

Bill leaned back, rubbing his chin thoughtfully.

"I'm fine with any of you swapping with the Guest House keepers," he said, sparking a surge of joy in the boys. "They've been quite negative lately, and I can't afford cranky people looking after my wealthy guests. It affects my business. The keepers will have to go through the same training you're doing and pass their tests. Anyone replacing them will need to complete the three-day Guest House training as well. As for the guard position - I'll need an answer by tomorrow after work."

Rising to his feet, Bill moved towards the door, a clear signal that their time was up. While the training requirement was a minor setback, the boys couldn't help but feel elated. They had secured what they had hoped for.

Grins spread across their faces as they thanked Bill and made their way out of the office. The moment Joe saw their expressions, he knew the meeting had gone well.

"So, one of you can become a guard, and the other can work at the Guest House?" Joe asked, trying to piece together what had happened.

"Not exactly," Roger corrected, his smile broadening. "Bill said 'any of you,' meaning anyone in our group can swap. At least, that's how I understood it."

He turned to Manu, his voice lighter.

"You should take the guard position. You're faster and stronger than I am, and you already have connections with the guard squad."

Manu shook his head.

"No, I can't. I've already made a deal with Imogen," he said. "You should take the guard position, Roger. You're the better fit. Joe and one of the girls can handle the Guest House job."

Roger hesitated. At first, the thought of joining the guards didn't sit well with him. The squad was cold, isolated, and ruthless. The idea of being associated with them, tasked with enforcing Bill's control over their fellow Voivokis, unsettled him. But Manu, always seeing the bigger picture, offered a different perspective.

"As a guard," Manu explained, "you'll have access to places others can't reach, more freedom to move around the village, and a chance to build a better relationship with Bill. You could even earn privileges we won't get in our current positions."

Roger mulled it over, the idea gradually taking root. The potential to trade favours with Bill or other guards was appealing. While it still wasn't his ideal role, the opportunity to improve their situation and help the group as a whole outweighed his discomfort.

"Which one of the girls should join us?" Roger asked, turning the conversation to their next challenge.

Joe groaned.

"Susan and Oli are definitely out. I can't handle being around them for twelve hours a day."

"Imogen's out too," Manu added, nodding.

Roger shot Manu a teasing look.

"Are you ever going to tell us what's really going on between you two?"

"She draws, I sell. Simple as that," Manu replied, expressionless.

"Right, of course," Roger laughed, rolling his eyes. "Why didn't I think of that?"

Manu smirked, then turned to Joe.

"So, Mai?"

Joe's expression soured.

"No way. She's as dull as a rock."

"Perfect match, then," Manu quipped. "You can talk about your video games all day, and she'll never interrupt."

Both Manu and Roger burst into laughter.

Taking a more serious tone, the boys agreed that separating Imogen and Leila wouldn't be good for Leila, leaving Sina as the best candidate.

"Sina's cool," Joe said thoughtfully, nodding. "I wouldn't mind it. Plus, she's probably the fastest weaver out of all of us."

Roger raised an eyebrow.

"We still have one more problem," he said. "The Guest House keepers need to go through four weeks of training."

"Bugger!" Manu exclaimed, slapping his forehead. "I almost forgot about that."

The three of them fell into a heavy silence, each deep in thought, trying to figure out how to overcome this expected obstacle. Unsurprisingly, it was Manu who came up with a few ideas.

"I see three options," Manu began, counting them off on his fingers. "First: we ask Bill to allow them to take the test after three days. If they pass, great. If not, they can retake it every three days until they do. That way, they won't waste a full four weeks."

Joe and Roger nodded, following his reasoning.

"Second option," Manu continued, "we ask Bill to waive their training fees, arguing that they've been working for him for a long time. But even then, the Guest House keepers wouldn't earn anything for those four weeks, so we'd likely need to pay them ourselves to make it worthwhile."

Roger scratched his chin thoughtfully, weighing the idea.

"And finally," Manu raised his third finger, "if neither of those work, we ask Bill for a 50% discount on their fees. Worst case, we cover both their course and wages, though it'll be tough without an income of our own."

Joe's eyes widened with optimism.

"Sina and I will get paid from the fourth day, remember?"

"True," Manu conceded, nodding.

"And guess what?" Roger grinned, his face also lighting up with excitement. He paused for effect, enjoying the moment.

"What?" Manu and Joe asked in unison.

"No training for the guards!" Roger announced, breaking into an impromptu celebratory dance, cracking up the others. "I'll start making money in just a couple of days!"

"That will definitely help us," Manu said, grinning.

Roger, still beaming, stopped his dance and turned to Manu.

"You could submit whatever Joe and Sina produce through Maria. We might have to share some of the income with her, but it's worth considering."

Manu's eyes narrowed thoughtfully.

"Yeah... that could work."

As Manu and Roger revelled in their enthusiasm, Joe's mind shifted to more practical concerns. He started mentally crunching the numbers, calculating their anticipated financial standing over the coming weeks. The lively conversation faded into the background as his focus intensified on the logistics of their situation.

"It wouldn't make sense," he said finally, his eyes wide with the weight of his conclusion. "We don't know how much debt Sina has, but based on my rough estimates, we wouldn't be able to wipe out our debts with Bill before Manu's test. Sharing our income with Maria wouldn't work for us."

Manu shrugged, unfazed.

"Then we stick to the original plan - keep whatever we produce hidden."

Reaching their hammocks, their minds were spinning with possibilities, but before long, the fatigue of the day caught up with them, and they were ready to call it a night.

The next morning, before dawn broke over the canopy, Imogen was already up, absorbed in her drawings. By the time the first rays of sunlight peeked through the trees, she had completed a couple of striking pieces. Eager yet anxious, she paced the village, clutching her notebook, anticipating Manu's reaction.

When she finally spotted him in the distance, her excitement couldn't be contained. She rushed to meet him, her face glowing with pride.

"I can definitely sell these," Manu said, inspecting the work. He was genuinely impressed.

Imogen's smile wavered slightly, her eyes searching his face.

"Don't you feel bad taking their money, knowing it only pushes them further from their freedom?"

Manu hesitated, his gaze flickering for a moment before settling on her. He understood the sentiment, but the pragmatic part of him knew that sometimes, survival came first.

"Not at all," Manu replied confidently. "First of all, I'll make sure they understand these drawings are investments. With only a few pages available, the scarcity alone will drive up their value. One day, they'll be able to sell your work to a wealthy Voi passing through. From that perspective, it's not just a purchase - it's an investment for them.

Secondly, these guys are going to spend their Lapes anyway. If it's not with us, it'll be on something else - probably food or drinks at the restaurant. They're content with the simplicity of their routine and the security of knowing exactly where their next Lape is coming from. They're not interested in the challenges of building wealth or the risks of living off the land. For them, it's easier to show up, earn a few Lapes, and spend a chunk of it right away."

He leaned in slightly, his tone laced with a mix of amusement and disdain.

"Honestly, Voivokis like them don't even mind being financially trapped. They work for Bill, get paid by Bill, and end up giving most of it back to him for food and lodging. Bill's got the whole system rigged perfectly for himself, which makes me wonder why he's always so grumpy."

Imogen chuckled at his candid observation.

"Alright, alright, no need to hype yourself up. Let's focus on getting to the factory before we're late."

The day at the factory dragged on, each moment blending into the next in an unbroken loop of monotony. The repetitive tasks dulled their senses, leaving Manu and Joe restless. Their thoughts kept circling back to the deal with the Guest House keepers. What if they back out? What if it doesn't work? The questions tormented them, feeding their impatience and a simmering desire for something more than this relentless grind.

Finally, the sharp, rhythmic drumming signalled the end of their shift, snapping them out of their daze. The boys wasted no time pulling Sina aside, eager to present their business proposal.

Sina was caught off guard. Why had they chosen her? Was there some hidden motive? Memories of being used or taken advantage of by her classmates flooded back, and her guard went up instinctively. While the prospect of a more versatile job intrigued her, the idea of spending twelve hours a day working alongside Joe - someone she struggled to connect with - gave her pause.

Her thoughts whirled, uncertain and conflicted.

"I'll need some time to think about it," she responded. "I'll let you know after dinner."

Sticking to her new routine, she grabbed an extra portion of food for Sika. As she approached Sika's hut, an unfamiliar voice floated out, halting her in her tracks. She waited, listening for a natural pause in the conversation before stepping inside.

"Excuse me, Sika. I brought you dinner," she said softly as she entered.

Sika greeted her with a warm smile and gestured towards her guest, an older Voivoki sitting cross-legged on the bamboo floor.

"This is Broko," Sika introduced.

Broko's face bore the heavy lines of hardship, his sunken eyes reflecting years of sorrow and defeat. Like Sika, he had been cast aside by fate, left with no money, no job, and no hope in Bill's village.

Sina sat down beside them, crossing her legs as she divided the meagre meal she had brought. Though it was barely enough for two, she didn't hesitate to share with Broko. The grateful elders ate slowly, savouring each bite as if it were a rare luxury. Their gratitude was palpable, but it only deepened the ache in Sina's chest.

The elders' conversation was steeped in resignation, their words heavy with despair. They spoke of debts that could never be repaid and futures that seemed to shrink with each passing day. Their days in the village were numbered, and they knew it.

Sina's thoughts wandered, Vaipor's cryptic words echoing once more:

"Your subconscious will show you the way."

And then, in an instant, everything fell into place. The meaning of his message hit her like a bolt of lightning, flooding her with a surge of clarity and elation.

"I've got it!" she thought, her heart pounding with excitement.

Without a second thought, she leapt to her feet, murmured a quick excuse, and took off towards the restaurant. Her pulse thundered in her ears, each beat driving her forward. The world around her dissolved into a blur of shapes and colours, her focus consumed entirely by the thrill of her revelation.

"Is everything okay?" Olivia asked, stopping her mid-stride.

"Yeah, why?" Sina asked, her confusion growing as she sensed the negativity behind her words.

"It's just… we've never seen you run before, and we thought your type never runs," Olivia sneered, dripping with mockery.

Although Olivia's jab could have stung, Sina's pure and kind nature won out. She chose not to dwell on the insult and hurried on her way, seemingly unaffected. Yet Olivia's comment left a shadow of doubt in her mind, planting seeds of insecurity.

All day, Sina had waited for a sign from her subconscious, and when she finally understood Vaipor's words, a surge of hope had flooded her. The boys' offer now seemed like a golden opportunity – a chance to break free from her current struggles, not just for herself but for Sika and Broko too. The thought of increasing her earnings and securing a future for them filled her with excitement.

But her brief encounter with Olivia and Susan, though only lasted seconds, started to affect her enthusiasm. Could she really make enough to save them? A week's worth of earnings wouldn't be enough. Even saving for a month seemed insignificant. But what about a year? A whole year? She wasn't ready to stay away from her family for that long. But even a whole year's worth of savings could be negligible if they ran through it too quickly? Could they manage their expenses, prioritise what mattered? Decades of grinding didn't seem to teach them. And there are the other Voivokis too. What if someone found out about their money and took it all?

Luckily, as soon as she spotted the boys, her worries melted away. Her enthusiasm shone as she approached them, a broad smile lighting up her face. With renewed confidence, she accepted their offer.

Relieved, Roger and Joe eagerly shared the full extent of their plan, pride swelling in their voices as they recounted their success in negotiating a discount for the Guest House keepers' training fees. Their excitement was undeniable - until Manu arrived.

"Wait, so Bill only gave them a 20% discount?" Manu asked, clearly unimpressed. "That's still going to cost us 2,528 Lapes."

"Yup. We tried our best," Roger replied.

"Then you have to improve your best," Manu snapped and stormed off.

Joe and Roger exchanged bewildered glances. They couldn't comprehend why Manu was so upset. Negotiating with Bill was no small feat, and to them, securing any kind of discount felt like a victory.

Seeing their disappointment, Sina stepped in to lift their spirits.

"Honestly, I wouldn't have had the courage to negotiate anything with Bill," she admitted. "You two did really well! Besides, what does it matter whether the discount is 20% or 50%? We'll manage to cover their training fees, especially if we work a little faster."

***

As the sun set, casting a breathtaking golden glow across the village, Imogen was captivated by the scene. She rushed to her usual spot, eager to capture the beauty in her notebook. Armed with only a graphite pencil, she took on the challenge, her talent once again shining through as she rendered the sunset in stunning detail.

Always up to something, running from one group to another, engaging with everyone along, Manu paid her a visit.

"How did it go?" Imogen asked, amused by Manu's restless energy.

"450 Lapes each, for a total of 900," Manu said, grinning.

"What?!" Imogen gasped in disbelief.

She leaped up and hugged him, her gratitude spilling out in an uncharacteristic display of emotion. Earning money from her art had been beyond her wildest dreams, marking a monumental moment in her life. For years, she had created her drawings without ever imagining they could be sold, always assuming she wasn't good enough.

"Why didn't my parents ever tell me that I could sell my drawings and earn some pocket money?" she wondered, reflecting on her childhood.

Though her parents had always been loving and supportive, they lacked an entrepreneurial mindset. It dawned on her that, in some strange way, being stuck in the Jungle with Manu had been a blessing in disguise. He had opened her eyes to the opportunities her talent could bring. Earning 450 Lapes for something she loved doing felt like a fairytale come true.

For Manu, though, it was just another deal. While he too was excited about the quick profit - over two and a half days' worth of factory wages – his mind was already on the bigger picture. He recognised that selling Imogen's drawings in Bill's village had its limitations, given the small number of Voivokis with savings. To access a larger community and expand their business, they needed to find a way out of Bill's village – a challenge he was determined to tackle.

"Don't forget to put aside your taxes for the Vilais," he reminded her, a hint of sadness creeping into his voice.

"What do you mean?" Imogen asked, puzzled.

"Remember our terrifying run-in with the Vilais and Vaipor's story?" Manu asked.

He briefly scanned the surrounding mountains as if looking for Vilais to show up before continuing:

"I don't fully understand how things work here, but apparently, Bill is handing over a third of everyone's wages to the Vilais. We haven't seen them around, but it doesn't mean they won't come. I assume it's like at my mum's company: they withhold her taxes and send them to the government. She doesn't need to worry about it. The money we got today had nothing to do with Bill, so to be safe, I think we should leave a third of it near our shelter for the Vilais. If they never show up, maybe we'll get to keep it."

"I don't want anything to do with them," Imogen said, hoping Manu would be willing to take care of their tax matters. "Can I leave it in your capable hands?"

Manu thought for a moment.

"No worries," he said. "By the way, have you thought of a name for our promising business?"

Imogen's face lit up. Naming their venture made it feel real, like the start of something big – something she never imagined she'd be part of. Owning a business? It felt surreal, but also empowering.

"How about Imoart?" Manu suggested.

Imogen beamed, her excitement bubbling over.

"I love it!" she exclaimed, instantly embracing the name that now seemed to define not just their business, but a new chapter in her life.

"From now on, you're the big boss of Imoart!" Manu declared with a playful grin.

"Yeah, the big boss of nobody except my pencils," Imogen laughed.

Manu pointed at the sunset drawing she was working on.

"Are you drawing this for anyone in particular?"

"No, I just wanted to capture this beautiful sunset. But then you showed up, and it's slipping away."

Manu smiled awkwardly, a slight blush warming his cheeks – something rare for him.

"Make it as detailed as possible," he said. "Oh, and one last question: how are you with portraits?"

"I haven't done many, but I feel I'm decent enough," Imogen replied, intrigued.

"Great. I'm going to convince Bill he needs a portrait of himself," Manu said with a mischievous grin. "And I want one of Susan too. But don't tell her what it's for. How long do you think you'll need to finish this one?"

"About half an hour, unless you keep talking."

Manu's smile widened as he quietly settled onto a nearby rock, watching Imogen bringing the sunset to life on the page.

✿ ✿ ✿

Back at the village, Olivia and Susan enjoyed the warmth of a flickering campfire, watching the flames dance as they waited for time to pass. In the City, their evenings were filled with exciting events, leaving them longing for more time. But in the Jungle, their entertainment was simply spending time together. They used to talk about fancy fashion and luxury holidays, sharing thrilling stories of their privileged lives. However, after spending two weeks in the Jungle, their perspectives began to shift. Instead of discussing superficial things, they opened up about their feelings of being trapped and the difficulties they faced.

"I am certain my dad's deployed a search crew by now," Susan said with a hopeful gleam in her eyes. "We have a helicopter that could fly us home."

Susan's assumption was likely correct, although she was unaware of the challenges that such an expedition would present. The location of the tribe they intended to visit was well documented but that's not where they were. The dense vegetation and thick canopy of trees obstructed visibility from the air, making it difficult to spot individuals on the ground unless they were in clearings, such as Bill's village. However, such villages were often hidden in the valleys and could only be seen from the sky directly above it.

Advanced technologies and search strategies allowed search crews to divide the area into grids and systematically cover each one, but even with these methods, the search could take a long time, and hope for finding survivors waned with each passing day.

The possibility of failed search mission didn't cross the girls' minds. As the fire crackled, they envisioned the moment Susan's dad's helicopter would swoop in to rescue them.

"It can carry eight people, including two pilots," Susan said thoughtfully. "Who would we take?"

"Well, there are only nine of us," Olivia pointed out. "Josh is gone, Asim is locked up. We could take Roger, Manu, Imogen and Leila."

"I would rather take Sina than Leila," Susan replied quickly. "I don't want Leila freaking out mid-flight. She can deal with her problems on her own when she sees us leaving. As for Manu… I'm not sure about him either. He's been quite bossy lately, and I still haven't forgiven him for embarrassing us after the market. Gee, I can't believe it's already been a week."

❧ ❧ ❧

Meanwhile, up on the mountain, Imogen shifted her eyes from her notebook to Manu.

"Done," she said, her voice tired but satisfied.

She had poured every ounce of her energy into the sunset drawing, adding as much detail as possible with the limited tools she had. The result was mesmerising – even Imogen felt proud of it. For a moment, she was tempted to keep it, imagining the day she might show it to her parents. But memories of their difficult journey, especially the gruelling days before they stumbled upon Bill's village, reminded her that keeping the drawing safe from the elements was nearly impossible.

"What are you planning to do with it?" she asked as she tore the page from her notebook.

She carefully folded the jagged edge of the paper, running her fingernail along the crease to create a sharp fold, and then tore away the unwanted edge, leaving a clean, straight line.

"I am planning to give it to Bill for free," Manu said casually.

Imogen's eyes widened in disbelief. Why would Manu offer her artwork to Bill without asking for anything in return? Her hands trembled slightly as she stammered, struggling to express her confusion. The idea of giving away something she had poured her heart into for free felt both shocking and disappointing.

Seeing her reaction, Manu quickly explained:

"Roger, Joe and I struck a deal with the Guest House keepers and Bill. Joe and Sina will swap places with the keepers. We were hoping Bill would either waive the keepers' training or at least give them a significant discount. But Roger and Joe only managed to negotiate a 20% discount. Even with that, the fees are still 2,528 Lapes. I'm hoping to use your beautiful sunset drawing to cover the training fees."

He paused before adding:

"What I am offering to you is this: you keep the 900 Lapes we earned today, and in exchange, you let me have this drawing. I'll use it to try and settle the fees with Bill. From your perspective, it's like I sold the drawing for 900 Lapes."

Imogen considered his words.

"I'm okay with that, but how does that benefit you? If you succeed, you'd be saving on the training fees, but isn't that split among the four of you?"

"Exactly. It would be 790 Lapes each," Manu replied. "So if I succeed, it's like I'm getting 790 Lapes for your first three drawings. Plus, since Bill wouldn't pay us in cash, we wouldn't have to hand over a third of it to the Vilais."

Imogen frowned, still puzzled.

"You totally lost me. Why wouldn't you have to give any of it to the Vilais?"

"It's simple," Manu said, slightly opening his hands. "If Bill waives the training fees instead of paying us directly, no money changes hands. That means there's no income to tax. If he paid us, say 3,160 Lapes for the drawing, we'd owe the Vilais 948 Lapes in taxes, which would leave us short in covering the fees. But if we skip the payment and use the waived fees to settle with Bill, we avoid the taxes entirely."

"And if you don't succeed?" Imogen asked, concerned. "Do we go back to splitting profits 50-50 after each sale?"

"No," Manu replied firmly. "That's a risk I have to bear. You'll still get your 900 Lapes, regardless. If this plan fails, I'll hold onto your sunset drawing and eventually find another buyer."

Imogen smiled. Though she didn't understand Manu's explanation about the taxes, she trusted him. Besides, from her perspective there was nothing to lose: she received more money for her first three drawings then she ever imagined.

"I hope it works out," she said. "Sounds like a massive gift for Roger, Joe and Sina."

"You're spot on. It's like giving them 790 Lapes each," Manu agreed. "But I am happy with that because working as a team will benefit all of us in the long run."

Manu snapped his head towards the village.

"Come on, we got to go before it gets dark," he urged.

He quickly led Imogen back to her hut, reminding her to leave a third of her Lapes by the entrance, before racing towards Bill's office. Just as he reached out to knock, the door swung open. Surprised, he blinked rapidly, needing a second to gather himself.

"What do you think of this?" he asked, holding up the sunset drawing.

Bill took the art, his eyes narrowing with curiosity as his fingers traced the unfamiliar texture. The paper felt strange to him – thin yet firm – and the pencil marks looked like nothing he had seen growing up in the Jungle. He turned it over, puzzled.

"It's from the City," Manu explained, catching Bill's bewilderment. "It's called paper. And this" – he tapped the dark lines – "was made with a piece of hollow timber, filled with graphite. We call it pencil. It's non-existent here. Incredibly valuable."

Manu grinned, sensing Bill's intrigue.

"You won't find anything like it in the Jungle. The material's expensive, and this drawing? It's the work of a true artist. The subtle shading gives the drawing depth and dimension, capturing one of the most striking villages in the Jungle. This is one-of-a-kind piece."

Bill stared at the drawing, still trying to wrap his head around the foreign material in his hands. Manu, reading Bill's body language, knew he had piqued his interest. The time was right.

"Would you like to have it?" Manu asked.

"How much do you want for it?" Bill asked, his tone cautious.

"I'll give it to you for free - if you waive the training fees of the Guest House keepers." Bill raised an eyebrow.

"That's 3,160 Lapes worth. That's way too much."

"The training costs you nothing, so you have a chance to make an incredible investment by providing free training for two of your loyal workers," Manu countered. "But if you don't see the value, no worries. I'll find another buyer."

Manu, recalling his past negotiations, understood the power of leaving someone wanting more. The tactic – tempting the other party with something valuable, only to pull back – had worked well with the kids he often bartered with. But Bill was no kid. He was a businessman, and Manu couldn't be sure whether the same trick would work on him. What he did know, however, was that often, letting silence do the work was the best approach.

"Why does it matter to you whether they pay for their training or not?" Bill asked, confused.

"Because we will be covering their fees," Manu explained.

Bill nodded slowly.

"I see. You've got some sharp negotiating skills, kid. We can make a deal, but I'll only waive half of their fees. No more."

Manu recognised that this was just the starting point. He knew Bill's initial offer was a baseline, and from here, the only direction was up.

"That would be an insult to the artist," Manu said, unflinching, his boldness catching Bill off guard.

"Seventy per cent, then," Bill countered.

Manu smiled and shook his head, pretending to reach for the drawing.

Bill quickly pulled the paper closer to himself, narrowing his eyes.

"You're really pushing it, aren't you?" Bill chuckled, amused by Manu's persistence. "Okay, I'll waive 80%. Final offer."

Manu shook his head again, the playful smile fading, but inside, he felt the thrill of victory approaching.

"It's 100% or no deal," he stated firmly.

Manu stepped closer, pointing at the intricate details of the drawing.

"Look at this," he said, tapping the paper gently. "The way every palm leaf is sketched, how the bamboo nods sway in the wind, the vines holding the huts together... This is one-of-a-kind. You won't find anyone in the Jungle who could capture your village like this. It's value will only go up every time someone looks at it. Your legacy, right here."

Bill smirked, clearly entertained by the young Voivoki's bravado.

"Alright, alright, I get it. No need to keep selling me on it."

He lifted the drawing closer to his face, inspecting it with newfound appreciation, letting the silence stretch before finally saying:

"Deal."

Manu had to fight the excitement bubbling inside him. He'd struck many deals, but none of them were as important as this. It wasn't just about him – this provided a much needed boost for his friends too.

Riding the wave of success, Manu glanced around, his eyes settling on a blank wall in Bill's office. Without missing a beat, he asked:

"Mind if we step inside for a moment?"

Curious, Bill gestured for him to enter. Manu walked over to the empty wall and ran his hand over it.

"In the City, great businessmen like you all have portraits of themselves on display," he said with a burst of enthusiasm. "You should have one right here. It would cement your legacy long after you're gone."

Manu paused, watching Bill's reaction carefully. The idea clearly piqued his interest.

"Would you like my artist to draw one of you?" Manu asked smoothly.

Bill chuckled, shaking his head in amusement.

"You've got guts, kid. You just walked off with over three thousand Lapes from me, and now you're asking for more. Everyone's got a limit."

Bill stroked his beard, casting another glance at the bare wall. Manu could see the thought of having his own portrait tickled Bill's ego, but the seasoned businessman wasn't going to jump in just yet.

"I'll think about it and let you know," Bill said, stepping towards the entrance – a clear sign the conversation was over.

Manu grinned. He had planted the seed.

Victorious, Manu joined Joe and Roger at the hammocks, a triumphant grin plastered across his face as he recounted the deal he had pulled off. The other two sat in stunned disbelief. They knew Manu had a knack for negotiations, but his audacity to push Bill beyond multiple generous offers left them speechless.

"It's all about creativity," Manu said, his eyes gleaming. "You find what they truly value, then use that to build a win-win."

With their plan unfolding, surpassing even their own expectations, the three boys finally settled into their hammocks, grinning, content as the gentle sway lulled them towards sleep.

The sunset had been breathtaking, casting a peaceful glow over the village, but soon the calm gave way to the familiar rage of the Jungle. Thunder cracked, and rain pounded down, turning the night into a stormy blur that repeatedly broke their rest.

In the early hours, with lightning flashing across the sky and the storm in full fury, a sudden, faint, but blood-curdling scream tore through the air, snapping Roger out of his dream.

His heart raced. He sat up in the hammock, eyes wide, pulse quickening.

Something had gone terribly wrong.

CHAPTER 5

A week earlier, at a market, a fight erupted between two Voivokis right next to Josh. Up until then, he had clung to the belief that they were all part of some elaborate reality show – that the Voivokis and Vaipor were actors meant to make things more dramatic. But the fury in the Voivoki's eyes shattered that illusion. The punch that followed was so real it made Josh's stomach churn. The Voivoki crumpled to the ground, blood pouring from his mouth as he spat out broken teeth, writhing in agony.

Fights weren't new to Josh – he grew up in a rough neighbourhood where brawls were more frequent than sunsets. Normally, it wouldn't have fazed him. But this fight wasn't just about fists flying; it was about his busted conspiracy theory. As soon as he saw that punch land, he knew: nothing about this place was fake. The Jungle was as real – and as brutal – as it gets.

Instinctively, he scanned the area and spotted a Voivoki's bow and quiver leaning against a stool. Hunger gnawed at him. He'd been hungry more times this past week than he cared to admit. At home, hunger was familiar – a regular reminder of his parents' neglect – but at least, there were corner stores and bakeries to sneak food from. Here, the Jungle didn't care if you were starving. No handouts, no second chances – just survival.

A strong bow and arrows – far better than the makeshift ones they'd crafted with Asim's lead – could be his ticket to food and safety. With that, he wouldn't have to rely on others or risk going hungry again. Or so he thought.

Just days ago, he'd caught a small crocodile with his bare hands. He was sure he could've killed it on his own and have it all to himself, but he had to share it with ten other kids. He assumed it would have lasted him nearly two weeks – more than enough to make it out of the Jungle.

"I am sick of catching food and climbing voku trees for everyone else," he thought bitterly, the weight of the group pulling on his desire for freedom.

He saw the other kids as a bunch of spoiled brats, with the exception of Asim, though their mutual stubbornness made it impossible for them to get along. Josh believed he stood a much better chance of making it back home on his own. His relentless drive and fearless personality would allow him to walk faster, catch enough food for himself, and collect Mapa seeds to barter at the markets along the way. With a high-quality bow and arrows, survival would only become easier. He was determined to take it into his possession.

The Voivoki was twice his size, his muscles bulging with enough power to crush Josh in an instant. But Josh was not thinking about the possible consequences. He had been fighting and surviving for as long as he could remember, and to him, the world was a battlefield. He was the lone wolf against everyone else.

As the chaos from the nearby fight continued to unfold, Josh planned his move. The distraction provided the perfect cover. He'd sneak up to the Voivoki, take his hunting gear, and disappear into the Jungle on the far side of the market. The crowd of shoppers would shield him just long enough to make his escape.

He was ready.

With an innocent expression, he wondered towards the Voivoki, head turning side to side like a tourist in a busy city. When he reached the bow and quiver, he didn't hesitate. As if they belonged to him, he grabbed the gear and casually walked away.

What happened next was a blur. All he could remember was the chaos of the moment, with shouts and angry voices echoing behind him. He sprinted with all his might, desperately trying to reach the safety of the thicket, just a mere soccer field's length away. Spears flew past him, striking the ground, while arrows buzzed perilously close to his ears. The realisation that a single poisonous arrow could end his life within minutes intensified his fear and propelled him to push his limits even further.

Reaching the edge of the thicket, he dove headfirst into the dense brush, ignoring the sharp thorns that tore at his skin. The angry voices were closing in – he had to find cover fast. The open trail he'd created would make it easy for his pursuers to follow.

Then, to his great luck, he spotted a wild boar trail, barely visible at knee level. Without a second thought, Josh crawled beneath the dense undergrowth, silently slipping into the shadows.

He could hear the Voivokis talking, their voices only a few dozen steps behind him as they debated which direction he might have gone. Luckily, the dense thicket overhead shielded him from their view. He kept crawling as quickly as he could until he reached a section where the towering prime forest blocked much of the sunlight, thinning the undergrowth.

Here, he felt like he finally had the upper hand. It didn't matter which way he went; the labyrinth of massive trees offered ample cover, allowing him to vanish from sight with ease. He sprinted, his heart hammering in his chest, until he decided it was safe enough to stop and catch his breath. The only sounds he heard were the relentless buzzing of insects and the rhythmic pounding of his own heartbeat. No signs of the Voivokis.

He was just about to sit and calm his racing pulse, the stolen hunting gear clutched tightly in his hand, when the fading adrenaline sharpened his senses. That's when it hit - an intense, searing pain in his right thigh. Glancing down, he saw a foot-long, razor-sharp thorn embedded deep in his flesh. Acting on instinct, he yanked it out, wincing as blood oozed from the wound. He quickly pressed his hands against it, applying pressure to stop the bleeding, while the reality of the Jungle's brutal dangers set in once again.

He knew that such injury in the Jungle could quickly become infectious, often leading to fatality, so he tore his spare t-shirt into makeshift bandages to tightly wrap around his wound.

"I must get to clear water," he thought to himself.

Standing up proved more challenging than he initially thought. The intense pain caused him to clench his teeth and clutch his thigh. The rawness of the wound throbbed with every heartbeat and dizziness threatened to pull him back to the ground. With a deep breath and trembling determination, he steadied himself, pushing through the waves of pain, knowing that he had to continue his journey despite the excruciating aftermath of the spike's extraction.

His goal was to venture back into the valley, where the likelihood of finding a stream or a river increased. However, he soon faced the harsh reality of his situation and his lack of experience navigating the treacherous Jungle. As the daylight rapidly dwindled, the similarity of the surrounding trees blurred his sense of direction. Lost and disoriented, he had no choice but to seek refuge at the base of a towering fig tree, huddling there throughout the long, eerie night, waiting for its passage.

Without any form of shelter to shield him, the incessant rainfall made it nearly impossible to find respite and obtain more than a few fleeting moments of sleep here and there.

The following morning, he didn't need an alarm to rouse from his uneasy rest. As soon as enough light filtered through the towering canopy above, he pressed forward, disregarding the throbbing pain in his injured leg. Without a clear sense of direction, he chose to descend, hoping to find his way back to lower ground. However, the treacherous terrain often led him uphill, draining him both physically and mentally. To compound his struggles, the deep cut on his thigh had swollen, intensifying the agony with each step. He paused intermittently to collect rainwater, attempting to cleanse his wound, but the relief was minimal at best.

"I must get to clear water," he kept repeating it.

After hours of exhausting struggle, he was greeted by the distant sounds of a cascading waterfall. It was music to his ears, giving a glimmer of hope to his weary heart. Aware of the dangers that lurked near water sources, he also recognised the vital importance of water for survival. His desperate need for clear water to cleanse his wound, quench his thirst, and possibly shoot down an unsuspecting thirsty animal propelled him forward.

The waterfall and its surroundings were so breathtaking that, if not for its location deep within a treacherous Jungle, it would surely be featured on the covers of travel magazines. The cascading water spilled into a crystal-clear pool, a rare moment of serenity in an otherwise hostile environment.

Josh followed the river downstream, hacking through the dense foliage before finally arriving at a spot where he could kneel at the riverbank to tend to his wound. His stomach growled with increasing urgency, reminding him of the 24 hours he'd gone without food.

Thinking of making a spear, he eyed a nearby clump of bamboo, but breaking off a stem proved nearly impossible. He longed for Asim's dad's elusive bush knife - something he had once doubted even existed. Left with no better option, he got creative. He broke a rock in half, using its jagged edge to weaken the bamboo's fibres, one by one, and eventually, separating a piece from the cluster.

With his makeshift bamboo spear in hand, Josh perched on a rock overhanging the river, scanning for fish. But his patience wore thin quickly. His hunger, fatigue, and the persistent rain sapped what little focus he had left. Frustrated, he moved further downstream, hoping for better luck.

He was in a miserable state - cold, drenched, and limping on his injured leg. Exhaustion clung to him like the humidity in the air. All he wanted was to lie down and sleep, to block out the relentless rain and aching hunger. What kept him going was the fear of having to spend another night without cover, soaked to the bone.

Drawing from his recent experience in the Jungle with the other kids, Josh knew the basic steps to building a shelter. However, without proper tools and a team around him, the task proved much harder than he anticipated. With only a sharp rock to cut through vines and branches, progress was painstakingly slow. By the time he finished with a barely standing shelter, the Jungle was already shrouded in near-total darkness.

The aesthetics of the shelter didn't matter to Josh. As soon as he was sure the rain couldn't penetrate the makeshift roof, he collapsed onto the elevated floor and instantly fell into a deep, dreamless sleep. He was so exhausted that even a tiger munching on his toes wouldn't have stirred him.

When he finally woke, the sun was already high, its rays dancing on the river's surface. For an adventurer, the spot might have been paradise, but for Josh, it was just another day to survive. His body, weakened from a day and a half without food, resisted as he tried to rise from his temporary bed. Every movement was an effort, a reminder of how dire his situation had become.

He tried again to catch fish, peering into the crystal-clear water, but once more, the river offered him nothing. Desperation drove him downstream, hoping for better luck. As the hours passed, hunger made his legs wobble beneath him. Hallucinations flickered at the edges of his vision, and in his desperation, he began eating whatever insects and ants he could find. By early afternoon, his body could no longer sustain him. He collapsed onto a smooth rock by the riverbank and fell asleep instantly.

He might have slept until morning - perhaps even permanently - had it not been for the piercing screams of a troop of monkeys in the lower canopy. The noise jolted him awake. He opened his eyes to see the agitated monkeys shrieking at something near another rock close by. He tried to get up, but his body remained unresponsive. Straining to see, he turned his head and squinted at the blurry shape that had captured the monkeys' attention.

As his vision cleared, dread settled in his chest. A dark, sinuous form was draped across the sun-warmed rock - a massive cobra, its body easily twice Josh's height, basking in the afternoon heat.

"That could be my dinner," Josh thought, a sudden burst of adrenaline fuelling him. But doubt quickly crept in.

"What if I fail to kill it?"

He couldn't afford another day without proper food. His eyes flicked to the monkeys.

"Why not go for one of them instead?"

Testing his new bow on a smaller, less dangerous target seemed smarter.

"If I miss, I can still go after the cobra. But if I go for the cobra first, I'll scare the monkeys away for sure."

Carefully, he shifted into a half-kneeling position, drew his bowstring tight, and took aim at the nearest monkey. He held his breath as the stolen arrow sailed through the air, and in an instant, the monkey fell, snapping branches on its way down before hitting the ground with a dull thump. The rest of the troop scattered into the treetops, screeching in alarm.

Josh blinked in disbelief. His first arrow - his first ever - had hit its mark. And it meant dinner. Glancing back at the cobra, he saw it was still basking, undisturbed. Not wanting to push his luck, he decided to collect the monkey first.

After battling through thick undergrowth, he found the fallen creature lying still, the arrow embedded straight through its skull. The sight was gruesome, making him hesitate for a moment. He'd seen a lot in his short life, but this... this was different.

"I don't mind getting a piece of steak from the butcher, but this bleeding hairy monster is pretty disgusting," he muttered to himself.

Hunger, however, left no room for squeamishness. Steeling himself, he yanked the arrow from the monkey's head, grabbed it by the tail, and dragged it back to the rock. He checked on the cobra - still there, blissfully unaware.

"Time to catch that one too," he thought, gripping his spear.

Just as he was about to make his move, he paused, remembering that snakes can sense ground vibrations. By the time he'd get close enough, the cobra might have either slithered away or, worse, positioned itself to strike. A cobra that size could lift its head as high as Josh's, with a striking distance that could easily reach him.

He moved forward slowly, inch by inch, watching the cobra's every movement. When it stirred slightly, he froze. Holding his breath, he drew his bow, his arrow aimed at the coiled body. He waited for the perfect moment. Between two heartbeats, he let the arrow fly.

The cobra reared up, thrashing wildly before collapsing back down. Everything happened so fast, Josh wasn't sure if he had hit it or merely startled it. He grabbed his spear and scrambled over the rocks for a closer look.

Moving slowly, his body tense and his knuckles white from the tight grip on his spear, he peeked out from behind the last rock separating him from the cobra. His eyes widened at the sight of a small patch of blood staining the stone, but the snake itself had vanished. He exhaled, a surge of relief mingled with disappointment.

The search was on. Tracking the faint blood trail into the dense thicket, Josh knew he was heading into a dangerous game. The thick underbrush was the perfect spot for the injured cobra to either disappear or strike back. Every step was slow, methodical. He poked ahead with his spear, testing the ground, his senses on high alert. Time felt suspended as the thrill of the hunt consumed him.

At last, he found his prey at the foot of a towering tree. Blood marks on the bark suggested the cobra had tried to climb but was too weak to ascend. It lay coiled, a broken arrow lodged in its side, but its head still lifted menacingly, poised to defend itself.

Josh's pulse quickened. Hunger clawed at him, and the cobra was his lifeline. His spear swiped through the air in wild arcs, but despite its injury, the snake dodged his attacks with terrifying speed. Josh had gone two days without food, and the desperation to secure this meal drove him into a primal frenzy. His strikes grew faster, more reckless. He needed just one solid hit to ensure days' worth of sustenance.

The long battle finally ended when Josh's spear found its mark - striking about a foot below the cobra's head, causing it to buckle. Seizing the moment, he moved in, delivering blow after blow until the creature lay motionless at his feet.

The thrill of victory was intoxicating. Two kills in one afternoon felt like a miracle, and despite his exhaustion, Josh was brimming with excitement. Even the gruelling task of making a fire - a struggle that had frustrated him earlier - did little to dampen his spirits. He persevered until flames flickered to life in his palms. Once the fire was steady, he fashioned a makeshift knife from bamboo, gutted his dinner, and roasted some of the meat, while smoked the rest for later.

By the time dusk fell, Josh had eaten his fill, the taste of victory still fresh on his tongue. With a full belly, fresh water nearby, and the satisfaction of survival, building a shelter that night was far less of an ordeal than the day before.

The last of the daylight had faded from the sky as he pulled a thin vine tight, adding the final touch to his hut. Filled with pride, he settled down, savouring the solitude and the crackling of the fire while he waited for the meat to cure. His thoughts drifted briefly to the City - the destination he hoped to reach one day, when the serenity of his evening was shattered by the sudden rustling of bushes behind him. Instinctively, he grabbed his spear, springing to his feet, ready to defend himself, his food, and his shelter.

He held his breath as he spotted movement in the flickering light of the fire. First, an arm appeared, brushing aside the leaves, followed by a familiar face peeking through the vegetation, smiling.

Relieved, Josh greeted him.

"Good evening, mysterious wise man," he said with a smile, feeling the tension melt away from his body.

He had set out to break away from his peers, determined to find his own path to the City, but after days of isolation and near-starvation, the sight of another person was a welcome relief.

"Impressive shelter you've built here," Vaipor said, inspecting the structure with a gentle shake.

Josh made himself comfortable on the elevated platform – a few pieces of bamboo, serving as his bed.

"Thanks," Josh replied, his pride unmistakable.

Vaipor lowered his backpack and gestured towards Josh's makeshift bamboo bed.

"May I?"

"Of course," Josh said, signalling for him to sit.

Once seated, Vaipor's gaze softened.

"How come you're on your own?"

Josh leaned against the frame, his arms crossed.

"I got tired of carrying the weight for a bunch of freeloaders who expect others to do everything for them."

"And how has that decision worked out for you so far?" Vaipor asked with a raised brow.

Josh's hand rubbed his stomach.

"Now that I've eaten, I'd say pretty well."

Vaipor chuckled softly.

"I'll give you credit - you've got guts, walking away and handling things on your own. But I think you'd agree that maybe, just maybe, it wasn't the best decision this time. Right?"

Josh shrugged.

"They will probably wander this Jungle for years. I'm getting back home, and soon."

"And you're so sure of that because...?"

"Because I'm not looking after anyone else now. I've got enough food for three days, and I know I'll catch more before I run out. Finding the way is the easy part."

Vaipor's smile faded into a more serious expression.

"Confidence isn't something you lack, my son. But let's not forget – you nearly starved to death right here, all alone. The Jungle would have swallowed even your bones long before anyone found you. That's a steep price to pay for your freedom."

"I wasn't dying. I was just... resting," Josh retorted.

"And if those monkeys hadn't woken you?"

Josh shrugged again, unwilling to concede.

"I would've woken up eventually. There are plenty of animals coming to drink, and fish to catch. No big deal."

Vaipor's eyes lingered on Josh for a moment, his expression unreadable.

"My son, you may not realise it, but you were unconscious from starvation earlier today. I admire your confidence and trust in your abilities, but at some point, you need to accept that luck played a big part in your survival. Right now, your stomach is full, but you've still got a nasty leg wound. While you sleep, that injury could easily get infected by parasites. By the time you wake up, the infection might be in your blood, spreading, paralysing you. Who would take care of you then?"

Vaipor paused, allowing his words to sink in.

"Being a lone wolf can make sense in some situations, but it's always wiser to have a safety net around you. Sure, you might make it home faster on your own, but your chances of survival are slim. The risk you took was far too high.

You longed for freedom, and now you have it – absolute freedom to do whatever you want, whenever you want. But there is a catch: this kind of freedom will gradually drive you insane. With no connection to anyone or a structure to hold onto, you'll become like a wild animal trapped in a human body. You'll end up fighting even your own thoughts and lose the ability to think clearly."

Josh stared into the flames, feeling the weight of Vaipor's words.

"Isn't it better," Vaipor continued, "to have the safety net of human companionship? Yes, it means following certain cultural, legal, political, and ethical rules, but that's a small price to pay?"

Josh shifted, curious but sceptical.

"What exactly do you mean?" he asked.

Vaipor took a deep breath, taking a moment to gather his thoughts.

"Let me break it down, because this could save your life if you ever see another human."

He began calmly.

"Let's start with the cultural boundaries. I can't speak of the culture in the City, but the Voivokis? They're proud of their traditions. They care about how they dress, their hygiene, how they speak to one another. And their society values success — those who rise above others earn respect. The cultures of the Nokonais - the real tribesmen - are vastly different. If you ever stumble across them, you'd better adapt quickly or you'll be dealing with their spears before you know it."

He paused, watching Josh absorb the information.

"Next, the legal boundaries. Here, the Vilais are in charge. They make the rules, and they punish anyone who steps out of line. They're probably like your government in the City.

Which brings us to political boundaries. The Vilais can change the rules as they wish. Occasionally new groups of Voivokis try to challenge their power, but the Vilais are too strong. I hope in your City, the power is more balanced, allowing the people of the City to have a say in setting the rules.

Finally, there are the ethical boundaries. Now, that's complex."

Vaipor reached for Josh's bow, causing him tense up.

"Did you make this?" Vaipor asked, inspecting it with admiration.

Josh hesitated, unsure of Vaipor's intentions.

"No," he admitted.

"Did you find it?"

Josh's eyes flicked to Vaipor.

"I… took it," he said, his voice flat but unapologetic.

"From someone else?" Vaipor pressed, raising an eyebrow.

"Yeah," Josh replied, a hint of pride creeping into his tone.

Vaipor sighed and shook his head.

"That's stealing. It doesn't fit within the Voivoki's ethical or legal boundaries, and I doubt it does in your City either. Ethical boundaries are blurry and far-reaching, making them the hardest to recognise, but stealing is unquestionably wrong. How did you take it?"

Josh felt a surge of pride and defiance swell within him. He had no remorse for what he'd done, despite knowing it was wrong. In his mind, survival justified the theft. He recalled the chaos of the market brawl - how it shattered his illusions that he was part of some harmless reality show. The fight had jolted him awake, igniting a fierce survival instinct. He knew, then and there, that to stay alive, he needed a strong weapon. And he had taken one.

"And then?" Vaipor urged, eager for more details.

"I ran like crazy," Josh said, his chest puffing with pride. "Arrows and spears whistling right past my ears. I zigzagged so they couldn't hit me. Once I hit the thicket, I was out of their sight."

Vaipor watched Josh's excitement, shaking his head with a mix of pity and concern.

"You've already nearly died twice," he said quietly. "It's not often that one receives three chances. Don't take more reckless risks. Do the right thing. If you want something, find a way to get it within the boundaries I mentioned."

Josh's pride deflated, the gleam in his eyes replaced by an awkward smile. His friends in the City would've cheered him on for his fearlessness, but Vaipor saw only the recklessness in his actions. Stealing had overshadowed his bravado.

"Tell me about this reality show," Vaipor said, his tone even more serious. "What is that?"

Josh reminded himself that Vaipor hadn't been to the City and knew nothing of its technology. Concepts like television, the internet, and social media were alien to him. Josh began explaining the idea of television.

"We have these magical boxes that let us see all sorts of things, even people who are far away from us in both time and distance. A lot of what we watch is just acting, entertainment. Reality shows, though, are like games where regular people compete for a goal. Sometimes the contestants don't even know what's coming, and they have to figure things out while millions watch them. They often go to places to test their survival skills."

"And you thought you were in a reality show here?" Vaipor asked, genuinely surprised.

Josh's cheeks burned.

"Yeah… some things didn't make sense to me."

"So you created a story based on your own beliefs?" Vaipor asked, his voice steady.

Josh remained silent.

"That's what we call a conspiracy theory," Vaipor said. "Sometimes Voivokis spread stories for attention, to prank others, or because they know things others don't. But paying too much attention to such theories distracts you from reaching your true goals. You and your friends all want the same thing: to return to the City. Yet, you let your own made-up story derail you from the path."

He paused, taking a deep breath, as if weighted down by the mistakes Josh had made.

Lifting Josh's bow, he squinted, testing its strength.

"Is this your strongest weapon?" he asked.

"Yeah," Josh replied, the memory of his first successful shot flickering in his mind.

"Many Voivokis would say the same, but the truth is, your words are far more powerful than this bow. Think about how you feel when someone says something hurtful to you."

Josh remained silent, his gaze drifting beyond the fire, lost in thought.

"And when you receive compliments or praises?" Vaipor continued. "It lifts you up, doesn't it? Just as words can affect you, they also impact others. Some people are so sensitive to what they hear or how they're treated that if you're not careful, you could cause wounds far deeper than any weapon. You must learn to stay level-headed, do the right thing, and if you ever meet another person, let kindness guide your words and actions. Build stronger relationships with those around you, and you'll find doors of opportunity opening – more than you could ever uncover."

Vaipor's voice softened, yet remained firm.

"Look at the troubled individuals around you, like your mother. Observe their destructive behaviour and learn from it - don't replicate it. Do the opposite.

You have incredible drive and confidence, but the noise in your head is blocking you from using that energy in a constructive way. Once you start spreading love and accepting different personalities, you'll attract the people you need to help you grow, smooth your path, and ultimately achieve your goals."

Vaipor rouse to his feet, gently placed his right hand on Josh, and added:

"But of course, first you must survive your journey as a lone wolf."

Josh felt a lump rise in his throat as he looked up at Vaipor, his words hanging in the air like a solemn promise. He managed a quiet 'Thank you,' but it felt too small for the weight of what had just passed between them. As Vaipor disappeared into the thicket, the flickering firelight catching brief glimpses of his retreating form, a surge of emotion washed over Josh. Gratitude, fear, and determination swirled inside him, tightening his chest. For the first time, he truly understood the gravity of his path ahead, and the warmth of Vaipor's guidance lingered long after he was gone.

He wanted to go to sleep, but his duties required him to stay awake. Just days earlier, Asim – ironically, the person he clashed with most – had taught him about the delicate balance between smoking and cooking meat. In the Jungle's humid heat, cooked meat spoiled quickly, but smoked meat could last for days. The process was long and meticulous, and he couldn't afford any mistakes, forcing him to fight off exhaustion.

The next morning, after enduring a few gruelling days, he decided to stay at his makeshift camp, resting, and allowing his wound to heal. All day, he remained alert, hoping to catch more prey, but luck evaded him.

Rising early the following morning, well-rested but aimless, he decided to follow the river downstream, certain he'll stumble upon a community. Now and then, when he deemed it safe, he tried fishing along the riverbank, but again came up empty-handed. By mid-afternoon, he set up camp, dried his clothes and shoes by the fire, and with nothing to do and no one to talk to, he resigned himself to call it a day.

Lying on his makeshift platform, the rough branches pressing into his back, Vaipor's words echoed in his mind with increasing intensity.

"Maybe he's right," he thought. *"Maybe running away was a mistake. I've got the freedom I always wanted, but this isolation is torturing. I would rather put up with the others."*

Then his thoughts drifted to his mum. Her behaviour was awful, but was she truly a bad person? Surely she knew he should've been home by now. Did she even care? If he made it back, could he help her change, or would he have to forget her for good? Maybe she was glad he wasn't home.

Despite his doubts, Josh felt a deep calling to escape the Jungle and help his mother get back on the right path. He was convinced that, one day, they could rebuild their relationship, move to a better neighbourhood, dress well, and surround themselves with positive, supportive people.

His mind had also drifted to his abusive dad, a man he barely knew. If he made it out of the Jungle, he would still have to wait many years to see his dad released from prison.

It was a rather peculiar realisation for Josh to recognise how their fates mirrored each other; both were fighting for survival. Yet while his dad lost his freedom, he was fed multiple times a day, had a roof over his head, people to converse with, and a release date to look forward to. Josh, on the other hand, had all the freedom he wanted but felt imprisoned by the treacherous Jungle and his own thoughts.

Though his memories of his dad were bleak, in his isolation, he still longed to see him, to talk to him. Perhaps they could help each other turn their lives around. But what if prison made his dad even more abusive? Would Josh still want to reconnect and count down the days to his release? Josh would be thirty by then – a distant future.

Unable to relax his mind, Josh sat up, his chest heavy with the weight of his emotional turmoil, reflected by the eerie darkness of the Jungle and the relentless rain. It felt as though the Jungle had already swallowed him whole, robbing him of any chance to survive. He reached out, but in the pitch-black night, he couldn't even see his own hands.

"No!" he whispered, his voice cracking as his eyes welled up. "One more chance… please!"

He buried his face in his hands and let the tears flow.

The next morning, the squawking of vibrant parrots roused him from sleep. With fresh determination, he packed up his camp, resolved to catch something to eat and, ultimately, to find a community that could help him survive.

During his journey that day, he came across a slippery voku tree. Its smooth trunk reminded him of the Voivokis and their obsession with its seeds - a currency for them, but completely worthless to him now, struggling with hunger and fatigue. He recalled the last heated argument with his peers, the one that had pushed him to leave. It had seemed like such a big deal at the time, but now, after days of isolation, hunger gnawing at his insides, he felt regret. Had he really risked everything over a handful of seeds? Even if he had the strength to climb the tree, what would be the point? He couldn't eat the seeds. With a heavy sigh, he turned away, continuing his journey.

In the afternoon, much to his delight, he managed to catch a frog while building his shelter. It was a small victory, but deep down, he knew his body needed a lot more calories than the small amphibian could provide. His stomach continued to ache, a constant reminder of his dwindling energy. As night fell, he lay on his makeshift bed, haunted by the thought that his survival was a delicate balance he was slowly losing.

By the early hours of the next morning, driven out of bed by his hunger, he set off again, his steps unsteady. His legs wobbled as he stumbled over exposed roots, and his mind, weakened by exhaustion, began playing tricks on him. Desperation clouded his judgment, tempting him to eat plants he couldn't identify. It was during this wandering that he found himself climbing a pong pong tree, his limbs shaky but driven by need. As soon as he snapped off one of its fruits, it felt like the Jungle itself had fallen silent. The ever-present hum of insects seemed to vanish, as though nature was warning him. His heart pounded in his chest, his mouth watered, and sweat trickled down his forehead as he tore open the glossy, light-green fruit. Oddly, there was no smell.

"That's strange for a fruit," he muttered to himself, cautiously climbing down the tree.

Still clutching the fruit, he circled the base of the tree and noticed a few overripe ones scattered on the ground, untouched. His mind raced. There had to be a reason the animals avoided them. His hunger screamed at him to take a bite, but his survival instincts prevailed. With a frustrated groan, he tossed the fruit aside, resisting the urge to test his luck. The Jungle was full of dangers, and he couldn't afford to fall victim to a poisonous mistake - not after everything he'd been through. Despite the unbearable hunger, he moved on, determined not to let the Jungle claim him just yet.

Later that afternoon, building a basic shelter drained what little strength and patience he had left. As he tried to tie a sturdy bamboo pole to a tree to serve as part of the roof, something in him faltered. He'd done it multiple times before, yet now, with fatigue clouding his mind, he couldn't figure out how to make the knot tight. After multiple failed attempts, frustration boiled over. He slammed the bamboo into the ground and lied down, closing his tired eyes to calm his nerves.

"Tie a knot to the tree, then loop it around in the shape of an eight, both directions," came Asim's familiar voice, calm and clear in his head.

Josh opened his eyes, and there was Asim, crouched beside him, patiently guiding him.

"Come on, Josh! You can do it!" Manu's voice chimed in from the other side. *"Just make sure you leave enough for another knot before you weave the end through the last loop."*

He blinked in disbelief as the scene came to life around him. His entire group was there - each person busy with their own task, working together, their shared goal to survive another night. A sense of comfort washed over him for the first time in days. Maybe everything would be okay.

But then, as if something had shifted in the air, the vines began to writhe unnaturally. One of the thick ropes Asim had tied around a bamboo pole moved, slithering slowly. Josh's heart skipped a beat, and he shot up, eyes wide with panic.

"Asim, look out!" he shouted, pointing as the vine twisted, scales emerging along its length. It hissed, coiling towards Asim's hand.

Josh's pulse raced as he waited for Asim to react, but his friend just continued tying the knot, oblivious to the danger. Suddenly, the scene warped, the figures of his friends flickering and dissolving like smoke. The snake vanished, and Josh found himself alone, staring at the vine he'd been struggling with earlier, still motionless in his hand. His breath came in short, ragged gasps as the hallucination faded, leaving behind only the quiet rustle of the Jungle and the crushing weight of his isolation.

He slapped his cheeks, trying to shake off the remnants of his dream, and with a renewed sense of urgency, hastily threw together a makeshift shelter, cutting corners wherever he could. As evening descended and the rain and wind intensified, the flaws in his rushed effort became painfully clear. Water leaked through several gaps, soaking him through. Too exhausted to fix it, he lay there, shivering, his thoughts drifting back to his conversation with Vaipor. Just a few days earlier, he had boasted about making it home faster than the others, confident in his ability to hunt and move quickly. But now, as the cold rain seeped into his bones, he realised how wrong he had been. He missed the others more than he cared to admit, and his pride was no match for the harsh reality of survival.

Things took a turn for the worse when the weight of the downpour caused one side of his flimsy roof to collapse entirely. Rain now poured directly onto his legs and torso. Desperation flared, and in a fit of frustration, he jumped up, fists clenched, and screamed into the storm. His cries echoed through the Jungle, raw and primal, though he wasn't sure what he was raging against - his failure, the unforgiving wilderness, or his isolation. But screaming released something inside him, and he only stopped when his throat burned and his lungs gave out. Drenched and defeated, he sat under the only section of his shelter that still offered some minor protection. Pulling his knees to his chest, he wrapped his arms tightly around himself in a futile attempt to stay warm.

He wished, in the back of his mind, that someone had heard him - that help would come. But the Jungle was merciless. His chances of survival were slipping further into the red with every passing minute, and for the first time, he truly doubted if he would ever make it home.

CHAPTER 6

Sitting upright in his hammock, wide-eyed and with his heart racing, Roger glanced over at Manu and Joe, still sound asleep and seemingly undisturbed. Doubt began to creep in, convincing him that the screams that had jolted him awake were nothing more than a figment of his imagination. Sleep now eluded him, so his thoughts drifted to his new job as a guard. He knew the open-air post would leave him at the mercy of the elements, but anything seemed better than the stifling monotony of the factory floor, weaving in silence.

He shifted restlessly, his impatience growing as he waited for any sign of life from his friends.

The moment Manu's eyes fluttered open, Roger couldn't contain his excitement any longer.

"It's day one!" he announced with a grin.

Manu blinked at him groggily, clearly still half-asleep. With a long yawn, he rubbed his eyes and stretched as much as his hammock allowed.

"Hmm?" he mumbled.

"It's day one!" Roger repeated, his enthusiasm undeterred.

Manu sat up slowly, scanning the area as though searching for something, before locking eyes with his friend. A soft smile spread across his face.

"Every day is day one," he said. "Every morning we wake up, we're blessed with another 24 hours."

Roger chuckled, shaking his head.

"That's a bit deep for first thing in the morning, don't you think?"

Manu shrugged, his smile lingering.

"Might as well start the day with something good."

After breakfast, Joe and Sina received a quick rundown of their tasks. With newfound enthusiasm, they tackled their daily duties, finding them a welcome change from the drudgery of factory work. The few items they had to wipe down were a far cry from the endless dust-collectors cluttering homes in the City, often kept as memorabilia. Well-versed in cleaning, Sina found joy in the simplicity of the Guest House. There were no harsh chemicals to handle or shiny surfaces demanding perfection.

Joe, however, had little basis for comparison. Back in the City, his housekeeping experience was limited to tidying his room once a week. By the time they finished their work - well ahead of lunch - Joe grew restless with the idle hours ahead.

"I'm going to check on the others," he announced.

Despite Sina's warning that they weren't allowed to leave the Guest House until their shift ended, Joe ignored her and left.

His unexpected arrival sent a ripple of shock through the workers. Everyone knew he wasn't supposed to leave the Guest House until the evening, and this was exactly why the previous keepers were keen to swap jobs for factory work. If Bill saw him wandering around during work hours, who knew what kind of punishment awaited? Manu, especially, felt a surge of anxiety as soon as Joe walked in.

"We're done with our work," Joe announced proudly, oblivious to the tension. "I came for some raw materials."

Manu froze in disbelief.

"Why on earth is he unable to keep his mouth shut?" he fumed internally. His eyes narrowed, and he subtly nodded towards the door, trying to signal Joe to leave without making a scene. But Joe, not catching on, repeated louder:

"I need some raw materials."

Manu's patience snapped. He stood up, puffing out his chest and flexing his shoulders in an attempt to look intimidating.

"You're a Guest House keeper now," he proclaimed, shoving Joe out of the factory.

Grabbing Joe's arm, he pulled him further from the entrance, raising his voice just enough to make sure everyone inside could hear him.

"You have nothing to do with the factory anymore. You agreed to swap, and there's no turning back."

"But…" Joe stammered.

"What on earth are you doing?" Joe asked, bewildered.

"What am I doing?" Manu hissed, barely containing his anger. "No, what are you doing? Our plan is a secret, you idiot."

"I thought it was only a secret until last night," Joe protested.

Manu clenched his fists, his frustration boiling over.

"Don't you remember that we have to hide the materials and the products until I pass the test? Now get back to the Guest House before someone starts asking questions!"

Meanwhile, Roger also received a brief training as a guard and was assigned a territory adjacent to Lightning's. Each guard was responsible for their own area, which varied in size depending on the complexity of the terrain. Roger's territory, though smaller than some, was among the more challenging, with thick, impenetrable vegetation, large rocks, and steep slopes. The guards with less demanding terrains had larger areas to patrol, but Roger's youth and fitness made him well-suited to handle the difficult landscape.

Being ever-curious, Roger took the opportunity to learn about the lives of the guards. What did they do when nothing was happening? How did they pass time? He rarely saw them interact with the other villagers, so he was eager to uncover what they did in their spare time.

Lightning, excited to have a new team member, seized the moment to share his stories. He proudly recounted his encounters with the local wildlife, describing how he had fended off dangerous creatures to protect the village, often earning a rewarding meal from Bill for his efforts and bravery.

"Speaking of the beasts," Lightning added with a smirk, "I heard faint screaming off in the distance last night."

"I heard it too," Roger replied, surprised and excited.

Expecting an adventure, he asked:

"Are we going to check it out?"

"What for?" Lightning asked, diminishing its significance. "Nobody screams in the middle of the night unless they're under attack. And by then... it's usually too late for a rescue."

The matter-of-fact response left Roger disturbed. Stationed at the edge of the wilderness, with no experience fighting anyone - let alone a wild beast - the reality of his exposure to danger sent shivers down his spine. He felt as if he was facing a double-edge sword: the financial trap of being stuck in Bill's village, far from home, and the physical risk of a deadly encounter, his life hanging by a thread.

"Do you often come across wild animals here?" Roger asked, inspecting the sharpness and sturdiness of his spear – a bamboo with a split rock tied to it.

"Oh yeah," Lightning replied, puffing up with pride.

Noticing Roger's discomfort, he patted him on his back and added:

"Don't worry. You'll be alright!"

Roger glanced briefly at the endless greenery, its shadows concealing untold dangers, as his mind raced to evaluate his next steps.

"Thanks. But I still think we should check the area and see if the Voi we heard is still alive and needs help," Roger insisted.

"Alright, I'll go," Lightning said with a shrug. "But because you owe Bill, he won't let you come with me."

Roger stared at him in shock.

"What? You have no debt and you're still working for him?"

"Yeah. What else would I do?"

Roger frowned.

"I don't know. Don't you want to go back to your family?"

Lightning chuckled, shaking his head.

"My family's in the same boat - working long hours just like me. What's the point of being together if we're not working? Eventually, we'd run out of money and end up either living off the land or back to work again." He shrugged, a resigned look crossing his face.

"Do you see them sometimes?" Roger asked.

"Oh, I catch up with them and old friends when I can," Lightning said, his tone casual. "But honestly, after working for Bill so long, the other guards have become my closest friends. It's just easier, you know? We share the same experiences, understand the grind. Kind of like family in its own way."

Roger nodded slowly. It all made sense. He thought of his mom, who often preferred spending time with her co-workers over family dinners. It wasn't that she didn't care, but work became her life, and the people around her filled the gaps. Roger had always been puzzled by it, but now, hearing Lightning's explanation, he started to see it differently.

And then, his thoughts shifted to his companions. He had been with them for so long, facing every danger together, that they had slowly become his family too. The connection they shared wasn't just about surviving the same trials - it was about living through them, day after day. In many ways, they understood him better than his real family back home.

"Did you go daydreaming in the middle of our conversation?" Lightning teased, snapping Roger out of his thoughts.

Roger smiled.

"No, just reflecting on what you said."

"All good, mate! We've got to start our work anyways. I'll check out the surrounding mountains after my shift, see if there's any sign of a Voivoki in trouble."

He reiterated the rules to Roger one last time before heading back to his territory, leaving Roger alone to officially begin his new role as a guard. At first, the freedom was exhilarating. He wandered through his assigned area, taking in the fresh air and the sense of autonomy. No more weaving or cramped spaces – just him and the open wilderness.

But as time passed, the novelty wore thin. His excitement slowly faded, replaced by creeping boredom.

How am I supposed to get through an entire day of just watching for wild animals or Voivokis trying to escape?" he thought to himself. *"What about a whole week? Or a whole month? Or perhaps many years, like Lightning?"*

Disheartened, he sat on a rock, staring into the dense trees. The stillness around him only made time drag on even more.

Just as his thoughts began to spiral, he felt a few raindrops on his skin. He glanced up, spotting dark clouds sweeping over the valley. After weeks in the Jungle, he knew how quickly storms could roll in, but this time, it felt like the last straw.

Grumbling under his breath, he searched frantically for something to shield himself with. Finding a large leaf, he curled up beneath it just as the storm broke. The downpour soaked everything around him within moments. Huddled under his makeshift umbrella, Roger watched the seconds crawl by, his patience wearing thin as the rain relentlessly hammered down.

"How lovely is the sound of rain?" asked a familiar voice next to him.

He turned to his right, startled, and there he was - the ever-mysterious Vaipor, exuding his usual vibrant energy, seemingly untouched by the storm.

"Good morning, sir!" Roger greeted him, pleasantly surprised. "It's always great to see you. You never seemed to worry or stress about anything."

Vaipor smiled, his gaze following the raindrops as they splattered against the leaves.

"Why would I need to stress?" he asked calmly.

Roger hesitated. The question was simple, but the answer felt far more complicated than he could articulate. He had read countless self-development books, listened to every motivational podcast he could find, yet here he was, huddled beneath a leaf, feeling the weight of boredom, anxiety, and uncertainty disturbing him.

"A quarter moon ago, you showed me what a book looks like and the kinds you enjoy. And yet, you're still stressing?" Vaipor asked again, his tone light but direct, cutting through Roger's thoughts.

Roger nodded slowly, knowing exactly what Vaipor was getting at. The knowledge was there, tucked away in his mind, but applying it – that was something else entirely. How often had he read about controlling his thoughts, staying calm under pressure, or finding joy in the present moment? Yet, now, faced with the isolation of his new guard post, the endless unknowns of the Jungle, and the constant fear of failure, all that wisdom seemed to slip through his grasp like water through his fingers.

"What good is knowledge without practice?" he asked, a glint of humour in his eyes.

"I know," Roger admitted with a twinge of guilt. "I'm just not sure I made the right decision, agreeing to take this position."

"Why's that?" Vaipor asked.

"Because I am already bored out of my mind. Time seems to crawl by, slower than ever. And then, just when I thought it couldn't get worse, the rain hit out of nowhere, and I don't even have an umbrella."

"You sound quite negative. Haven't you learned to focus on the positives?"

"Yes, but what's so positive about sitting out here alone, rain or shine, every single day?"

Vaipor's smile widened.

"Let's start with the rain. Have you actually paid attention to the sound of it? Have you thought about its impact on life – the way it nourishes the earth, cools the air, and sustains the Jungle around you? Imagine the scorching heat you'd be enduring if the rain hadn't come. Maybe, instead of resisting it, you could appreciate it."

Roger blinked, caught off guard by the simplicity of Vaipor's perspective. He hadn't thought about it like that. He'd been so focused on his discomfort that he hadn't stopped to consider the beauty in the storm, the life-giving force it brought, or the relief it offered from the suffocating heat.

"Take a moment," Vaipor continued. "Really listen. Feel the rain, not as an obstacle, but as something necessary. You might find your mindset shifts when you embrace the things you can't control."

Roger fell silent, allowing Vaipor's words settle in his mind like the raindrops that softly tapped against the leaves. He closed his eyes and listened. The cool air kissed his face, and for the first time, he stopped resisting the rain. He didn't huddle under the giant leaf or wish the weather away; he simply accepted it. And with that acceptance came a small, unfamiliar sense of peace, one that was only briefly interrupted by the low rumble of thunder echoing through the valley. Every time it cracked, shivers raced down his spine, a stark reminder of the Jungle's raw and unpredictable power.

"What's on your mind?" Vaipor asked quietly, sensing Roger's unease.

Roger opened his eyes and sighed.

"The rain is calming, I can admit that, but the thunder… it keeps breaking my focus."

Vaipor smiled.

"What if, instead of fighting the thunder, you allow your mind to accept it? Let it resonate inside you. Feel the depth of its roar in your chest."

Roger hesitated but then closed his eyes again, doing as Vaipor suggested. At first, the thunder jolted him, but minute-by-minute, something gradually shifted.

"I see your point," Roger said, his eyes still shut and a faint smile creeping onto his face. "The thunder has so many layers, like it's… singing, almost. I can feel it in my whole body. When it hits my head, it feels like an explosion of energy that travels down to my toes. It's so powerful that I'm almost waiting for the next one, just to feel that rush again."

Vaipor nodded approvingly.

"Good. Now, with your eyes still closed, picture a plant you've nurtured, one that you hope will bear fruit for the rest of your life."

Roger's mind shifted effortlessly into the visualisation. His mother had introduced him to various meditation techniques when he was younger, hoping they would help him process the trauma he'd endured. Even though he was only fourteen, he had already learned to quiet his mind and explore his inner world – a skill that had been vital in managing the heavy burden of his past. But sometimes he needed a reminder. Now, with Vaipor's gentle guidance, it felt almost natural to let his imagination take root.

"What do you see?" Vaipor asked.

"A small plant," Roger whispered, "just about the size of my palm. It's soaking up the rain. With every drop, I see it stretch taller. The thunder makes its roots dance deeper into the earth, searching for more nourishment."

"Isn't it beautiful?" Vaipor asked, his voice soft but full of meaning.

Roger nodded.

"Yes, it is. But…" His brow furrowed, the contentment in his voice fading. "It doesn't change the fact that I'm still sitting here, all alone, waiting for time to crawl by."

Vaipor's eyes glimmered with understanding. "Perhaps," he said gently, "but what if this moment isn't just about waiting? What if it's about planting seeds - within yourself? You can spend your time wishing it away, or you can use it to grow something meaningful. The loneliness, the boredom – they're like fertile soil, Roger. And you, my son, decide what will grow in it."

Roger frowned, still doubtful.

"But how does this help me and the others leave Bill's village? How does it get us back to our families?"

Vaipor nodded patiently.

"Well, let me unpack it for you," he began. "Think about your situation. You're working off a debt, the same trap many fall into. You got caught up in it, and now you're here. But – " Vaipor held up a finger – "you've been given an opportunity. This boring guard post that nobody else wanted? It's your way out, and if you're smart about it, you'll be free sooner than most."

Roger mulled over the comparison.

"So, it's like this rain. It just keeps falling, hour after hour, and while it seems dull, it's helping the plants grow, providing food for everyone, including me."

"Exactly," Vaipor said, pleased. "Your 'boring' job is the same. It's the foundation. It may not be exciting, but it's what will help you and the others grow, giving you a path out of this place."

Roger nodded, seeing the connection.

"Okay, I get that. But what about the thunder? How does that fit in?"

Vaipor smiled, tapping Roger on his back.

"I'll let you figure that one out."

Roger thought for a moment, the pieces falling into place. His smile grew wide as he spoke.

"I think I understand. I've been avoiding situations or conversations that seem intimidating - like how I tried to tune out the thunder. But once I let myself hear it, even feel it, I started to enjoy it. Maybe it's the same with life's uncomfortable moments. I need to embrace them and..."

"...the doors of opportunity will open," Vaipor finished with a warm laugh, giving Roger a friendly pat on the back. "I knew you'd get it. You're a sharp kid. Remember this metaphor - the rain, the thunder - wherever life takes you."

Roger smiled, a weight lifting from his chest.

"I will."

Vaipor rose to his feet, brushing off his knees as if readying himself for the next journey.

"Wait! Please," Roger blurted, scrambling to stand. "You seem to know everything, but you never show us the way back home. I get it, I do! But... can you at least tell me - will I ever see my mum again?"

Vaipor's expression softened, his gaze steady and kind. He placed a hand on Roger's shoulder, the gesture both grounding and reassuring.

"Focus on the positives in everything you experience. Embrace the challenges, and you'll uncover paths you never imagined. Those paths will lead you where you need to be."

For a moment, Roger felt an ache in his chest but also a flicker of hope.

"Thank you," he whispered.

Vaipor nodded, his comforting smile lingering as he turned to leave, disappearing as quickly as he had appeared.

Roger sat back down, curling up under the large leaf once again, feeling the weight of solitude settle around him. But this time, instead of letting the loneliness drag him down, he closed his eyes and began to meditate, letting the rhythm of the rain and the lessons from Vaipor guide him inward. As he listened to the sounds of the Jungle, his mind opened to the idea that maybe - just maybe - the way home wasn't a single road, but a series of discoveries waiting to unfold.

❧ ❧ ❧

At the factory, things shifted noticeably after Roger, Sina, and Joe left, replaced by two middle-aged Voivokis. They mostly kept to themselves, exchanging only brief words with the kids, as if they felt out of place among a group so much younger. But their goal wasn't to fit in - it was to have a job more fulfilling than their previous post, watching over a mostly empty Guest House.

At lunchtime, Manu hung back, waiting for the others to head to the restaurant before he made his move. Today was perfect for smuggling raw materials to the Guest House. He grabbed a half-full bag, cautiously poking his head out the entrance and scanning the village for Bill. The rain had driven everyone to take cover, and aside from the bustling restaurant where the workers were enjoying their break, the village seemed deserted. Normally, on a sunny day, Bill might be out and about, but Manu knew that on days like this, Bill preferred the warmth of his house to braving the rain.

It was the ideal moment. Manu moved quickly, bag slung over his shoulder, and made his way towards the Guest House. Just as he neared, heart racing with anticipation, the very last person he wanted to see emerged at the gate - Bill.

"What's going on here?!" Bill's voice was sharp, his eyes narrowed with suspicion.

Manu forced a calm smile, though his heart pounded in his chest.

"Just bringing some raw materials to Joe and Sina so they can keep producing during their quiet times," he replied smoothly, trying to mask his nerves.

"And who gave you permission to take things from my factory?" Bill's tone was edged with anger.

Manu took a deep breath.

"We thought we'd surprise you by producing more than you expected," he said, as confidently as he could manage.

Bill paused, caught off guard. On some level, he appreciated the kids' initiative, but his pride and control over the village gnawed at him. No one, especially a group of kids, could think they were better at running his operations. His mind raced through the implications - if workers started making more money, they'd pay off their debts faster, and that meant leaving his village. The last thing he wanted was to lose workers, especially the kids, who were always scheming for their freedom. Maybe it wouldn't apply to everyone, but the ripple effect was too dangerous. He couldn't afford to let this get out of hand.

Bill's face hardened, and he stepped closer to Manu.

"Listen, kid," his voice was cold and deliberate. "Everything in this village is under my jurisdiction. Don't for a second think you can sneak something past me. Nothing – nothing - moves here without my permission. What makes you think you could pull this off right under my nose?"

Manu's heart raced, but he held Bill's gaze, though fear prickled in his chest.

"Taking my raw materials from my factory without my permission is stealing," Bill continued, his words dripping with control. "And I could lock you up for it. But," he added with a twisted smirk, "I like sharp Voivokis, so I'm willing to give you a choice - bail yourself out for ten thousand Lapes, or I'll lock you up."

Manu's eyes widened in shock, his stomach sinking. That number was staggering. It was like being hit with the reality that they were, once again, just pawns in Bill's game. A week ago, he had realised they were all trapped, but this felt different - personal, like his ambition had betrayed him. Until now, his entrepreneurial thinking had always been praised. He'd been encouraged to solve problems creatively, but here, that very skill had backfired.

He swallowed hard.

"We thought you'd appreciate the extra Lapes we'd be earning for you," he said, his voice laced with disbelief.

Bill's expression hardened.

"Lock up or ten thousand Lapes?" The ultimatum hung in the air like a noose.

Manu's dreams of fast-tracking their way to freedom shattered in that moment. Ten thousand Lapes? It seemed impossible. But he knew what being locked up would mean - at Bill's complete mercy, no options, no way to help the others. At least this way, even though the debt was massive, it was a path forward. Unlike Asim, who had been locked away without a choice, Manu still had a sliver of control.

"Ten thousand Lapes," he whispered, the weight of the decision pressing down on him.

Bill nodded curtly.

"Take all the raw materials back to the factory," he ordered, his voice cool once again. "And don't you ever step out of line again."

Manu joined his peers at the restaurant for the first time since arriving in the village and ordered the cheapest meal on the menu. He sat silently, disengaged from the lively chatter around him, replaying his encounter with Bill over and over, searching for answers about what he could have done differently.

Noticing his uncharacteristic silence, Imogen leaned in.

"What's the matter?"

Manu sighed deeply.

"We were planning to smuggle raw materials into the Guest House so Joe and Sina could start weaving clothes and shoes. The idea was to hide whatever they produced, submit it all after our test, and regain our freedoms right away. But then Bill caught me. He offered to let me bail myself out for ten thousand Lapes instead of locking me up. I had no choice but to accept."

"So, what does that mean?" Imogen asked, confusion creasing her brow.

"It means he just added ten thousand to my debt." Manu rubbed his temples in frustration. "I don't understand how he found out so quickly. He's usually in his office, especially when it's raining."

"I saw the guard talking to Bill when I stepped out of the factory," Leila chimed in innocently.

Manu turned to Joe, his gaze sharp.

"You told the guard when you came over, didn't you?"

"He asked me where I was going," Joe defended himself.

Manu was ready to jump on Joe.

"You've got to be kidding me! Your stupidity cost me ten thousand Lapes, and I should consider myself lucky he didn't lock me up for who knows how long!"

Sensing the tension, Leila quickly intervened.

"Guys! We've escaped a terrible accident and survived in the Jungle for weeks without our parents. We're in this together, and we'll share the burden of the extra ten thousand Lapes."

"She's right, Manu," Imogen added firmly. "We came together, and we will leave together."

Sensing the support from his peers helped Manu calm down, but Joe remained troubled by his recent mistake. He realised that his inability to know when to withhold information had placed a significant burden on them all. Being included in conversations and activities of such weight was new for him. In the City, his hardworking parents had provided everything and made decisions on his behalf. He'd lived a comfortable life, spending hours each day playing video games, but that had left him ill-equipped to grasp the consequences of his words and actions. Overwhelmed with shame, he wished the ground would swallow him whole then and there.

While the others moved on to discuss their feelings about their new colleagues at the factory, it was the sudden arrival of Roger that prevented Joe from sinking further into his spiral of self-pity.

"I found Josh!" Roger announced, his eyes wide with excitement.

CHAPTER 7

With each passing day, the kids learned from Maria to recognise an increasing array of sounds made by the creatures of the Jungle. Having spent 46 years at Bill's village, the sounds of the surrounding Jungle became her clock. The first sound she introduced the kids to was a distinct calling of the macaques, which reverberated through the air every afternoon, signalling the approaching moment when Bill would beat his drum.

That afternoon, when the highly anticipated calls pierced through the air, the kids exchanged cheeky smiles, eagerly waiting to see Josh. While none them were particularly close friends with him, the knowledge that he was still alive brought them all a sense of relief.

Having eaten and drunk twice that afternoon helped Josh regain a good portion of his depleted energy by the time the rest of the kids finished their work and rushed to meet him.

They surrounded him, showering him with admiration and hugs. Surviving a week on his own was no small feat for any stranger to the Jungle. Even Mai and Joe embraced him, despite feeling awkward about hugging the troublemaker who had teased and embarrassed them for years. The moment felt surreal; the very boy who had often made them the butt of his jokes was now standing before them, vulnerable and alive. As Mai stepped forward, her heart raced with a mix of resentment and relief, but when their arms wrapped around each other, warmth surged between them, bridging the chasm of past grievances. Joe watched for a moment, wrestling with his own conflicting feelings, yet he couldn't ignore the bond they shared in that moment. With a deep breath, he stepped up and pulled Josh into a fierce embrace.

Manu was the last in line. When his eyes locked onto Josh's, a wave of emotions surged through him. He didn't smile; instead, he stared intently, his heart weighed down by a mixture of relief and lingering frustration. The silence was thick, holding everyone in suspense.

"Is he holding a grudge?" some wondered, exchanging uneasy glances.

But then Manu stepped forward, slowly opening his arms and pulling Josh into a tight embrace.

"Why on earth did you take off?" he asked, his voice carrying both exasperation and concern.

"I know I was stupid," Josh admitted, his voice barely above a whisper. "But I've learned my lesson."

Manu's voice softened, though the edge of his worry remained.

"Someone told us you'd been shot. We thought you were dead this whole time."

Josh's eyes shimmered with unshed tears as the weight of his recklessness settled over him. To fight back the rising tide of emotion, he leaned on the one thing no hardship could take from him: his humour.

"Well, even the spirit world rejected me," he quipped, making the group burst into relieved laughter.

Sensing the encouragement, Josh launched into an animated recounting:

"There were arrows and spears whistling past my ears, landing inches away. Their sharp, gleaming edges could've turned me into Edam cheese - you know, the one with all the holes - but not a single one hit me! It had to be the spirit world intervening. I guess they weren't ready for me. Not yet, anyway."

Roger, wiping tears of laughter from his eyes, shifted to a more serious tone.

"Alright, Josh. No more reckless theories, okay? They might be funny, but they're also dangerous - and could cost us our lives. That's not a joke."

Josh nodded, his tone turning sincere.

"I know you're right. I'm sorry for what I did. I won't put us at risk again."

Sina, eager to shift the focus, interjected.

"Okay, enough of the past. What's next? Are you staying with us?"

Josh nodded resolutely.

"Yeah. I've learned my lesson. We were thrown into this treacherous world together, and we'll leave it together."

Manu stepped forward, drawing everyone's attention as he moved towards the spot where Josh's bow and quiver rested. Bending down, he picked up the weapon and held it up, his gaze sharp.

"Is this yours?" he asked as he picked up the weapon.

Josh nodded proudly. Watching Manu inspect every inch of his bow, he realised he hadn't taken the time to assess it himself. From the moment it came into his possession, he had been in survival mode, with no room for contemplation.

The bow was crafted from a sturdy piece of teak, shaped over a fire into a sleek, symmetrical curve. Its taut string, woven from yucca fibres, was so tight that it required nearly all of Manu's strength to draw. He didn't need to unleash an arrow to recognise its lethal potential.

He nodded approvingly at Josh, eyes wide, eyebrows slightly raised, and a faint smile playing at the corners of his lips.

"I killed a monkey and a cobra with it," Josh grinned, eager to recount the details of his survival.

He was a natural storyteller, and whenever he spoke, his words effortlessly captivated his audience. He spoke rapidly, as if racing against time, eager to share everything he had experienced. He only paused when he realised that Susan, Olivia, and Asim were missing.

"Where is my good old friend, by the way?" he asked, prompting a ripple of laughter.

Everyone understood he was referring to Asim and assumed it was just his trademark sarcasm, given the tough battles they had fought over the years. But Josh meant every word. His near-death experience and encounter with Vaipor had ignited a newfound determination within him to become the person he always aspired to be.

"Seriously, where is he?" Josh asked again, his tone shifting.

The laughter dissolved into uneasy silence.

"He's locked up," Manu said quietly.

Josh's face drained of colour, concern flashing across his features.

"Locked up?" he repeated, unsure if he heard right.

"There's more you need to know," Manu said, watching Josh's reaction closely.

Taking a deep breath, he explained their precarious entrapment in Bill's village and the grim turn of events that had led to Asim's imprisonment. Every word weighed heavy as he described how Asim had become a casualty of forces beyond their control.

Josh's initial disbelief quickly gave way to anger, his jaw tightening as a fire sparked in his eyes. His gaze shifted to the bow lying nearby, a storm of emotions building within him.

"Don't even think about it," Roger interjected, his voice steady but firm. "Violence only generates more violence. We need to regain our freedom through hard work and unity, not through reckless actions that could cost our lives. You could channel that energy into helping us instead."

Josh understood the truth behind Roger's words; retaliation would only spiral into chaos. Yet, the desire to fight back against their captors was strong.

"What do you have in mind?" Josh asked, his curiosity piqued. "Collecting Mapa seeds?"

"No, that would take too long," Roger replied, shaking his head. "As we mentioned earlier, we had a plan to weave clothes in the Guest House. But Manu was caught trying to smuggle raw materials from the factory and almost ended up locked up. As punishment, Bill slapped us with a debt of ten thousand Lapes, which, when added to what we already owe, could take us years to pay off before we can even think about which way to go."

"Why not just sneak away in the middle of the night?" Josh suggested, his eyes glinting with the thrill of the idea.

"It's too risky," Roger cautioned, a frown creasing his brow. "We can't afford to be caught again. But if you could help us source materials, we could make more clothes and shoes, and pay off our debts quicker."

"That would be just the first step," Manu added, his voice steady. "While it would help, it wouldn't give us the momentum we need. We need to find a way to sell whatever we make instead of handing it over to Bill, letting him rake in the profits."

"You mean cut out the middleman?" Roger asked, a spark of understanding igniting in his eyes.

"Exactly," Manu confirmed, his voice rising with conviction. "I don't know how much money Bill receives for what we produce, but I guarantee you he's making a lot more than we will once we pass our tests. Consider this: he pays us 125 Lapes for clothes and 212 for shoes. If he sells the clothes for 200, he makes a profit of 75 Lapes on every piece we produce. But if we could obtain our own materials and sell our products for the same price, we could pocket an additional 75 Lapes per item."

As Manu spoke, the air around them buzzed with anticipation. The kids exchanged excited glances, their expressions a mix of hope and determination. While not everyone grasped every detail of Manu's plan, his infectious enthusiasm lit a spark within them. They had seen Manu navigate challenges before, and his unwavering belief in the possibility of success inspired confidence.

"If Josh is on board, he could help us figure out where to source the raw materials and where to sell the finished products," Manu continued, his eyes glimmering with optimism. "Of course, in return, we'd have to buy food for him."

"I'm in, of course," Josh said, a grin spreading across his face, energised by the prospect of being part of something greater than himself.

"Don't get me wrong, I agree with Manu. But how are we going to buy him food if we don't even have any money?" Leila questioned, her brow furrowing in concern.

"On credit," Manu replied, his tone confident.

"With all that debt, we will never get out of here," Leila sighed, frustration lacing her voice.

Having grown up in a sheltered environment, Leila lacked exposure to entrepreneurial thinking, making it difficult for her to grasp the broader vision. She was fixated on their mounting debt and focused solely on paying it off rather than considering the potential benefits of taking on a little more in hopes of future gains. This mindset had been ingrained in her by her parents, who had missed out on numerous investment opportunities due to their obsession with paying off their mortgage. While their cautious approach provided them with a sense of security, it also kept them tethered to their jobs, leaving little room for growth or freedom.

"On the contrary," Manu assured. "If we succeed, we'll be making significantly more than we are now, allowing us to pay off our debts much sooner. Bill is probably selling what we produce for at least double or even triple what he will pay us."

"Yeah, I can definitely see that," Roger chimed in. "He is so loaded that he doesn't even bat an eye at the fact that his Guest House sits vacant most of the time."

"Does that mean we'll need to build our own factory and stop working for Bill?" Imogen asked, slowly grasping Manu's vision.

"I doubt he'd let us construct anything in his village," Manu said thoughtfully. "But we can easily use the huts were you all sleep. Rica started her business right in her hut. We're paying rent anyways."

As this realisation dawned on them, a sense of possibility began to swell within the group. They were trapped in Bill's village, but he had never explicitly said they had to work for him. The reason everyone toiled for him was that no one had dared to create their own opportunities. The only Voivoki they had heard of who had broken free from Bill's grasp was Rica, and she had done it by seizing her own chance at success. Now, with newfound hope igniting their imaginations, they couldn't see any reason why they couldn't follow in her footsteps.

"What about the training?" Mai asked seeking clarity. "Don't we need to be qualified?"

"That's a bucket load of rubbish," Manu laughed, shaking his head. "We don't need any formal qualification to produce the same quality as Maria. Let the market decide if our products are good enough. The training is just Bill's way of tying his workers to his ecosystem."

"What do you mean?" Mai pressed, clearly puzzled.

"First, some Voivokis get ensnared by falling into debt with him," Manu explained. "He offers everyone a chance to repay their debt through work. But before they can even start earning, they're forced to pay for training. During that time, they don't get paid, which means they have to buy food and cover rent on credit. By the time they finally pass their tests, they're buried in debt that takes years to pay off. To keep them there even longer, Bill throws all kinds of entertainment their way - like that festival last week - encouraging them to spend even more. This is exactly what happened to us. What's worse is that many of them accept their situation as normal, thinking it's just how life is meant to be."

"Like Maria," Roger chimed in, nodding thoughtfully.

"Or Sika and Broko," Sina added, her voice heavy with the weight of their shared experiences.

"Well, circling back to our plan, the key challenge is for Josh to find suppliers of raw materials and buyers of the finished products," said Manu. "Let's be honest; he could easily get lost in the Jungle before he even meets anyone relevant."

"If Asim came with me, it would be way easier to navigate and carry stuff," Josh replied. "What did you say his bail is?"

"Twenty thousand," said Manu.

"Twenty thousand Lapes?!" Josh exclaimed. "I was able to collect about 300 Mapa seeds on the way, which would get us roughly 30 to 40 Lapes. I can't even imagine 20,000 Lapes worth of Mapa seeds."

"You'd need a few trucks for that amount," Joe chimed in.

"Oh, absolutely! I'll just bring my toy trucks next time," Manu quipped, making everyone laugh.

"Guys! Seriously, what are we going to do about Asim?" Leila asked. "We can't let them take him to the Kilisi."

"Can't you bail him out on credit?" Josh suggested.

"We haven't asked, but it's a possibility," said Manu.

"The challenge is that even if Josh — and let's say Asim - find suppliers and buyers, it could still take ages to complete those round trips," Roger pointed out. "However, if we establish a regular route, we could potentially consolidate our debts under one person and have multiple pairs of transporters."

Roger's idea sparked a new wave of excitement, fuelling their imaginations. They quickly realised that if only one of them stayed indebted to Bill, they could drastically cut their collective expenses. Only one person would have to cover the training fees and accommodation, while the rest could focus on building their new business. It was a breakthrough, a lesson they discovered on their own, and they were rightfully buzzing with excitement.

"Manu, can you speak to Bill?" asked Roger.

"I can't," Manu replied, shaking his head. "After what happened today, it's better if I stay under the radar for a while."

"Okay, I'll handle it then," Roger said, remembering Vaipor's words. "But who should we consolidate our debts with?"

A few awkward glances were exchanged, and slowly, many pairs of eyes landed on Mai. She was the least fit for any physical work, making her the most likely candidate.

"You guys want to transfer all your debt to me?" Mai asked, alarmed, her voice rising in disbelief.

Her heart pounded as the enormity of her peers' proposal sank in. Taking on everyone's debt meant shouldering a burden that terrified her, a responsibility so massive it felt like it could crush her. What if they abandoned her after they regained their freedom? The idea churned in her insides. Without them, she would be stuck here forever, never seeing her family again. The thought alone was suffocating. Filled with panic, she felt an overwhelming urge to vanish into the darkness, away from the pressure, away from the impossible weight. A couple of the girls tried to stop her, calling out her name, but their words couldn't reach her. She slipped away, leaving them standing helpless as the night swallowed her. Mai's abrupt departure left the group rattled, a silence hanging over them as tiredness began to creep in.

They decided to postpone any decisions and call it a night, the excitement of their planning fizzling into exhaustion. Josh flopped onto an empty hammock, a wide grin spreading across his face as he swung lazily a few times before settling down. The soft fibre cradled him, a comfort so sweet it was hard to believe that just the day before he had feared he'd never see daylight again. Within moments, his snores filled the air, drawing chuckles from his companions, particularly the boys. They, too, had felt that same relief when they first slept in these hammocks just a week earlier.

As the night deepened, the Jungle's symphony of sounds lulled the weary group into a peaceful slumber. One by one, the kids drifted off, their worries momentarily forgotten. The gentle sway of the hammocks rocked them into a deep, restful sleep, and before they knew it, the soft glow of dawn began creeping through the trees, bringing with it the promise of a new day - and fresh challenges.

The gruelling days of isolation, battling for survival, had left Josh completely drained. While he remained fast asleep, Roger had already made the trek to the restaurant and back, returning with breakfast in hand.

"We've got to wake him," Manu suggested, glancing at the village. "Our shift commences soon."

Standing beside the hammock, he gently shook Josh's shoulder, snapping him out of his dream. Josh blinked groggily as Roger handed him his portion.

"Jungle service," Roger grinned.

Josh sat up, rubbed his eyes and asked:

"How much?"

Manu and Roger exchanged amused glances, anticipating his reaction.

"Twenty," Roger replied casually.

"Twenty Lapes for this?!" Josh blurted out, staring at the meagre meal in disbelief.

"Yup," Roger said, smiling.

Josh shook his head in frustration.

"We seriously have to find a way to cut our expenses."

"I know," Roger agreed, his tone growing sombre. "But we don't have many options until we can execute our plan from last night. It's only a matter of time. I can feel it."

He glanced at the dark clouds.

"Anyways, what are you planning to do today in this rain?"

"I guess I'll just wait for Voivokis to turn up with raw materials – maybe stand on the far side of the village with an umbrella," Josh shrugged. "That way we can keep our eyes on this place from two sides."

"Why don't you ask Bill if he's got any work for you?" Manu suggested, eyeing Josh over his breakfast.

Josh's face twisted in disdain.

"I don't want to become his slave."

"You won't," Manu reassured him. "Take a job that lets you keep an eye on the village, gives you flexibility, and doesn't require any training. Becoming a guard sounds like a good option."

Josh sighed.

"I'll see," he muttered, focusing on his food.

He was in no rush, but the rest? Their clock was ticking. The relentless grind of working day in, day out under strict rules was eye-opening. It dawned on them that their parents had faced the same battle: large bills, mounting debt, and endless hours just to stay afloat. Did they have a choice? Unlikely. They were trapped in a cycle the kids were only beginning to understand.

Roger was determined to make the most of his second day as a guard. Inspired by Vaipor's words, he approached it differently. To kill time, he set about constructing a makeshift shelter at a vantage point where he could monitor both the village and the Jungle. As he wove palm leaves for the roof and lashed timber together for the frame, his mind spun with scenarios. The kids had big plans to launch their business, but too many uncertainties lingered, and Bill still held most of the cards.

Meanwhile, at the factory, the rest of the group worked in a silence heavy with unspoken thoughts. Their conversation from the previous night still weighed on them, sparking questions and ideas they couldn't freely share. It was hard for them to stay focused on the mundane tasks without overthinking.

Mai, though, was the most distant. Not a single smile crossed her face that morning. In the City, someone in her state would call in sick or take paid leave. But here, in Bill's world, no such luxuries existed. The idea of paying someone who wasn't working was alien to him. Lunchtime couldn't come soon enough for her, and the moment the rhythmic drumming signalled the break, she bolted from the factory, desperate for a moment alone.

Josh sat at the restaurant, watching the factory workers spill out one by one. The sight struck him as pathetic, reminding him of the rigid discipline teachers in the City tried to enforce. He couldn't imagine himself becoming that brain-numbingly robotic, especially not in the heart of the Jungle, where freedom was within reach for those who knew how to survive.

"How did it go with Bill?" Manu asked, eager for any news.

Josh shrugged.

"He offered me the same factory job you guys are stuck with. I politely declined and asked him to keep me in mind if anything else comes up."

"That's actually a good sign," Manu said, his expression thoughtful.

Sina raised an eyebrow.

"How so? He didn't end up getting a job."

"Think about it," Manu explained. "If there wasn't significant demand for what we're producing, Bill wouldn't have wanted to hire another person for the same role. He's not the type to pay anyone to sit around."

His words resonated with the group. Bill wasn't someone who employed people out of pity. Every worker in his operation had a purpose, and every product had a price. If he was willing to add more hands to the factory, it meant one thing: business was booming. And while that might not have been the escape plan they wanted, it meant their strategy had potential. Still, it required patience, which after a couple of days of rain was wearing thin.

While some of the villagers spent their downtime sleeping, others found comfort in conversations or hobbies. Imogen was intently focused on sketching a portrait of Susan by the unsteady light of flickering torches. The shifting shadows made it difficult to capture Susan's features, but Imogen pressed on, determined to create something remarkable.

Mai had never been much of a talker, but since the discussion about her possibly taking on everyone else's debt, she had become even more withdrawn. Seeking refuge from the village's noise, she found a secluded spot beneath a large leaf, her thoughts heavy with worries about her family.

Each day was a battle against the whispers of self-doubt, memories of taunts and judgments from her past resurfacing to erode her confidence. They made her feel like an outsider - not just within the village itself but also amongst her peers. As raindrops softly drummed on the leaf above, Mai's emotions churned inside her. She longed for acceptance and understanding, a break from the invisible weight she carried within. Yet while the leaf shielded her from the rain, it couldn't protect her from the storm of thoughts that raged within.

"What are you doing here all by yourself at this time of the day?" came the voice she had longed to hear for days.

"Nothing," Mai replied, her voice a mixture of surprise and hesitation.

"Nothing?" Vaipor echoed, raising an eyebrow.

"Yes. Really, nothing," Mai repeated, her gaze distant.

"Can I join you in doing nothing?" Vaipor asked, a playful note in his voice.

"Sure," Mai said, the faintest hint of a smile tugging at her lips.

With another large leaf in hand, Vaipor settled beside her without a word, allowing the silence to stretch between them. He sensed the coldness in her responses, knowing she wasn't ready for conversation yet. So he waited, patient, giving her the space to adjust to his presence.

"Still into doing nothing?" Vaipor eventually asked, breaking the quiet after what felt like hours.

This time, Mai responded with a small, genuine smile, the first warmth in her eyes since their meeting.

"I guess that smile means you are really into doing nothing," Vaipor teased lightly. "When you do nothing, do you normally do it by yourself or with others?"

A soft laugh escaped Mai, the tension breaking as his gentle persistence cracked through her defences.

"There we go," Vaipor said with a hint of triumph. "I knew you could laugh. So, why are you sitting here all by yourself, trying so hard to look upset?"

She hesitated for a moment, then let out a soft sigh.

"Because… it feels like everyone's always picking on me."

"Tell me what makes you feel that way."

Mai explained how the others wanted to shift their debts onto her, so they could be free and leave her behind, believing she was slower and less capable.

"Do you really think they'd leave you behind?" Vaipor asked gently.

"Yes. None of them are really friends with me... so why would they care?"

"You're in a group of ten, and none of them are friends with you?" he asked, his tone full of genuine curiosity.

"That's right."

Vaipor paused thoughtfully.

"Why do you think that is?"

"I don't know," Mai said, frustration creeping into her voice. "It's not like I'm mean to anyone. We've just never been close, and being stuck here didn't change that. I just want to get back home to my family... and be left alone."

Vaipor's eyes searched hers, then he asked quietly:

"What would you do if you were home?"

Mai didn't immediately answer. She looked to her left, as if searching for the answer in the darkness. Her mind drifted back to the comfort of home. She pictured herself lounging on their soft couch, legs up, a bag of crispy potato chips in one hand, a fizzy drink in the other. The TV was on, playing something indistinct - it didn't really matter what. Her phone buzzed beside her, and she glanced at it to see a message from one of her closest online friends, someone she'd never met in person.

Snapping back to the present, she turned to Vaipor.

"I would probably just watch TV."

"Is that the magic box where you can see all sorts of things?"

"Yeah."

"What would you watch?" he asked, his tone gentle but curious.

"I don't know. Whatever is on."

Vaipor chuckled lightly, trying to ease her into the conversation.

"And how long would you watch… whatever is on?"

"Until I get bored, I guess."

"And after that?"

"I would probably eat something and text my friends."

She paused, a flicker of suspicion crossing her face.

"But what's with all the questions?"

"I came to help you," he replied. "But first, I wanted to get to know you a little better. Sorry if it feels like too many questions… but are you open to my help?"

Mai sat quietly, mulling over his words. She didn't think she needed help - aside from someone just taking her home, so she bluntly asked:

"Are you going to take me home?"

Vaipor laughed.

"I'm here to guide you on your journey," he replied, his tone steady and reassuring. "But first, can you explain to me what texting means?"

His question caught Mai off guard, shattering her assumption that he knew everything.

"Well, we use these small, magic boxes – what we call phones - to send messages to our friends through social media, no matter how far apart we are," she began, her voice gaining confidence.

"Interesting," Vaipor mused, his gaze fixed on her. "So, you don't actually see them?"

"You can, but you don't have to," Mai clarified.

Vaipor squinted, contemplating her response.

"Hmmm…"

Unsure how to interpret his reaction, Mai felt her confidence begin to wane.

"Do you have any real friends?" he asked, surprising her with the directness of the question.

"They are real friends who truly care about me," Mai protested, her tone sharper.

"How can you be so sure about that?" Vaipor pressed gently.

"Because they are always there when I need them," she answered, her defensiveness rising.

"Do you know what body language means?"

"No," Mai replied, her brow furrowing in confusion.

"Well, it's the most important part of communication," Vaipor explained. "It encompasses your attitude and feelings, conveyed through your posture, movements, facial expressions, and even the look in your eyes. In fact, about 70% of communication is based on body language, while only 10% comes from tone. That leaves just 20% for the words themselves. So, to me, it seems relying solely on your magic boxes and social media can be risky. Don't you think?"

Mai's heart sank at Vaipor's words, each syllable striking a nerve she had hoped to avoid. The idea that her friends from social media might not be 'real' cut deeper than she anticipated. As she sat there, her mind raced with images of the laughter and support she had received through her phone, but doubt gnawed at her. She felt the urge to argue and defend her connections, yet insecurity clamped down on her voice.

"You must learn to socialise with real humans and form real friendships," Vaipor continued, his tone gentle yet firm. "Here in the Jungle, your heightened sense of desolation is due to your inability to connect with your social media friends and your reluctance to build authentic relationships with your peers and the Voivokis around you."

"I tried," Mai protested again. "But they still want to leave me behind."

"Isn't that just your misperception? Be careful not to let it deceive you. They want to work as a team, to free everyone from Bill's grip including you."

"Then why did they single me out and expect me to take on all their debts?"

"Don't you want to return home as soon as possible?"

"Of course I do," she replied.

"Exactly. And their plan is brilliant - they need to make fast progress, traveling through the Jungle and carrying heavy loads. The quicker they complete their trips, the quicker you'll all be free. Are you the fastest in the group?"

Mai hesitated, well aware of the answer.

"Not really," she admitted, her thoughts drifting to how she often struggled to keep up. The village, despite its hardships, was a relief compared to the exhausting treks through rough terrain or climbing voku trees.

"Are you the slowest?" Vaipor pressed.

"Maybe."

"Maybe or yes?"

"Yes! I'm the slowest!" Mai snapped, her frustration boiling over. "You said you came to help, but all you're doing is criticising me - just like everyone else!"

"Do you think help is just about getting praise to make you feel good? If that's what you're after, you don't deserve my time. I'm here to help by giving you honest direction and feedback, to open your eyes to what you're not seeing. You need to understand yourself better if you ever want to turn your life around and be truly happy, surrounded by real friends - not just random people on social media you've never met.

But if you keep defending your weaknesses instead of working on self-improvement, I won't waste my time here. I'll leave you to your misery."

Vaipor's tone was unwavering, and it shook Mai to the core. Her parents, though loving, had always showered her with kind words, never wanting to spoil the little time they had with her due to their long work hours. Even when they saw her mistakes, they avoided confrontation. But this was different. For the first time, someone seemed to care enough to confront her with the harsh truth. It felt like staring into a mirror she had long avoided.

"I'm sorry," she said quietly, the sincerity in her voice undeniable.

"Your physical well-being has a profound impact on your overall life," Vaipor began. "The better you take care of your body, the better you feel. And when you feel good, you radiate positive energy that naturally draws people to you. Have you ever noticed how certain people energise you while others leave you feeling drained?"

Mai nodded, listening closely.

"That's because people emit unique energy," Vaipor continued. "Some people uplift you, while others deplete you. And just like you sense their energy, others pick up on yours. When you're not feeling good about yourself and your energy is low, your subconscious pulls from the people around you. They sense this - often without even realising it - and they may distance themselves to protect their own energy."

"How do they do that?" Mai asked, her curiosity evident.

"There are many ways," Vaipor replied. "Some people lash out, saying hurtful things to regain control over their energy or feel powerful. It's rarely about you - it's about their own struggles."

"But I don't hurt anyone," Mai said, missing his point. "So why are people still so mean to me?"

"In most cases, you don't know what others are going through. Sometimes, causing someone else pain gives them a twisted sense of relief from their own suffering. But instead of focusing on why they're mean, focus on what you can control - your energy. Build a strong, positive energy shield that protects you."

Mai frowned.

"I don't get it."

"That's okay," Vaipor reassured her. "You will one day. Let me give you an example: think about how you usually react when someone says something hurtful. You feel upset, right? But instead of letting their words hurt you, you can twist them into something funny or let their negativity slide off you like water. If they see their words don't bother you, they will likely stop - or even try to befriend you. Don't let their negativity define your reality."

Mai let out a deep sigh.

"But how will a positive energy shield help me get back home?" she asked.

"By focusing on your physical and mental well-being," Vaipor explained, "you'll start to see paths you never imagined were there."

He stood, his movement deliberate yet gentle, and placed a firm but reassuring hand on Mai's shoulder. She felt a tremor ripple through her, though she wasn't sure if it was from his touch or the weight of his words.

"You'll form authentic friendships," he said, his voice calm but resolute. "And those connections will carry you through even the hardest times. Trying to change others leads to frustration. But creating harmony within yourself? That attracts success. Carry this advice with you, and what you're seeking will eventually reveal itself."

With that, he wished her well and disappeared into the darkness, leaving Mai alone to process his words. The night felt strangely still in his absence, yet his voice lingered in her mind, echoing like a distant melody. She wasn't angry or disappointed. Instead, his message struck deeper than she had expected, planting seeds of doubt and hope alike. If her isolation and frustration were rooted in something within herself, that meant she had the power to change it.

She closed her eyes, inhaling the cool night air, and silently promised herself that she would change. The thought filled her with a curious mix of determination and relief. Yet as quickly as it came, the comfort faded. Thoughts of her family crept in, turning her newfound resolve into a sharp ache of desperation. The idea of getting home felt as distant as ever.

With these thoughts pressing down on her, she made her way back to the hut, her steps slow and heavy. The Jungle's quiet only amplified the storm inside her. By the time she saw the flickering light of her hut, Sina was already waiting at the entrance, her face drawn with worry. A stab of guilt hit Mai - she hadn't meant to worry anyone - but the weight of Vaipor's words kept her silent. She wasn't ready to talk yet, still unsure what this new realisation even meant.

"Is it about your family?" Sina asked, her voice soft and caring.

"Yeah, I miss them dearly," Mai replied, tears welling in her eyes.

That night, for the first time, Sina and Mai truly opened up to each other. The conversation began hesitantly, but soon the dam broke, and their thoughts and feelings poured out. Mai spoke of her doubts, her fears of not fitting in, and her growing realisation that she had been looking at things the wrong way. Sina, on the other hand, shared her own insecurities - the pressure of keeping up with others, the constant second-guessing of her decisions, and the weight of expectations that sometimes felt suffocating. As the night deepened, they found comfort in each other's vulnerability, the shared burdens that they never realised were so similar.

By the time they finally let the conversation wind down, it was late, and they drifted off to sleep with a newfound bond between them. But the rest was short-lived. A cacophony of shouts, clanging, and banging abruptly woke them. It was as if a construction site had sprung to life right outside their hut, the sounds so loud and chaotic that they could barely think. They exchanged groggy, bewildered glances, their brief night of peace quickly replaced by confusion and the promise of yet another long, unpredictable day.

CHAPTER 8

Bill's village hummed with an unusual energy that morning. Unfamiliar Voivokis scurried through the narrow pathways, their voices ringing with urgency as they barked orders and hurried to complete their tasks. Emerging from their hut, Sina and Mai were immediately approached by a neatly dressed Voivoki who delivered an unexpected proposal: she was seeking extra hands to help set up and manage the bustling market Bill had arranged to promote his various businesses.

"We're already tied up with other work," Mai said, politely declining.

The Voivoki's expression remained calm, but her offer took an enticing turn.

"It's your decision," she said evenly, "but I'm willing to pay 450 Lapes for today's work. It's a fair deal for both of you."

Sina and Mai exchanged surprised glances. The offer was more than double what Bill paid Sina, a tempting sum that was hard to ignore. Yet, knowing all too well the grip Bill held over their lives, they hesitated. Breaking away from their obligations could provoke trouble. With a reluctant sigh, they turned down the offer.

The Voivoki, undeterred, swiftly moved on to oversee her workers, leaving Sina and Mai standing near their hut, drawn in by the scene unfolding before them - the hustle and intensity of the market preparations.

Just then, Imogen and Manu appeared, their faces lit with excitement.

"Hey! Before breakfast, would you two like to pose for caricatures?" Manu asked, barely able to contain his eagerness.

Sina tilted her head.

"What's a caricature?"

"It's like a funny portrait - where your features are exaggerated, like giving someone a big nose or huge lips," Imogen explained, grinning.

Sina and Mai exchanged amused looks, unsure how to respond to the odd but intriguing offer. Sensing their hesitation, Imogen's voice grew more urgent.

"Come on, you in or what?"

Sina, though wary of stepping into the spotlight, decided to embrace the invitation. But Mai hesitated, her internal struggle far more pronounced. For someone as introverted and burdened by insecurities as Mai, the thought of standing in front of others was daunting. Every step towards action felt like an uphill battle, with persistent self-doubt and the fear of judgment shadowing her every move. The mere idea of being laughed at or ridiculed weighed heavily on her, making even the simplest decisions feel like monumental tasks.

But as she stood frozen, she recalled her recent conversation with Vaipor.

"The more positive I am, the more others will like me," she reminded herself.

That brief moment of insight gave her the strength to push back against the negativity swirling in her mind.

Summoning all her courage, she finally responded, though her voice carried a hint of apprehension.

"Where are we doing it?"

Her question was met with an outpouring of encouragement from her friends.

"Right next to all the action," said Manu, grinning. "Let's go! We don't have much time."

Mai felt a strange mixture of nerves and excitement bubbling inside her. Her palms grew clammy, yet her smile widened. As they moved towards the market, each step lightened the weight on her shoulders. Slowly, her fear began to give way to something else - a growing sense of anticipation. For the first time in her life, she felt a surge of confidence, a quiet but powerful victory over the self-doubt that had held her back for so long.

As they approached, it became clear that the market was being set up in the open space between the plantation fields and the village huts. The flat area, now cleared of vegetation, was a perfect spot for the bustling event. Though smaller than the previous market the kids had attended, it still had ample room to accommodate a couple hundred Voivokis and featured around 20 stalls, each filled with the energy of last-minute preparations.

Mai took a deep breath, feeling the warm breeze and the hum of excitement around her. This was more than just a market - it was a moment of transformation, a step towards embracing herself, insecurities and all.

A few robust Voivokis were busy stacking large pieces of timber in the middle of the field, while others dug holes with precision and speed, setting the groundwork for what would soon become the heart of the market.

"They're building the stand for the drum," Manu remarked confidently, as if he had been part of similar events countless times before. A few steps away from the edge of the market, he pointed out a sizable rock, smooth and flat, perfect for someone to sit on.

"That's our spot. We need to get to work right away."

Without hesitation, Imogen set up her materials and began sketching her first caricature, capturing Leila's features with quick, deliberate strokes. The rest of the boys arrived shortly after, carrying bundles of timber, vines, and napier grass, their arms full with the tools they needed to bring their stall to life.

Josh, unburdened by any constraints, darted back into the bush to gather more materials. Meanwhile, Joe and Roger wasted no time. They mimicked the techniques of the Voivokis nearby, using sharp sticks to dig holes for the posts. Luck was on their side - the recent heavy rains had softened the ground, making it easier to dig deep enough for their structure to stand firm.

Sina and Mai, working with quiet determination, began weaving together a roof made from the vines and grass, carefully crafting a protective shelter that would shield them from the unpredictable weather. The memories of the torrential rains from days prior lingered in their minds, and they wanted to ensure that neither the models nor the artist's delicate work would be ruined by another downpour.

As the group moved with focus and purpose, their stall began to take shape, standing in contrast to the chaotic flurry of activity around them. There was an unspoken sense of camaraderie in their efforts, and with every stroke of Imogen's pencil and every carefully placed beam, they inched closer to becoming part of the bustling marketplace.

Manu crafted a simple frame to display Imogen's portrait of Susan. He split two thin bamboo sticks three-quarters of the way, creating grooves to hold the edges of the paper. Next, he carefully stripped the bark from a piece of timber and softened it by hammering it with a stick. Once the bark was pliable, he used it to tie the ends of the split bamboo together. He repeated the process on the opposite side of the paper and finished the frame by securing two more bamboo pieces along the top and bottom. While it may not have been the sturdiest frame, it served its purpose well, allowing them to hang the drawing inside their stall and draw the attention of passing Voivokis.

As their stall neared completion, Imogen's nimble fingers had already brought Leila's and Sina's caricatures to life. She was carefully adding the finishing touches to Mai's when a pair of curious Voivokis approached, intrigued by her creations. Without missing a beat, Manu stepped in, diplomatically informing them that the artist was focused on her work and couldn't be interrupted. However, he graciously offered his help.

"How much would it cost to get a drawing of myself?" one of them asked.

Manu hesitated for a moment, unsure of the right price, and decided to playfully negotiate. "Well, given her remarkable talent and the unique canvas she uses, how much are you willing to pay?"

"50 Lapes," replied the younger one.

Manu shook his head.

"I'm afraid you might not fully appreciate that her art goes beyond a simple drawing. She is the finest artist in the Jungle, and she works on paper - something that simply doesn't exist elsewhere. The final artwork holds significant value. A more generous offer would better reflect its true worth."

The other kids gathered around the stall, their excitement palpable as they opted to delay breakfast to witness the negotiation unfold.

"250 Lapes," declared the older of the two Voivokis.

Imogen struggled to contain her enthusiasm, tempted to step forward and accept their offer herself. The prospect of earning 250 Lapes for something she loved was incredibly enticing. Yet, she trusted Manu's talent for securing the best deals and held her tongue.

"Let's not waste each other's time," Manu said, causing Imogen to nearly drop her pencil. "As I mentioned, she's the finest artist you will ever encounter, and her artwork is crafted on a material you won't find anywhere else. The value of her creations will only appreciate, promising substantial returns. You strike me as an intelligent and perceptive Voivoki who understands the remarkable potential in this opportunity. So, wouldn't it be wise to propose a more reasonable offer?"

As the negotiation progressed, more onlookers gathered, eager to witness the unfolding drama. Even Susan and Olivia joined the growing crowd. Amidst the atmosphere of anticipation, another voice rang out:

"650."

The kids exchanged incredulous glances, the prospect of earning 650 Lapes - a sum that required days of hard labour under Bill's employment - for a single caricature left them stunned. They couldn't fathom how some Voivokis could afford to spare such a hefty amount for an artwork that Imogen could easily complete in half an hour.

All eyes were fixed on Manu as he paused, scratching his temple, carefully weighing his next words.

"Well," he began with a grin that mirrored the surprise on Imogen's face, "that's quite a bit lower than our usual rate, but since it's my birthday, you can secure your spot for just 650 Lapes today." His smile widened as murmurs of excitement rippled through the crowd.

In an instant, nearly a dozen eager Voivokis shot their hands into the air, each desperate to claim their place in line. One Voivoki, who had initially scoffed with an offer of just 50 Lapes, now pushed forward, arguing that he and his friend deserved to go first.

Manu, unfazed by the rising energy, held up a hand to quiet them.

"Since our talented artist can't get to everyone at once," he said, his voice calm but commanding, "my friend Josh will collect 50% deposits. He'll let you know when it's your turn."

A quick glance at Josh, and a nod of agreement followed. Without missing a beat, Josh moved through the crowd, gathering the deposits from fourteen eager Voivokis, all determined not to let this rare opportunity slip through their fingers.

As the excitement buzzed around them, Imogen leaned in close, whispering urgently,

"Manu! What about my work at the factory?"

Manu leaned closer to her.

"We all need to focus on what we do best," he replied. "And you, Imogen, are the best at drawing. By the end of today, you'll have earned enough to pay off your entire debt to Bill. You'll practically be free."

Imogen's eyes widened.

"But what about our agreement? We were supposed to split the profits."

Manu smiled, his gaze firm.

"We will, but think about it. Today's earnings could set a lot of us free. What's the point of you and me hoarding all those Lapes if we're still stuck here with the others? We don't leave anyone behind."

Imogen stared at him for a moment, her resolve growing stronger. She gave a nod, understanding the bigger picture. Their freedom wasn't just about money - it was about breaking free as a group.

Manu was just about to dash off for breakfast when a familiar voice stopped him in his tracks.

"Quite the salesmanship there, kid."

Manu turned to the sound and immediately recognised Rich, standing casually with a knowing smile.

"Rich!" Manu exclaimed, barely able to contain his excitement. He resisted the impulse to hug him, opting for a wide grin instead. "It's great to see you again! What brings you here?"

"I heard about the market," Rich replied with a glint in his eye. "Thought I'd come by and see if there were any good deals. You know us entrepreneurs - we're always on the hunt for the next big opportunity. But what about you? You haven't made much progress since we last spoke. I thought you were on your way home."

Manu's smile faltered slightly, a hint of embarrassment crossing his face.

"Well... we're kind of trapped at the moment, so leaving isn't really an option," he admitted, his awkward grin betraying his unease.

"Trapped? What do you mean, 'trapped'?" Rich's tone grew more serious, his curiosity piqued.

Manu sighed and launched into an explanation, recounting how they had wandered into Bill's village, drawn in by the promise of a proper meal. Hungry and exhausted, they'd accepted the offer without a second thought - a decision that quickly spiralled into a major blunder. He went on to describe how Bill not only forced people to work but also burdened them with unnecessary training fees before they could even start earning wages.

Rich shook his head, his expression a mix of disbelief and admiration.

"He's got this whole thing rigged in his favour, doesn't he?" he said dryly. "How much debt are you all in at this point?"

Manu's shoulders tensed. The weight of their situation hung heavy, but he knew there was no use hiding the truth from someone as savvy as Rich.

When Manu revealed that he alone had racked up over 11,000 Lapes in debt, Rich's eyes widened in astonishment. Manu continued, outlining their promising business plan - a plan that could have not only paid off their debts but generated a significant profit for Bill as well. Unfortunately, Bill's overinflated ego had gotten in the way, preventing them from moving forward.

"When he caught me with the raw materials," Manu explained, "he gave me an ultimatum - either he locks me up or I take on an extra 10,000 Lapes of debt. I chose the debt."

Rich shook his head.

"Real entrepreneurs don't let their egos get in the way of progress. This guy clearly doesn't know the first thing about long-term growth," Rich said. "Then again, if he'd let you go through with it, he'd risk losing all of you eventually. Quality resources are hard to find out here, so he's doing whatever he can to keep you chained to his operation."

Rich paused, his gaze drifting momentarily to the distant mountains before leaning in, his voice lowering with curiosity.

"So, what about this business idea you've got going? Tell me more."

Manu explained the arrangement he'd made with Imogen, detailing their plan to sell as many artworks as possible.

"We can charge a premium because of the scarcity," Manu added, a glimmer of excitement in his voice. "No one here has ever seen paper."

Rich's eyes lit up.

"Smart thinking! Supply and demand - you're already ahead of the game." He leaned in further, his tone now serious and calculating. "So, tell me, how much do you need to start that weaving business you mentioned?"

Manu froze. The idea of receiving seed money from a Voivoki he had met only once felt surreal, despite knowing that many successful entrepreneurs often relied on such support to launch their ventures. Yet, several key aspects of the plan were still murky, leaving him uncertain about how to respond.

"I don't know," Manu confessed, his voice dropping to a hesitant murmur. "I'm not sure where to even begin - where to get the materials, how much they'd cost, or where we'd be able to sell whatever we end up making."

Rich nodded.

"Well, figure it out and let me know when you're ready. You know where to find me," he said, giving a quick nod before turning to leave.

Manu stood still, feeling a surge of adrenaline coursing through him. An enormous opportunity had just unfolded before his eyes, but it came with an equally large risk. His skin prickled with goose bumps as the weight of the situation sank in. If they wanted to break free from Bill's stranglehold, he would need to act swiftly - and carefully. The need to gather information became urgent, but the slightest misstep could jeopardize everything. If Bill caught wind of their plans, it wouldn't just mean failure; it could mean lock up - or worse, a one-way trip to the dreaded Kilisi.

Manu's thoughts churned as he made his way towards the restaurant, barely aware of his surroundings.

"If we pull this off, Bill would lose his manufacturing business," he thought, his pulse quickening.

Later that morning, Bill paid a surprise visit to the factory. His trademark lack of pleasantries was on full display as he cut straight to the chase, informing the workers that he expected significant boost in productivity.

"For those of you on a day rate, I've increased the quota starting today," he declared, outlining the new expectations before striding away.

Maria, seasoned in the art of enduring such unwelcome news, remained unfazed. However, the two new recruits from the Guest House exchanged worried glances. They had initially welcomed the break from monotony, but the sudden pressure to work faster left them disheartened. Their quiet grumbling set a sombre tone for the rest of the morning.

"He doesn't give a damn about us. I bet he didn't even notice that Imogen's not here," muttered one of them.

Meanwhile, a good distance from the factory, a group of Voivokis was making their way down from one of the hills, each carrying a large basket on their back. Sensing an opportunity, Roger approached them to enquire about their business.

"We're the Totoli Group," one of them began, a sense of pride in his voice. "We trade in raw materials, shoes, and clothing. We're here for our usual full moon dealings with Bill."

Roger's heart raced at their response. This was the moment he had been waiting for ever since their business idea began to take root. While business wisdom suggested a measured demeanour, the thrill of this opportunity made it difficult to temper his excitement. The prospect of collaborating with the

Totoli Group felt like the key to unlocking their dreams and breaking free from Bill's grip.

"How much for the raw materials?" Roger asked, flashing a big smile.

"Two thousand," one of the traders replied, his tone neutral.

"And what do you pay for clothes and shoes?" Roger pressed, eager to glean more information.

"You do realise these are trade secrets we can't share, right?" the trader shot back, a hint of arrogance in his voice.

"I understand, but I'm pretty sure I can offer you a better deal than Bill," Roger countered, surprised by his own confidence.

"How so?" the trader asked, then added: "Listen, kid, I appreciate your enthusiasm, but we don't have time to waste."

He swung his bag over his shoulder and prepared to head straight to Bill's office.

"Wait!" Roger called out, stepping in front of them. He needed to think on his feet; if the traders made it to Bill, their plan would be delayed for at least a month, and he wasn't ready to let that happen.

"What you see on the surface is often misleading," Roger continued, his voice steady. "Sometimes I serve as a guard for Bill, and I actually enjoy being here on my own. It helps me declutter my mind so I can make better decisions when it matters. Don't you ever like to have a moment to yourself?"

His words hung in the air, creating a brief pause as the traders exchanged glances. Roger hoped to pique their interest and buy some time.

"Yeah," the trader replied, taken aback.

"I thought so," Roger said with a cryptic grin. "Successful people like us all understand the value of solitude, and for me, getting paid to be alone is just a bonus. I run a factory with more workers than Bill does. As a skilled trader, you know how to maximise your profits. Let's make a deal that will benefit us both. How much do you want to pay for clothes and shoes?"

With each word, Roger felt his confidence swell. While calling himself a successful entrepreneur might have been a stretch, his determination to forge a deal made it feel entirely justified. As he finished speaking, he marvelled at how quickly he had put into practice the skills Vaipor had imparted to him.

"Embrace the challenges, and you'll uncover paths you never knew were there," echoed Vaipor's words in his mind, fuelling his resolve.

Fortunately for Roger, the trader realised he had little to lose by sparing him a few minutes. If Roger was bluffing, the trader still had his deal with Bill as a backup. But if Roger spoke the truth, he could increase his profit margin by offering prices 25% lower than what he paid Bill:

"375 for clothes and 525 for shoes."

"That's well below what we're currently getting from other traders. Let me see what I can work out," Roger replied confidently. "I'll discuss it with my business partner and get back to you shortly. Make yourself comfortable in the hammocks over there."

Without waiting for a response, he sprinted down the hill towards the factory, urgency propelling him forward.

"Manu, come quickly!" he called, breathless as he reached the factory.

The workers glanced at him with concern, their faces etched with worry. Roger wasn't supposed to leave his post, and if Bill caught wind of it - or if anyone reported him - he could face serious consequences. The fact that he was risking so much hinted at something monumental.

Manu sprang up at Roger's frantic gesture and hurried outside, their shared urgency evident. Together, they darted into Imogen and Leila's hut, hoping to minimise the risk of being seen by Bill.

"What's going on?" Manu asked, his brow furrowed with concern.

"I found the traders. They call themselves the Totoli Group."

"Holy Jungle! Where did you find them?"

Manu's initial worry quickly morphed into excitement, the thrill of new possibilities coursing through him.

"Up on the hills. They're selling one bag of raw materials for 2000 Lapes and offering 375 for the finished clothes and 525 for the shoes."

"Do you remember Rich?" Manu asked, a wide grin spreading across his face.

"Of course! What about him?"

"He's here! I spoke with him, and he said to let him know how much we need to start our business. He'll help finance it! Let's figure it out."

Without a calculator or pen and paper, they relied on mental math, a challenge that felt both exhilarating and daunting. To keep things manageable, they assumed that each of them had a debt of 2000 Lapes to Bill, except for Imogen, whose popular drawings rendered her practically free. Josh was also an exception, but they had to add 10,000 Lapes for Manu and 20,000 for Asim.

"Okay, so that's 2000 Lapes multiplied by the eight of us, plus Asim's 20,000 and my 10,000. That totals 46,000 Lapes," Manu calculated. "How many bags did they bring?"

"Seven," Roger replied. "So that's another 14,000 Lapes. How long do you think that will last us?"

"I'm not sure, but the ten of us are only using about a third of a bag a day. That means it should last us around 21 days. That's nearly a month, considering the weekends when the others probably won't want to work," Manu said, his mind racing with possibilities.

"So how much profit would we make if we could buy all the materials?" Roger asked, his curiosity piqued.

"That's hard to say," Manu replied, furrowing his brow. "We end up with unfinished products every day and complete them the following day. But based on what I've seen, we could easily produce nine pieces of clothing and three pairs of shoes daily. So that's..."

They exchanged awkward smiles, feeling the weight of the calculations becoming a bit overwhelming.

"Gee, it would be great if Joe were here right now," Manu chuckled.

"Come on, Manu, we can do this!" Roger urged, his determination shining through. "You calculate the clothing at 9 times 375, and I'll handle the shoes."

It didn't take long for them to crunch the numbers, and their excitement went through the roof as the figures came together. Their estimated daily revenue soared to 4950 Lapes, and in 21 days, they could potentially amass an impressive 103,950 Lapes.

"That's huge!" Manu exclaimed, his enthusiasm infectious. "So basically, from 14,000 Lapes worth of raw materials, we can generate 104,000 Lapes worth of clothes and shoes in a month. That's not bad, ey?"

"Yeah, but let's not get carried away," Roger cautioned, his practicality surfacing. "We still need to strike the deal, and there are a lot of moving parts. What's next?"

They dove deeper into the details, piecing together the steps they would need to take if Rich keeps his word and back their venture. They carefully outlined their plan, exploring every angle. Yet, beneath their enthusiasm, a faint but persistent thread of doubt lingered.

The stakes were high: they needed 60,000 Lapes for the business and an additional 5,000 to cover food and essentials until the traders returned in about a month. For a group of kids, it was an ambitious ask - one they both knew few adults would take seriously.

To make their plan work, they agreed, sacrifices would be necessary. They'd have to convince everyone to leave the comfort of Bill's huts and give up the variety of delicious food at his restaurant. Cutting expenses was crucial, but persuading the others to return to their modest living arrangements would be no small feat. After all, adapting to abundance comes far easier than willingly stepping back into scarcity for the mere promise of a better future.

"Let's go talk to Rich," Manu said urgently, his determination clear. "We have no time to waste."

He leaped out of the hut and sprinted towards the market. Roger was no slowpoke, but keeping pace with Manu in a hurry was no easy feat.

Before long, they reached their market stall. Imogen was nearly finished with her fourth caricature, her focused strokes capturing the essence of her subjects. Meanwhile, Josh held a captivated crowd in thrall with his storytelling prowess. His tales were so engaging that even he sometimes lost himself in his own imaginative embellishments, weaving a tapestry of adventure and intrigue that left listeners hanging on every word.

Manu and Roger waited impatiently for Josh to take a breather from his animated storytelling. They were eager to ask him if he had seen Rich, but Josh's excitement seemed to stretch his tales into an endless stream.

Finally, unable to wait any longer, Manu and Roger decided to interrupt his performance, calling him over.

"Have you seen Rich?" Manu asked, trying to sound casual.

"I think so," Josh replied, barely breaking his narrative flow. "Check the bar on the other side of the market."

The market was alive with the sounds of vendors hawking their goods and shoppers bustling about, yet Manu and Roger paid little mind to anyone else as they swiftly zigzagged through the crowd.

Fortunately, Rich's presence was hard to miss. He occupied a stool at a round table with an air of confidence, surrounded by four Voivokis dressed as fashionably as he was. It didn't take a local to recognise that this group was distinctly different from the rest.

To attract more visitors, the bar featured a Voivoki playing his djembe, his rhythmic beats complemented by a soulful voice that filled the air with familiar melodies. Many of the Voivokis joined in, harmonising with the musician, creating an infectious atmosphere of camaraderie.

The conversation at Rich's table was intense, the kind that drew attention without revealing a single word. The hushed voices created an impenetrable bubble, leaving Manu and Roger uncertain about their next move. They exchanged hesitant glances before cautiously approaching the table, positioning themselves across from Rich.

They tried to catch his eye - small, subtle waves that grew increasingly awkward as Rich stayed focused on the discussion, oblivious to their presence.

Each passing second felt heavier, the boys' unease mounting. Their thoughts spiralled, preoccupied with the traders waiting for their return and the possibility that any further delay might test the traders' patience.

"We got to make a move," Manu urged, glancing at his watch.

"Not yet," Roger replied, his brow furrowed with concern. "What if he doesn't take it well? We could blow our chances in a second."

"Yeah, but we have nothing to lose."

"True," Roger conceded. "Let's wait another minute and then we move."

Just then, luck smiled on them. One of the Voivokis stepped away from the group to order more drinks, creating the perfect opportunity for the boys to catch Rich's attention.

At first, Rich stared at them, his expression blank as he appeared lost in thought. He didn't immediately register that he was locking eyes with two agitated boys sporting broad grins.

"Hi, Rich!" Manu called out confidently, breaking the silence and drawing the attention of the entire table.

"Oh, hey boys," Rich responded, his demeanour shifting. "What brings you here?"

"We have our business plan that we discussed this morning," Manu explained eagerly.

Rich raised a hand, politely asking the other Voivokis to temporarily vacate the table. It wasn't common for a seasoned businessman to prioritise young aspirants over a group of seemingly important adults, and the boys were keenly aware of that. But there was no time for pride or hesitation. Anticipating that Rich wouldn't have long to spare, Manu quickly briefed him on their business plan, his heart racing with each word.

"How much do you need?" asked Rich.

"65 thousand," Manu replied with as much confidence as he could utter.

"Wow… that's a hefty sum, kid," Rich said, clearly taken aback.

The boys exchanged glances, unsure of how to interpret his reaction. They figured that for someone like Rich, coming up with such a sum wouldn't be the issue; rather, he seemed surprised by their ambitious plan, underestimating both their combined debt and the scale of their proposed business. After all, they were still quite young to be embarking on such a venture.

"How did you arrive at that figure?" Rich probed, ready to dissect the boys' plan.

But Manu and Roger were prepared. With confidence, they presented their detailed calculations, weaving in often overlooked aspects like taxes, contingencies, and realistic margins. As Rich listened, a flicker of approval crossed his face - a subtle but encouraging sign that they had impressed him.

"I'll grab a few samples from the factory," Roger said abruptly, leaping up and sprinting off before Rich could even respond.

Rich turned back to Manu, raising an eyebrow.

"Where do you plan to produce them?"

"We'll build a hut near a river or lake to keep our expenses low by catching our own food," Manu explained. "Plus, transporting our goods on water would be much quicker than slogging through the mud of the Jungle."

Rich nodded thoughtfully, but his scepticism lingered.

"How certain are you that you can sell them?"

"Roger mentioned that the traders come this way every month with seven bags of raw materials and take the finished products with them."

"But how do you know you can trust them?" Rich countered. "They could just be bluffing to sell you their raw materials."

Just as he finished speaking, Roger returned with a pair of shoes and a couple of pieces of clothing in hand. Rich examined them closely, testing their durability by attempting to tear them apart. They held firm, a testament to their quality.

"Nice work," he said, a smile breaking across his face. "But how do you know you can trust these traders? They have plenty of ways to trick someone into making a purchase."

The boys exchanged worried glances, caught off guard by Rich's probing question. They understood the truth in his words; if they bought raw materials from the traders and couldn't sell the finished products, it would not only result in a loss for Rich but would also plunge them deeper into their existing troubles.

"I want to meet the traders," Rich said, offering a glimmer of hope. "If I can determine that I can trust them, I'll be willing to invest in you and your business. I'll provide the financial capital necessary to launch your venture. From that point on, you'll be responsible for everything - procurement, production, and sales. As for the profits, I'll take 50%. It's a mutually beneficial arrangement, provided everything is executed well. I'll also offer you my mentorship. Deal?"

Manu and Roger exchanged triumphant smiles. Although they hadn't expected Rich to take 50% of the profits, they quickly rationalised that earning half and receiving mentorship from a highly successful entrepreneur was infinitely better than receiving nothing under Bill's oppressive rule. The allure of working for themselves instead of as mere cogs in Bill's empire was a powerful motivator.

"Deal!" they exclaimed, their excitement brimming as they awaited Rich to seal it with a handshake.

But Rich didn't move to extend his hand. His gaze remained steady, his expression unyielding. For him, the deal wasn't done until every piece fell into place, and one critical element was still missing.

"Bring me the traders," he said firmly, his tone leaving no room for negotiation.

Grateful for the chance to proceed, the boys didn't waste a moment. They sprinted up the hill, weaving through the low-growth vegetation towards the spot where Roger had last left the traders.

Their breath came in short bursts as they reached the clearing - only to find it empty. The traders were gone.

CHAPTER 9

Despite the vibrant energy and chaos of the bustling market outside, Asim found himself utterly unable to appreciate any of it. For eleven agonizing days, he had been in isolation, trapped within the confines of a dimly lit hut that stood a stone's throw from the edge of Bill's village. The hut was more of a cage than a shelter, with its heavy wooden door sealed shut since the moment the guards had thrown him inside.

The hut had two other small openings: a narrow window, barely wide enough to fit a hand, through which meagre meals were served, and a foul-smelling hole in the floor, covered by a wooden lid, functioning as a crude toilet. The stench from the pit was unbearable, and it seemed to attract swarms of flies and mosquitoes. They buzzed incessantly around him, a maddening presence that might have driven him insane if he still had the energy to care.

His meals consisted of scraps - stale, leftover bread and murky water - delivered once a day by the indifferent guards. On the first couple of days, Asim had tried to stay active, doing push-ups and squats, clinging to the hope that he could maintain some semblance of strength. But by the third day, even that small glimmer of motivation had evaporated. His already slender frame had begun to wither away after weeks of minimal food in the Jungle, and now, with almost nothing to sustain him, his weight had plummeted alarmingly.

His lips were cracked and raw from dehydration, each attempt to open his mouth causing a fresh stab of pain. When he tried to peel the dry skin away, he only worsened the damage, leaving his mouth an agonising mess. Every movement felt like a battle against his own body, which was rapidly betraying him as the days dragged on in this miserable, airless prison.

During the early days of his confinement, Asim had been consumed by the desperate need to escape. At first, he tried to charm the guards, attempting to win their sympathy or strike some kind of deal. But without anything valuable to offer, his efforts were met with cold dismissiveness. Left with no other options, his thoughts turned to more extreme measures. He toyed with the idea of widening the foul-smelling hole in the floor - his makeshift toilet - envisioning an escape through the muck of urine and feces under the cover of night. Crawling through filth seemed a small price to pay for freedom. But by the third day, the idea became impossible. His body had weakened so severely that he could barely scratch the hardwood floor with his fingernails, let alone dig his way out.

As exhaustion and hopelessness overtook him, Asim resigned himself to lying on the filthy floor, unable to summon the energy to continue fighting. Despair gnawed at his spirit, and he found himself repeatedly asking:

"Why? Why me?"

From the very beginning, life seemed stacked against him. His father, a lazy, unskilled man, had been no help. His mother was always angry, always yelling, never showing any sign of warmth or care. It felt like no one had ever truly cared about him. Not his parents. Not his classmates, despite the fact that he had once saved their lives. And certainly not the Voivokis, who had treated him with nothing but contempt since the moment he stumbled into their twisted world.

They locked him up like a wild animal, now starving him because he refused to bend to their will, to become their slave. The hopelessness of his situation weighed heavily on him.

"What's the point?" he wondered, sinking deeper into his despair. *"What's the purpose of living if it's just to suffer like this?"*

He gave up. He couldn't see a way out.

The uncertainty made it worse - he had no idea how long he'd remain locked up or what fate awaited him. Unbeknownst to him, Bill had already decided to send him to the Kilisi - a brutal prison with little hope of return. His bail, set at an exorbitant twenty thousand Lapes, was far beyond what most Voivokis could afford. And even if anyone knew of his plight, why would they sacrifice their hard-earned money for a stranger?

Time was slipping away, and he was powerless to stop it.

"How did you end up here?" came a whispering voice, couldn't tell if it was real or just a trick his mind was playing on him. The suffocating darkness had begun to blur the lines between his thoughts and reality, between what was happening outside of him and what was unravelling within.

"How did you end up here?" The voice repeated, this time with a bit more force.

Asim barely opened his eyes, just enough to catch a glimpse of a shadowy figure sitting in front of him, legs crossed, staring quietly. His vision was hazy, exhaustion pulling at the edges of his consciousness, and he couldn't quite make out whether the figure was real or a hallucination born of his weakness. His eyelids felt unbearably heavy, and without a word, he let them fall shut again.

A soft creak echoed through the silence as the tiny window in the wall slid open. A guard, expressionless and mechanical, tossed a small piece of stale bread and a cup of water through it. Normally, that sound would have triggered a rush of hunger and thirst, but now, even the basic need for sustenance wasn't enough to stir Asim. His body screamed for nourishment, for even a single bite, but every muscle in his frail frame protested any attempt at movement. He lay still, unwilling to endure the agony of forcing his cracked lips open, knowing even the act of chewing would be a painful ordeal.

So he remained on the floor, his body limp, eyes shut, as if surrendering to the void.

The soft voice broke through the silence again. The mysterious figure leaned in, whispering words of encouragement.

"Don't give up, Asim. You're still young, with so many opportunities ahead of you. But if you let your hope die now, you may never get out of here. You must keep that hope alive! Eat, drink, and ask for more - regain your strength."

Asim's bitterness surged.

"That tiny, disgusting piece of bread isn't going to change anything," he thought, his stomach churning at the mere idea of swallowing it. *"Forcing it down would hurt more than the hunger."*

The mysterious figure hesitated, watching Asim for any sign of response. But Asim remained still, unyielding. Concerned, the figure spoke again.

"Can you hear me?"

Asim gave a small, reluctant nod. Taking it as a cue, the figure continued, his voice now carrying the weight of a story - one that, he hoped, would reignite Asim's will to fight.

"You know," the figure began softly, "I once knew a Nokonai family, one with many children, living in a beautiful village by a river. Life was good for them - peaceful, simple. The river gave them an abundance of fresh fish every day, and the land was so fertile, you could grow anything: fruits, vegetables, spices. They never went hungry, and their hut, sturdy and comfortable, shielded them from storms and the cold nights.

They didn't have much by the standards of the world outside, but inside that village, they had everything they needed.

It wasn't just about what they had, though. It was how they lived. Their community was tight-knit - everyone helped one another. If someone needed something, be it food or a kind word, there was always someone there to provide it. And the kids, they weren't just raised by their parents; the whole village played a role. The cultural rules were strict but fair, and they were built on respect. If a child misbehaved, any adult could step in, discipline them, guide them. It didn't matter if the child was theirs or not.

And yet, despite this closeness, there was an invisible barrier between the kids and their parents. The village's hierarchical structure made it uncommon for kids to have deep, meaningful conversations with their own mothers and fathers. Instead, when a kid sought advice or needed someone to talk to, they would approach whichever adult they felt most comfortable with. Parents were seen more as authority figures, and this created distance. Still, the kids never felt alone. The whole community acted as a family, even if that bond with their own parents was distant.

But then, war erupted, ripping apart their peaceful world. The idyllic village they had called home for generations was suddenly under siege. They were forced to abandon nearly everything they owned, fleeing into the unforgiving depths of the Jungle in search of safety. The journey was brutal, and not all survived. Some villagers, too weak or slow, disappeared into the darkness, while others fell into the hands of the rebels, their fates unknown.

The oldest son of this family was just seven years old, yet he bore responsibilities far beyond his years. Not only did he have to carry his own belongings, but he was also tasked with carrying one of his younger siblings. The weight was crushing - something that would challenge even a strong - able-bodied Nokonai - but this young boy's determination was unshakable. His will to survive and to protect his family gave him the strength to push through the Jungle, step by agonising step.

The villagers' fight for survival changed them. The warmth and compassion that had once united the community gave way to desperation. Nokonais who had once cared for each other were now forced to make difficult choices, driven by the instinct to protect themselves and their loved ones. In this harsh new reality, the boy learned a painful lesson: trust is a fragile thing, easily broken. He grew wary of everyone outside his immediate family, convinced that survival depended on self-reliance. And yet, despite the chaos and the loss of trust, one thing he never let go of was his hope - a flicker of light for a future that wasn't as dark as the one he was living through.

That hope, no matter how small, carried him forward.

After countless moons of misery, the boy and his family finally reached a large Voivoki community that, at first glance, seemed like a sanctuary. It had everything they had longed for during their perilous journey: a comfortable hut, fresh drinking water flowing through the village, and an abundance of food they had never even imagined. Yet, despite these newfound comforts, the scars of their past trauma lingered. They felt like outsiders, never truly at home in this new world.

Their way of thinking, cultural practices, and daily habits often clashed with the rhythms of Voivoki life. The strong bonds of their old community had dissolved, and the boy had lost access to the mentors who had once guided him. Over time, he grew increasingly distant, burdened by a deep mistrust of others and a well of anger that bubbled just beneath the surface. His behaviour became more disruptive, lashing out in frustration wherever he went. He often wondered if returning to the land they had fled, even at the mercy of the rebels, might have been a better fate than this hollow existence.

But one day, everything changed.

The boy was being tied by two guards after yet another fight, his top smeared with blood, when an elderly Voivoki from the village witnessed the scene. With swift, calm authority, the old Voi intervened, persuading the guards to let the boy go. Though the violence of the moment would have repelled most, the elder's compassion was unshaken. He invited the boy into his home, offering food and water. He then led the boy to a simple dugout tub, partially filled with water, and asked him to look into it.

'Tell me what you see,' the elder asked gently.

At first, the boy tried to brush off the question, offering a vague and shallow response. But the old Voi was patient, his kind yet probing questions nudging the boy to think deeper. Slowly, the boy found himself reflecting on the image before him. The more he stared, the stronger the sense of discomfort grew. The reflection - his own face, his bloodstained top - stirred something unpleasant within him, a deep-seated dislike that he could no longer ignore.

The old Voi, sensing the boy's internal struggle, broke the silence.

'I bought this for myself today, but you can have it,' he said, holding out a finely woven top. The boy blinked, startled by the unexpected gesture of kindness. Without a word, he accepted the gift, slipping into the new clothes. A quiet 'thank you' escaped his lips as he tried to process this sudden warmth from a stranger.

'Come with me,' the elder said, guiding the boy outside to his immaculate garden. They walked in silence, the gentle breeze hot but calming. The elder led him to a cosy outdoor lounge beside a small fire pit.

'Take a seat, my son,' he said, inviting the boy to sit down. The boy watched as the old Voi carefully added a pile of twigs to the ashes and, with practiced ease, coaxed the flames back to life.

What happened next left the boy speechless.

The elder took the boy's bloodstained top, holding it up for a moment as their eyes met. Without a word, he slowly lowered it into the fire. The flames licked at the fibre, hungrily devouring it until it was nothing but ashes. The boy's eyes widened in shock. Finely woven clothes like that cost days of hard work. Now it was gone, just like that.

'Why couldn't he wash it instead?' the boy wondered, unable to see the old Voivoki's logic.

But the old Voi's voice was calm, almost soothing.

'You've got a fresh start now, my son.'

For the rest of the day, they talked. The old Voivoki, through his gentle words and quiet wisdom, reignited something within the boy - something long buried under layers of anger and mistrust. It wasn't just the fire in the pit that was rekindled; it was the fire of hope, the very flame that had once carried the boy through his hardest days. And now, under the guidance of the old Voi, it was sparking to life once more. His loving and caring nature resurfaced, radiating through his interactions with everyone around him. He recognised that he had been spiralling down a dark path, allowing anger and frustration to overshadow the goodness within him. This turmoil only fuelled his negative emotions, trapping him in a never-ending cycle of despair.

With reinvigorated trust in those around him, he became the kind-hearted child he once was. His genuine actions and words fostered authentic friendships, and he blossomed into one of the most dependable and intelligent kids in the community. His remarkable change was contagious, positively affecting not just his own life but also the lives of his parents and extended family. His focus on the blessings in his life assisted him to emerge as a role model and source of inspiration."

The mysterious figure paused, letting Asim process his words.

"This boy didn't allow his hope to slip away. What about you?"

Asim didn't respond.

He remained still, waiting for the storyteller to continue, but the silence stretched on. When he briefly opened his eyes, he found himself completely alone. Had he been daydreaming, hallucinating, or was someone truly speaking to him?

"It's rather strange how that boy's story feels so much like my own," he mused, his mind racing. *"Except he ended up having a great life."* The weight of despair settled heavily on his chest, but a flicker of something began to stir within him - a small ember of defiance.

"If he could turn his life around, then so can I. But how did he do it? The boy had someone to guide him, someone who believed in him. But who do I have?" Asim wondered, the familiar pang of loneliness creeping back in.

"I have nobody... or do I?" His thoughts swirled like a storm, searching for clarity.

"Perhaps it wasn't even the old man that helped him, but rather his renewed hope."

As the realisation struck him, he felt a rush of warmth spread through his body.

"His hope!" he muttered, his eyes snapping open, his expression softening.

"That's it! It was his hope!" his voice grew louder, echoing in the emptiness of the hut.

With long-lost vigour and determination, he added,

"He was losing his hope, just like me, but he didn't let it slip away. And neither will I!"

The conviction in his words ignited a spark deep within him, burning away the shackles of despair that had held him captive for far too long. He tried to sit up, but his body rebelled - weak, dizzy, barely able to respond to his mind's reignited determination. Instead, he rolled onto his side, inching towards the stale meal that had been left for him. Each movement was a herculean effort, his muscles screaming in protest. The sun had visibly shifted across the sky by the time he managed to bring the small piece of bread to his lips. Yet, despite the struggle, each bite was a victory, a reminder that he was still fighting.

When he finished, he rested, gathering what little strength he had left. He knew he needed more food and water, but just the thought of speaking - forcing his cracked, parched lips to move and project sound loud enough - was agonizing. His throat was raw, his chest tight, but his determination fuelled him. He had to push through the pain.

"More food and water, please!" he called out, summoning every ounce of strength he had left. His voice echoed weakly in the silence, and for a moment, he wondered if anyone had heard him at all. The market sounds outside his hut, distant and muted, might have swallowed his plea. Despite giving it his all, doubt crept in - had his voice even reached the guards?

He couldn't afford to give up now. He repeated his request before exhaustion completely overtook him, drifting him into a restless sleep.

Suddenly, a loud shout jolted him awake.

"Here you go!"

His eyes snapped open, and to his great relief, another piece of bread and a cup of water were tossed into the hut. He stared in disbelief. For the first time in nearly eleven days, he had eaten twice in one day. All he had done was ask. It seemed so simple, so easy - but the struggle to reach that moment had been anything but.

Meanwhile, the marketplace buzzed with energy as sellers and buyers shouted over one another, each trying to outmanoeuvre the other in securing the best deals. Setting up this bustling market in his small village allowed Bill to charge vendors a modest fee for their stalls while drawing attention to his restaurant, Guest House, and, most crucially, his expanding manufacturing business.

At the heart of the market stood Bill's stand, run by a few seasoned Voivokis, promoting his clothing and footwear. The demand was considerable, with a steady stream of enquiries and purchases. To any outside observer, it would have seemed like Bill was on the brink of success few could boast about.

But for Manu and Roger, the scene unfolding below was a sign of impending disaster. They had been counting on an arrangement with traders that could provide the leverage they needed to liberate themselves and the other kids from Bill's iron grip. Yet, as they stood atop the hill, watching the market from above, the traders they were supposed to meet were nowhere to be found. The absence edged at their nerves. If the traders had gone directly to Bill instead of waiting for Roger, their entire plan could collapse, and worse - if Bill discovered their intentions, he would lock them up and send them to the Kilisi without a second thought.

"They must be at the market," Manu said urgently, his voice tight with tension. "Or they've already cut a deal with Bill. We have to find them now."

Without hesitation, the boys sprinted down the hill, their feet pounding against the earth as they raced towards the market. Weaving through the crowded stalls, their eyes scanned every corner, every vendor, hoping to spot the traders in the throng. But luck remained elusive; the traders were nowhere in sight.

"Let's check Bill's office," Manu suggested, his voice steady, but Roger felt a shiver run down his spine at the suggestion. Up until now, they had done everything in their power to avoid Bill's attention. Going near his office felt like walking into the lion's den, an act that could expose their plot to undermine his operations.

Seeing Roger's hesitation, Manu pressed,

"We've got the backing from Rich - this is our chance! If we don't act now, we're done for."

Roger swallowed hard, knowing Manu was right. If they failed to secure a deal with the traders, the consequences would be catastrophic. With their fate hanging by a thread, they bolted towards Bill's office. Just as they neared the entrance, their hearts leapt - the traders stood there, their backs to the boys, engaged in conversation with one of Bill's guards.

This was their moment.

"Wait!" Roger shouted, his voice filled with desperation as he summoned every ounce of courage.

The traders turned, eyes narrowing as they saw Roger and Manu running their way.

"We have a deal!" Roger gasped, trying to catch his breath. "We accept your terms."

But before they could seal their fate, Bill emerged from his office, his face dark with authority.

"What's going on here?!" his voice thundered, sending a shiver down the boys' spines. "Get back to your jobs, now!"

Turning to the traders, Bill offered them a disarming smile.

"I apologise for the interruption," he said smoothly, gesturing towards his office. Please, step inside. We've much to discuss."

Manu and Roger stood frozen, their opportunity slipping through their fingers like sand. It felt as though the ground had caved in beneath them. Their chance at freedom was crumbling right in front of them, and on top of it all, Bill's anger loomed large for abandoning their work.

But Manu, ever sharp, wasn't ready to give up.

"Wait!" he called out, his voice confident and cutting through the tension. "Rich wants to speak with you."

Manu, holding his gaze on Bill, whispered to Roger to get Rich immediately.

As Roger dashed off, everything stopped. The traders hesitated, curiosity flickering in their eyes. Bill turned sharply, his forced grin betraying a flicker of discomfort.

"Who's Rich?" Bill asked, his tone laced with false amusement, though Manu could sense the unease beneath his polished facade.

"Our business partner," Manu said, not flinching. "He's on his way. Roger went to get him."

The silence that followed was thick with tension, each second stretching into what felt like an eternity. Bill's patience was wearing thin.

"The kid's bluffing," Bill scoffed, trying to sow doubt in the traders' minds. "You don't want to waste your time with a couple of factory kids, do you? Let's head inside."

The traders exchanged uncertain glances, teetering on the edge of belief and scepticism. Their leader seemed ready to follow Bill's lead when suddenly Manu's voice sliced through the air once more.

"He's here!"

Rich strolled up with an air of quiet confidence, exchanging a polite yet loaded greeting with Bill. The tension between them was palpable, as their small talk dripped with sarcasm, making even the traders shift uncomfortably. Beneath the surface of civility, the mutual disdain was clear.

The leader of the traders, sensing the strange dynamic and pressed for time, cut through the awkward pleasantries.

"Let's get down to business. We're not here for chit-chat."

Rich flashed a calculated smile.

"Of course. The boys and I are ready to finalise the deal and iron out a few remaining details. How about we continue this over a drink at the bar? I've already reserved a table for us."

Bill, who had been struggling to maintain control, exploded.

"You can't just barge in here and derail my meeting!" His voice thundered, brimming with frustration.

Manu and Roger had seen Bill's temper flare many times before, but this time, there was something different. His usual outbursts were laced with domineering anger, meant to intimidate and crush anyone in his path. But today, as he yelled at Rich, there was a new edge - a tremor of concern that hadn't been there before.

Rich stepped closer to Bill, speaking in a calm, measured tone that carried more weight than Bill's bluster.

"You seem to forget," Rich said, his voice quiet but firm, "that you're three moons behind on your payments. I can enforce the terms of our agreement anytime."

For decades, Bill had poured his life into his weaving business. Finally, it had begun to turn a profit, but its success was fragile. Today's meeting with the traders was critical; losing them could destroy everything he'd built. Desperation gnawed at him as he turned his full attention to salvaging the deal.

"You don't want to do business with a Taua who rips everyone off, do you?" Bill said, trying to sway the traders. "Rich here has his hands in all sorts of shady dealings, but the only one who ever seems to come out ahead is him. You'd be taking a huge risk trusting someone like him. With me, you know what you're getting - respect, transparency, and a track record of good business. Why don't we head into my office? We can wrap up our usual transaction quickly and efficiently, and I've had your favourite dishes prepared for you, on the house."

The leader of the traders, unimpressed, shook his head.

"Sorry, Bill. The boys offered us much better terms. And besides, you've failed to deliver on your promises more times than I can count."

Bill's expression tightened.

"That won't happen again. We've increased our production capacity significantly."

"You increased your capacity by trapping kids in your schemes and using their lives as collateral. And you still sleep soundly at night?" Rich cut in sharply.

One of the traders raised an eyebrow.

"What do you mean by that?"

Bill, sensing the danger of the conversation slipping out of his control, tried to drown out Rich with more promises and reassurances. But the traders' focus had shifted. Rich, calm and unwavering, revealed Bill's deceitful methods - how he manipulated his workers into a state of perpetual debt, binding the kids to four weeks of labour without pay.

No matter how loudly Bill spoke, the traders were captivated by Rich's revelations.

"Well then," the leader of the Totoli Group said. "Why don't you show us to that table you reserved? Let's discuss business over drinks."

The group walked away, leaving Bill standing there, stunned. His mind raced as he processed the situation - his business, once on the verge of booming, was now teetering on the edge of collapse. Before his deal with the Totoli Group, he could only sell small quantities of his products through independent traders. He had made more money per sale back then, but the volume was meagre. Once he secured a contract with the Totoli Group, everything changed. They could reach a larger customer base, and their constant demand allowed his weaving business to take off.

The Totoli Group was like the large supermarket chains of the City. They dominated vast territories, and their reach was so extensive that manufacturers and farmers alike scrambled for the chance to work with them. But with that power came resentment - smaller traders and businesses couldn't compete with them. Yet for Bill, they had been a golden opportunity. Even though they paid less per item, they bought everything he could produce, putting him in a position where the potential for wealth seemed limitless.

Their pressure to increase production, however, had forced him into a tight corner. Desperate to meet their demands, he had scrounged for more factory workers, eventually trapping a group of kids into his labour scheme. With their help, he had finally reached the production capacity required to fulfil his agreement, and let the profits pouring in. He had visions of becoming one of the wealthiest Voivokis in the region, and clearing his debt to Rich, his ever-watchful financier.

But now, with the traders slipping through his fingers, all of that was at risk. His weaving business, the very thing he had poured decades into building, was on the verge of collapse. The Totoli Group had been his ticket to success, and without them, he had no way to maintain the volume of sales he had grown accustomed to.

And then there was the problem of his factory workers. Bill had advanced them credit to survive, trapping them in a cycle of debt they could only repay by working in his factory. But if he lost the Totoli contract, he would no longer need their labour. Worse yet, with no other job prospects available, they would have no means to pay off their debts. He faced the grim reality of having to either forfeit their debts and let them go or risk losing even more money.

Yet, Bill wasn't ready to give up so easily. Not after seeing how well his products had been received at the market. The demand was still there; the potential for profit still existed. All he needed was a new plan beyond the Totoli Group.

CHAPTER 10

The table Rich had reserved for the day was small, fitting only five: Rich, the boys, the leader of the Totoli Group, and one of Rich's trusted team members. To accommodate the rest of the traders, Rich instructed one of his associates to arrange refreshments, ensuring they were comfortable while he conducted business at the main table.

The bar was bustling with Voivokis, patrons filling every available space as bartenders moved swiftly to meet the growing demand. The drink selection was modest - toddy, fresh water, coconut water, and various herbal teas - but it was the cooling method that intrigued the boys. To combat the heat, the drinks were stored in deep holes dug into the shady side of the surrounding hills, bamboo tubes submerged in the earth acting as makeshift coolers. Several fire pits strategically placed around the area drew heat away from the storage, cooling the drinks. While they were far from ice-cold, the boys were grateful for the refreshing beverages in the scorching midday heat.

The meeting itself was brief but impactful. Rich skilfully negotiated a deal, agreeing to pay only 10% of the 14,000 upfront for the raw materials, with the remaining balance due in seven days. This strategy left the boys puzzled. They exchanged curious glances but waited until the meeting was over and the Totoli Group had departed to ask Rich to explain.

"In business, you always have to find the optimal balance between risk, reward, and time," Rich began, his voice steady with confidence. "By paying only a 10% deposit for the raw materials, we minimise our risk. We've secured 14,000 Lapes worth of materials for just 1,400. If the traders deceive us and don't follow through with the purchase, we'll be left with shoes and clothes that cost us next to nothing, aside from labour. However, if they return in seven days as promised, we can pay the balance using the finished products instead of cash. This strategy maximises our potential reward - we're leveraging 1,400 Lapes to generate substantial profits. I gave us that seven-day buffer to establish production and ensure we have enough goods to cover the debt."

The boys listened, wide-eyed, absorbing every word. Rich's strategic thinking left them astounded. In just a few minutes, their mentor had provided a crash course in business acumen that promised to reshape their approach to life. Any doubts they had about splitting profits with him evaporated, replaced by a reinforced understanding that the value of his mentorship far outweighed any financial cut he took.

"The next matter we need to address is your debts with Bill," Rich continued. "Come with me."

With a renewed sense of purpose, the boys followed Rich, heads held high. As they walked through the busy market, Roger caught sight of Bill by his stall, engaged in animated discussions with potential buyers. He carried himself with the polished ease of an experienced salesman, projecting optimism and enthusiasm. Yet, beneath that confident exterior, there was an unmistakable tension. Bill was desperate. The Voivokis he was speaking with weren't serious buyers; they were interested in small, one-off purchases, nothing close to the bulk orders he needed to replace the Totoli Group's business.

As Rich and the boys approached, Bill's expression shifted. His air of control faltered, giving way to a subtle unease. He knew that the presence of Rich - his creditor - meant his precarious situation was about to become even more complicated.

"We'd like to discuss the kids' debt," Rich began, his voice composed and professional.

"Get lost, Rich!" Bill spat, his voice shrill with rage. "First you steal my business, and now you want to take my workers too? You're out of your mind!"

"I understand your frustration," Rich replied, maintaining his calm. "You know where to find me when you're ready to talk."

Bill turned his attention to Manu and Roger, his face twisted in fury.

"You two still work for me. Get back to the factory, or you'll end up locked away like your big-mouthed friend!"

Rich interjected smoothly:

"They're my business partners now, Bill. From this day forward, they have nothing to do with you."

"That's impossible!" Bill exclaimed, his voice rising in desperation. "They owe me 25,000 Lapes! They can't leave until their debt's paid."

"Twenty-five thousand?" Rich raised an eyebrow, unimpressed. "You'll see them back at work for now, but if you've got a better offer, you know where to find me."

Without waiting for a reply, Rich turned on his heel, guiding the bewildered boys away from Bill's stall. Bill, seething, shouted after them,

"I'll be watching you!"

The short walk back to the bar was a blur for Manu and Roger. Just moments ago, they felt like serious business partners backed by a wealthy Voivoki, but now everything seemed to unravel. Confusion clouded their thoughts, and the excitement of their potential success was fading into doubt.

"Why'd you screw us over?" Manu asked bluntly as they reached the table, his voice a mix of frustration and disbelief.

Rich smiled, leaning back in his chair.

"I didn't screw you over, my friend," he said, pausing for emphasis. "Pardon me, my business partner. Take a seat."

The boys hesitated, glancing at each other. Despite the title of 'business partner,' they couldn't shake the feeling that they'd been outmanoeuvred. It weighed heavily on them - the idea that Rich had used them to craft a lucrative deal with minimal effort on his part. After all, they were the ones who had handled most of the legwork, from finding the right contacts to brokering the deal.

As they sat down, the question lingered in the air: Why would someone as experienced as Rich partner with two inexperienced boys unless there was more to his game than they could see?

Back at the village, the midday drumming signalled the workers' lunch break, offering them a brief respite to visit the bustling market and grab something to eat. They were buzzing with excitement as they hurried towards the lively stalls, eager for a taste of freedom, however fleeting.

But not Susan and Olivia. The market held no allure for them. They had a singular focus: meeting their Voivoki friends, Jane and Jess, who had promised them a way out, a path to freedom. The route to the City was unknown to them, but their faith in their friends held up. Their friends had assured them that someone in their circle could lead them home.

Yet once again, their hopes were dashed. Their friends were nowhere to be found, their absence a painful reminder of how fragile that promise had been. The shallow friendship they'd formed was like a lottery ticket, with freedom as the ultimate prize. But, as with any gamble, disappointment had come instead of the reward.

"They might come later," Olivia said, her voice tinged with optimism, trying to salvage their hopes. "And if not, we can always try to befriend other wealthy Voivokis. Surely someone would help us."

And so they did. During their lunch break, they put all their efforts into catching the attention of the well-dressed Voivokis around them, eagerly engaging in conversation with those whose clothes and jewellery screamed of affluence and status. They chatted and smiled, strategically positioning themselves in the paths of those with wealth and power.

But when less fortunate-looking Voivokis in shabby clothes and worn shoes approached, they dismissed them just as quickly, judging their worth by appearance alone. That's exactly what happened when one of them placed his patched-up bag on the girls' table with a sigh, trying to join them for his meal.

The girls, engrossed in shallow conversation, noticed his untidy state with a single glance.

"May I take a seat?" he asked, his voice lined with fatigue.

"This seat is taken," Olivia replied coldly, her eyes never lifting to meet his.

"I don't see anyone here," he replied, confused.

"Our friends are on the way," Olivia insisted, her tone flat.

"I'll be quick. I'll eat and be gone in a blink of an eye," he offered, trying to hold onto a shred of dignity.

The girls exchanged a knowing look and shook their head subtly before Olivia repeated:

"This seat is taken."

Though snubbed by the girls' blunt dismissal, the Voivoki slung his worn bag over his shoulder, turned without a word, and quietly disappeared into the bustling crowd. The girls, relieved, resumed their conversation, feeling they had avoided an uncomfortable situation. But as the minutes passed, their attention was drawn back to the same Voivoki emerging once more from the rowdy crowd, this time with a leaf tray in hand. Olivia and Susan exchanged nervous glances, both hoping to avoid another awkward encounter. Olivia subtly scratched behind her ear, pretending to be distracted, while Susan fixed her gaze on a nearby stall.

The Voivoki, undeterred by their coldness, approached again. This time, however, he carried their favourite desserts - treats they often craved but rarely indulged in. He gently placed the plates in front of them, his hands steady and his movements graceful.

"Kindness touches the soul of even the most wicked," he said in a calm, almost soothing voice.

The girls felt their confidence waver as they glanced up, meeting his eyes for the first time. His smile was soft, disarming in its sincerity. He gave them a respectful nod, a silent farewell, and turned to leave. Before the girls could process the unexpected gesture or utter a response, he was already gone, blending into the crowd like a ghost, leaving them with a lingering sense of discomfort and confusion.

"That was strange," Olivia muttered, her brow furrowed. "Why would he buy us our favourite desserts after we brushed him off like that?"

"I don't know," Susan replied, her voice tinged with caution. "But I wouldn't touch them. Who knows what he might've done to them?"

"Yeah, good point," Olivia said, unease flickering in her eyes.

Susan, still staring at the untouched treats, sighed.

"I do feel a little bad about how we treated him, though."

Olivia shrugged, dismissing the guilt.

"Don't overthink it. He wasn't exactly the kind of person we're trying to connect with."

Meanwhile, just a dozen steps away, Mai and Leila weaved through the crowded restaurant, grabbing food for not just for themselves, but for Josh, and Imogen as well. They headed straight to Imogen's stall, where Josh, as energetic as ever, entertained passers-by with stories while collecting deposits for Imogen's caricatures.

Despite being immersed in her favourite activity, Imogen was clearly fatigued. After four and a half hours of intense drawing under pressure, the sight of her friends arriving with food felt like a lifeline.

"Siesta time, my friends!" Josh declared, raising his voice above the chatter. "Can't have our artist entering the spirit world because she's starving!"

The crowd burst into laughter.

"We'll be back in business soon," he added with a grin.

Most of the crowd dispersed, but a few lingered, waiting for Imogen's return. Imogen, stretching her arms to the sky, finally stood up from her seat, exhaustion etched on her face.

"How many have you drawn so far?" Leila asked, her tone a mix of concern and admiration.

"Nine," Imogen replied, stifling a yawn.

"And how many more are left?" Leila pressed.

"I lost track," Imogen admitted, looking towards Josh for the answer.

Josh, savouring every bite of his meal, responded between mouthfuls.

"We've got another 11 lined up, but more could show up."

"Wow!" Mai exclaimed, her eyes wide with excitement. "They love your stories, huh?"

"Yeah," Imogen agreed, managing a tired smile. "He really knows how to keep them laughing."

Josh, appreciative of the praise, nodded gratefully, still chewing.

A few bites later, Leila's expression turned serious as she leaned in closer.

"Have you seen Manu and Roger? They've been gone for ages."

Josh swallowed his bite and shrugged.

"I saw them with Rich earlier, but that's about it."

The brief lunch break felt even shorter that day for Leila and Mai. As they returned to the factory, resuming their usual spots, the weight of daily targets and Bill's ever-growing wealth pressed down on them. They longed to stay at the market, where the vibrant energy, the laughter, and Imogen's art seemed like a glimpse into a forbidden paradise for those trapped in Bill's world.

Just as a quiet sadness began to settle over them, Manu's sudden appearance jolted them to attention. Their curiosity sparked, they bombarded him with questions, eager to know what he had been up to. But Manu, like a seasoned politician, deflected their enquiries with vague answers, leaving them both intrigued and frustrated.

Maria, watching from her position, smiled knowingly. She had seen that look in Manu's eyes before - the same steely desire, drive, and determination that reminded her of Rica, her old friend she regretted not sticking with. Manu's absence from the factory spoke volumes. She could sense he was onto something significant this time. The fire in Manu's eyes, burning with purpose, was a spark she hadn't seen in years.

✹ ✹ ✹

In the heat of the afternoon, Joe and Sina's boredom at the Guest House was shattered by the unexpected creak of the gate. They perked up, eager at the prospect of finally having a guest to attend to. But when the guards stepped inside, carrying someone on a stretcher, their jaws nearly dropped.

"Asim!" Sina cried out in shock and joy, rushing towards him. "Are you alright?"

Asim, bruised and battered, was barely conscious, lying on a stretcher carried by the same guards who had mercilessly beaten him when he tried to escape Bill's clutches. Leading the group was a finely dressed Voivoki, his demeanour warm and calculating as he motioned towards Asim.

"Prepare a bath for him and clean his clothes," the Voivoki commanded, his voice sharp.

Joe and Sina exchanged bewildered glances. No one had informed them about Asim's arrival, let alone that they would be taking orders from a stranger. But the weight of the Voivoki's authority stifled any questions, and they scurried off to obey.

"You look awful," Joe muttered as he helped Asim, feeling utterly awkward.

The comment sparked a wheezy laugh from Asim, but it was cut short by a painful coughing fit that wracked his body. His face contorted in agony as his condition painfully reminded them all of what he had endured.

He forced a faint smile through his discomfort.

"You guys can go now. I'll manage from here."

He braced himself for the bath, his body screaming with aches, but his spirit unbroken.

Just as Joe and Sina stepped onto the porch, they were greeted once again by the finely dressed Voivoki.

"My name is Rich," he introduced himself, his voice both smooth and commanding. "I want you two to look after Asim. Make sure he gets sufficient food and water - we need him to regain his strength as soon as possible. He'll sleep in one of the rooms tonight, and I'll take the other. If you need me, I'll be at the market. The guards have been told to let you out whenever you need to speak to me. You shouldn't have any problems."

With that, Rich turned and exited through the gate, leaving Joe and Sina standing there, stunned by his authoritative presence but bubbling with excitement at Asim's arrival.

"Do you think this is the same Rich that Manu and Roger spoke to before we ended up at Bill's village?"

Joe gave her a blank look, so she elaborated.

"You know, the one with the really nice house and the waterfall in his garden?"

Joe nodded. "Could be. But I don't get the connection between him and Asim."

"We can ask Asim when he's done with his bath," Sina replied, her curiosity now fully piqued.

Asim was in no hurry with his bath. He savoured the rare luxury after nearly two weeks of neglecting his basic needs. Every moment was a balm to his bruised and battered body. After his bath, he managed to eat a little, but he was way too weak to sit up or engage in any meaningful conversation. Joe and Sina helped him to his bed and left him alone, continue burning with curiosity.

Outside, the market had begun its usual noisy wind-down. The macaques' evening calls blended with the distant pounding of drums, signalling the end of the workday and the market's closure. All around, merchants hurried to pack up, eager to leave. Only Bill's stall remained active, his temporary salespeople desperately calling out, trying to make one last sale despite the dwindling crowd. Bill himself paced nervously, scanning for any potential traders he hadn't spoken to, his anxiety building with every passing second.

But the true excitement lay at the other end of the market, where Manu had drawn the crowd's attention. Standing atop a rock, he reminded the gathering that the auction for Susan's portrait was about to begin. The energy was electric, the anticipation thick in the air. The first bid shot up almost instantly, followed by a volley of counter-bids as over 50 eager participants threw their hands in the air, vying for the piece. The bids climbed rapidly, the pace quickening, and the voices rose louder and louder.

Manu kept the momentum, playfully guiding the auction with the same cool confidence that had helped him sell caricatures earlier for a solid 650 Lapes. But this auction was different. The competitive spirit was intense, driving the price higher and higher. It wasn't long before the bidding crossed into the thousands, the energy pulsating like a drumbeat. Manu had anticipated a strong turnout, but even he could hardly believe it when the price soared to an astonishing 18,740 Lapes.

As the announcement rang out, the crowd erupted into cheers, their applause echoing through the market. Manu quickly got Josh and Roger to verify the payment, and once the transaction was confirmed, they handed the portrait over to its delighted owner. The proud Voivoki who won the auction beamed with excitement, waving Susan's portrait high above his head for all to admire. In the midst of the commotion, he called over a musician, who immediately struck up a lively tune on his djembe, setting the crowd into motion. Soon, everyone was clapping and singing along as the Voivoki danced joyously, his energy infectious.

Roger, still grinning from ear to ear, stepped up to Manu and gave his arm a squeeze.

"Wow," he said, his voice filled with awe. "A total of 31,740 Lapes for the day. Can you believe it?"

Manu flashed an equally wide grin. The success of the auction, combined with the earlier caricature sales, was more than he could have hoped for. Around him, his peers and even some strangers approached to congratulate him, offering pats on the back and words of admiration. His pride swelled as he took in the recognition. He had orchestrated both the auction and the caricature sales, and though he revelled in the success, he never lost sight of the contributions from Imogen, Josh, and the others. Their teamwork had made this remarkable day possible.

As the last well-wisher drifted away, Manu felt a pair of eyes on him. Turning, he found Imogen standing nearby, her dark brown eyes glistening. She stepped towards him, her voice trembling slightly as she spoke.

"Is this the path you wanted me to draw?" she asked, her words thick with emotion.

Manu wrapped her in a tight hug, chuckling softly.

"Not exactly," he admitted, "but it'll do for today."

They held each other in tight embrace before Imogen sank to the ground, covering her face with her hands. Concerned, Leila quickly settled beside her, draping an arm over her shoulders. But when Imogen lifted her head, she was smiling with watery eyes. It had been an exhausting day for the young artist - the pressure, the relentless pace - but she knew it had all been worth it. The reward of seeing their efforts pay off in such an extraordinary way was enough to push aside her weariness.

"What are you going to do with all that money?" Josh asked, breaking the moment with a grin.

Before Manu could respond, a handful of Voivokis appeared, their expressions stern as they approached. Without hesitation, they demanded 30% of the Lapes the kids had earned that day. Manu's stomach dropped. It was obvious who they were - Vilais, notorious for taxing everyone. A wave of frustration hit him like a punch in the gut. He hadn't even had time to sit down and catch his breath, let alone enjoy their success, and here they were already demanding their cut. It was infuriating.

His gaze hardened as he met the Vilais' eyes.

"We still need to do our calculations," he said, struggling to keep his voice even. "Please come back later.

One of the Vilais smirked.

"That's fine. But you better have our 30% ready when we return," he warned and moved on to harass other vendors.

The moment they were out of earshot, Manu huddled with Josh and Roger, and they quickly divided the pile of Lapes.

There was no time to waste. They had to count their Lapes and portion out their tax.

"Eighty-four fifty," Josh muttered, eyeing the small fortune in front of them. He glanced at the thinning crowd, watching as vendors packed up and began slipping into the forested hills. A dangerous temptation sparked in his mind - to take a chunk of the money and disappear until nightfall. It was so simple. The thicket wasn't far.

Leaning in, he whispered,

"I can hide some of the Lapes in the bush. It'll save us on taxes."

Manu's pulse quickened. For a brief moment, the plan excited him - it could work. But then Roger, ever the cautious one, spoke up, his voice low and firm.

"If you get caught, it's game over," he said, glancing at Josh with warning in his eyes. "They'll throw you straight into the Kilisi, and we won't ever see you again. It's not worth the risk."

They all stared at the departing crowd, watching the silhouettes disappear into the hills, the idea of freedom flickering in their minds. It was tempting to believe those vendors were luckier, walking away from the market without a care. But in reality, they all had to pay their fair share of taxes before departing.

Imogen, noticing the boys' tense expressions, whispered, her voice laced with concern.

"What's going on?"

Manu sighed heavily.

"We have to pay 9,522 Lapes in taxes."

Imogen's shoulders slumped, her eyes growing wet with frustration.

"Nine thousand five hundred Lapes? For what?" Her voice trembled, barely containing her outrage. "I've been drawing all day, and now they just want to take it?"

Manu's fists clenched, his anger building. It wasn't just unfair - it was robbery.

"There has to be a way to minimise our taxes," Manu said, his voice tight with determination. His eyes flicked towards the fading daylight. "I need to find Rich, urgently."

Fortunately, Manu didn't need to search long. Just as he took a couple of steps, Rich emerged from the crowd, a warm smile on his face as he congratulated them on their success. Manu thanked him but wasted no time diving into their dilemma, venting about the 9,522 Lapes the Vilais were demanding.

Rich listened patiently, then smiled knowingly.

"What expenses do you have?" he asked, his voice calm and steady.

The kids exchanged confused looks, clearly at a loss. Rich could see the confusion and it reminded him of the moment one of his own mentors had asked him that same question decades earlier. Now it was his turn to share this critical piece of knowledge - a financial truth that many overlook, keeping them trapped in endless cycles of poverty.

"When you run a business, you deduct your expenses first and pay taxes on what's left. Employees, on the other hand, pay taxes upfront and cover their expenses from what remains. Once you fully grasp this, you'll be light-years ahead of those who don't. It's a game-changer."

Manu, Roger, and the others exchanged more puzzled glances, clearly struggling to wrap their heads around it. Rich wasn't surprised, and continued, simplifying his explanation.

"Let me give you an example. Say you earn 100 Lapes as an employee. You have 50 Lapes in expenses. You'll pay 30% in taxes on the full 100, which leaves you with 70. Subtract your 50 Lapes of expenses, and you're left with 20 Lapes."

"100 minus 30% is 70, minus 50 equals 20," Roger muttered, doing the math aloud.

He looked up, making sure everyone else was following. The others nodded in agreement, the numbers finally starting to make sense.

"That's right," Rich nodded. "Now, let's look at it from a business perspective. As a business owner, you spend your 50 Lapes first, then pay taxes on what's left. So, 100 minus 50 leaves 50 Lapes. You then pay 30% tax on that 50, which is 15 Lapes, leaving you with 35."

"100 minus 50 equals 50, minus 30% leaves 35," Roger repeated, his voice sharper now with clarity.

Rich smiled.

"Exactly. You end up with nearly double what you would as an employee. That's the advantage of running a business."

Manu's eyes widened, his brain racing as the numbers clicked into place.

"So what we did today - selling caricatures and holding the auction - that was clearly business, right?" Manu asked, a spark of realisation lighting up his face.

"Exactly," Rich confirmed. "Now, instead of handing over a chunk of your hard-earned Lapes to the Vilais, we need to find a way to account for your expenses. The more you spend on legitimate business costs before paying taxes, the less the Vilais can take from you. Let's go through your numbers and figure out what you can deduct."

Manu, Roger, and the others suddenly felt a renewed sense of hope. Instead of being at the mercy of the Vilais, they had options - and with Rich's guidance, they might just find a way to keep more of what they'd earned.

"First things first," Rich continued, his voice steady. "You spent 14,000 Lapes on raw materials today. Deduct that from the 31,740 Lapes you made, and you're left with 17,740. Now, I'm going to charge you 20,000 Lapes for consultancy services - on record, that is. This will show a loss of 2,260 Lapes, which means you won't owe the Vilais a single Lape."

His words hit the kids like a sudden jolt. They had trusted Rich up until now, but the mention of a 20,000 Lape charge for 'consultancy' made them question everything. Was he really helping them, or was this just another trap? They began to wonder if it wouldn't have been simpler to just hand over the 9,522 Lapes to the Vilais and be done with it. That would have been much less than Rich's supposed 20,000 Lapes fee.

"What exactly is 'consultancy'?" Roger asked, scepticism creeping into his voice.

Rich chuckled, flashing a knowing grin.

"It's just a fancy term for chatting."

Manu blinked, still not fully understanding.

"So you want 20,000 Lapes for talking to us today?"

The group held their collective breath, tension hanging in the air. They had worked too hard for their money to give up two-thirds of it for a few minutes of conversation. It seemed like no matter how hard they tried, they were always at the mercy of Bill, the Vilais, and now even Rich? It felt as though every step forward was met with someone ready to snatch away their gains.

Rich's expression softened.

"No," he said, his tone reassuring. "I said 'on record,' which means no real money is exchanging hands. It's a legal way to lower your taxes. The consultancy fee is just an agreement, something to help you show a loss. We'll sort out the actual fees when the time comes - if it even does."

The kids barely registered the last part. They were too relieved to hear the answer they'd been hoping for. A collective sigh of relief escaped them, their tense bodies finally relaxing. Rich's plan might have seemed overwhelming at first, but now they understood that, for the moment, they wouldn't be losing anything to the Vilais - or to Rich.

"But how do we explain this to the Vilais?" Manu asked, his brow furrowed with concern.

"Leave that to me," Rich replied calmly. "Let's find them, and I'll do the talking."

Manu and Roger followed Rich through the thinning crowd, leaving the rest of the group behind with a swirl of emotions. Relief mingled with doubt. They wanted to believe that Rich had their best interests at heart, but experience had taught them to be cautious. Trust was a rare currency in the Jungle, especially among the Voivokis, who often prioritised their own prosperity over anyone else's well-being. Was Rich really any different? Would he truly help them break free from Bill's hold and, eventually, assist them finding the way back to the City? He spoke a language they didn't understand. How could they trust him?

Not far away, Rich's conversation with the Vilais was brief. His years of dealing with their tax demands allowed him to navigate the situation with ease. Though the Vilais were displeased to learn that the kids wouldn't be paying taxes, Rich's explanation left them with little room for argument. He had followed their own rules to the letter: businesses were taxed on their profits, and since the kids' venture appeared unprofitable on record - thanks to the hefty 20,000 Lape consultancy fee - they owed nothing.

The Vilais, departed with tight-lipped expressions, their frustration visible but powerless to change the outcome. For Manu and Roger, it was a huge relief, even if their confusion lingered.

"We made 31,740 Lapes today," Roger whispered, almost disbelieving. "And somehow, we're still unprofitable?"

Manu nodded, equally bewildered. They just learned that businesses deducted their expenses before paying taxes, but Rich's 20,000 Lape 'fee' hadn't been a real transaction. In their minds, it didn't count as an actual expense. And yet, here they were, with no taxes to pay and all of their Lapes intact.

"I guess this is how the system works," Manu muttered, trying to make sense of it. It was a game they were keen to understand, one that clearly had loopholes - if you knew where to look.

Rich, grinning ear to ear, watched the Vilais disappear into the crowd, his chest swelling with pride. He turned to the boys and clapped his hands, as if dusting them off after another successful round of negotiations.

"We'll talk about the next steps tomorrow," he said, clearly satisfied with how things had gone.

Before Manu or Roger could ask any questions, Rich strode off towards the village, his long, confident strides leaving no room for doubt. His purposeful pace echoed his authority, each step weighted with a presence that seemed to command attention. He headed straight for the Guest House, eager to refresh himself before dinner.

As he swung the gate open, Joe and Sina jumped to their feet, greeting him with icy-cold water from a deep well and a basket of fresh fruit. Rich settled at the dinner table, his fingers reaching for a rambutan.

"Can we get you anything else before we leave you to enjoy the comfort of the Guest House?" Sina asked, ready to serve.

"No, you can go," Rich replied. Then, turning to Joe, he added, "But you, stay. I want to have a word with you before you leave."

Joe's heart skipped a beat, and unease crept into his chest. His mind raced, trying to figure out why Rich would single him out. Had he done something wrong? Did something happen at the market? Each thought seemed more troubling than the last.

Seeing Joe's discomfort, Rich chuckled softly, his smile warm but teasing.

"What's got you so nervous? Relax, I don't bite. Come sit with me, have some fruit - it's on me."

Still unsure but unwilling to appear rude, Joe slowly sat down. He picked up a rambutan, his hands shaking slightly as he peeled its hairy skin, fighting the rising tension in his chest. Each second felt heavier, weighed down by the growing sense that whatever conversation awaited him might be more than just casual.

"How is Asim?" asked Rich.

"He's good," said Joe, briefly meeting Rich's gaze.

A few moments of silence passed as Rich waited patiently for Joe to elaborate.

"Is that all?" Rich prompted.

"He ate a bit without talking and has been asleep ever since," Joe added quietly.

"Hmmm," Rich nodded, engrossed in his thoughts.

Manu and Roger had spoken to him about Joe, but he wasn't expecting him to be so different. He was timid and introverted, barely speaking unless directly addressed, and even then, his answers were clipped. He was the polar opposite of Manu and Roger, whose confidence seemed to fill any room they entered.

To ease Joe's tension, Rich decided to steer the conversation towards himself.

"You see, I am an investor," he began smoothly. "I invest in various ventures. Some pay off handsomely, while others don't. When I heard one of you was locked up, I took a gamble. I paid the twenty-thousand-Lapes bail, trusting that my investment would yield loyalty and reliability. I envisioned your friend working alongside me for many moons to come."

Rich spoke with charisma, weaving stories of his entrepreneurial triumphs, each more dazzling than the last. But Joe's attention faltered. A single phrase had caught him off guard, and his thoughts spiralled.

"Many moons to come?" he wondered silently, his hand tightening around a piece of rambutan. *"Do Manu and Roger know about this?"*

Rich, ever perceptive, noticed he lost Joe's attention. He relished challenges and saw potential in Voivokis like Joe - potential often buried beneath layers of insecurity and self-doubt.

Adapting quickly, Rich changed course.

"Roger and Manu mentioned you're great with numbers," he said, watching Joe carefully. "Is that true?"

"I guess so," Joe mumbled, his face blank.

"Every business needs someone great with numbers. So why aren't they involving you in theirs?" Rich asked.

"Those two are close friends," Joe replied, shrugging. "They wouldn't want me in their business. Back in the City, we barely even talk to each other."

"Why is that?"

Joe hesitated, then admitted:

"All they usually do is play sports, talk business, and trade stuff. I am not good at sports, and don't care about business."

Rich leaned in, intrigued.

"So, what do you like to do?"

"I play video games," Joe said, assuming Rich wouldn't know what it was.

"What kind of games are those?" came the expected question.

Joe's eyes lit up at the opportunity to talk about his passion, but the challenge quickly dawned on him. How could he explain video games to someone unfamiliar with even the simplest technology of the City? He glanced around, searching for something to spark an explanation.

"It's like… looking through a window, which we call screen, and what you see always changes," Joe began, his excitement growing. "It's not real. It's a virtual world – just moving drawings to your commands. For example, the game could be about you walking through this village, clean this Guest House, or use your arrow to hunt for food, or protect yourself with a knife if someone attacks."

Rich nodded slowly, his brow furrowing even deeper as he tried to grasp the concept.

"So… you're walking through the screen?" he asked, still puzzled.

"No," Joe replied, suppressing a chuckle. "You just look at it, sitting down, and use a controller to move around."

"A controller?" Rich echoed.

Joe nodded, then grabbed two pieces of rambutan from the basket and placed them side by side on the table. He leaned forward, using the fruit to illustrate his point.

"Okay, imagine this," Joe began, gesturing towards the rambutan on the right. "If I touch this one, the view through the window shifts to the right, like I'm moving left to see what's on the other side. And if I touch the other, it shifts the other way."

Rich leaned in, his curiosity piqued.

"So, you control what you see without walking?"

"Exactly," Joe said, encouraged by Rich's engagement.

Rich tilted his head, still fascinated.

"Interesting... but how do these games help you become successful?"

Joe blinked, caught off guard by the sudden shift.

"What do you mean?"

"Exactly what I asked," Rich replied, his gaze sharpening as he studied Joe's reaction. "You've got this skill, this passion - but how does it translate into something that will make you thrive?"

Joe fumbled for an answer, suddenly feeling exposed. It wasn't just a casual question - it was a challenge. He shifted uncomfortably in his chair, feeling the weight of Rich's expectation pressing down on him. He was only fourteen - why was he being pushed to think about success? What did that even mean for someone like him? His mind went blank, the words sticking to his throat.

Rich, sensing Joe's discomfort, leaned back slightly. He had no intention of pushing too hard. The success of his venture with the kids depended on their trust, and unlike Bill, Rich understood that fear wasn't the way to build connections. Joe, with his quick mind and talent for numbers, was a crucial piece of his puzzle. Rich needed him to stay open and engaged, not retreat into silence.

He softened his tone.

"Forget it. Tell me about your favourite games instead."

Joe's relief was palpable, and he quickly launched into an animated description of his gaming adventures - talking about strategy, levels, and his proudest moments in-game. The tension in his shoulders eased as he spoke, his excitement taking over.

Rich listened, a faint smile tugging at the corners of his lips, but behind his amusement was a growing concern.

"How much time do you usually spend playing these games?" he asked.

"Just a couple of hours," Joe replied, trying to sound casual.

"A moon?"

Joe hesitated, then sighed.

"A day."

Rich kept his expression neutral, though inwardly he felt alarms going off. He could see the deeper issue now - this wasn't just a hobby. Joe's casual admission masked something more serious, and Rich understood he had to tread carefully if he was going to help the boy without shutting him down.

Joe wasn't just a casual gamer; he was ensnared in a cycle of addiction. The games offered him an escape, a realm where he felt a sense of control - something life had rarely granted him. But this illusion of mastery came at a steep price. The better Joe became, the deeper he craved that fleeting sense of accomplishment, fuelling a relentless need to return to the virtual world. What Joe failed to see was the trap he was caught in - one that, bit by bit, was drawing him further away from reality.

"What are your parents doing?" Rich asked, wanting to understand how Joe ended up on this dangerous path.

"Probably looking for me," Joe shrugged.

"I can imagine that," Rich said, leaning forward slightly, "but what do they do for a living?"

"I don't know," Joe replied, his voice distant.

Rich raised an eyebrow.

"You don't know?"

Joe shook his head.

"They're always working. We don't really talk much."

Rich's eyes narrowed as he gauged Joe's body language.

"And your friends? Do you spend much time with them?"

"Not really. I'm fine on my own," Joe said with a faint edge of defensiveness.

Rich paused, letting the silence linger before steering the conversation into deeper waters.

"What are you planning to do when you grow up? When you become an adult?"

"I don't know," Joe blinked and looked away. "I've never really thought about it."

Rich hummed softly, as he observed signs of Joe retreating inward.

"I think your addiction is hurting you," he said.

Joe looked into his eyes.

"What do you mean?" he asked, seeking clarification. "What's an addiction?"

"It's when something takes over so much of your life that it becomes harmful - like eating too much, which makes you overweight and unhealthy," Rich explained.

"I don't play that much," Joe protested. "Some of my friends play way more than I do."

Rich's smile was thin and calculated.

"Using wrong benchmarks can lead you down dangerous paths. You said you play for a couple of hours a day, but you also mentioned playing an hour or two before school. Then after school, you said you play until your parents get home - early evening, right? By my calculations, that's four hours after school alone."

Joe shifted in his seat, the unease creeping back into his posture.

"And then," Rich continued, "you said that sometimes after dinner, you cover the gaps under your door so the light doesn't show, playing late into the night while your parents think you're fast asleep. Add all that up, and we're talking about six, maybe even eight hours of gaming a day.

It seems like you rather play than spending time with your friends. Am I wrong?"

Joe hesitated, his eyes flicking up to meet Rich's for a brief moment before dropping again. His silence was louder than words.

Rich, sensing the weight of the moment, carefully measured his next words.

"Listen, Joe, addictions can ruin lives. Trust me, I know this firsthand - I was addicted to chewing betel nuts."

Joe raised his head and met his eyes.

"Betel nuts? I don't even know what that is."

Rich gave a small nod.

"That's good. That means you've never tried it. It's bad for you. Every time I chewed it, my mind would go numb in a way that felt... euphoric. I wanted to chew it all day, every day. It got to the point where I couldn't focus on anything else - my friendships fell apart, my business ventures began to crumble. I was losing everything because I was chasing that feeling.

My business partners stopped trusting me, and my employees didn't respect me anymore. I was heading towards rock bottom, Joe. But then something happened - a wake-up call that made me realise how much I was destroying my life. I quit. Cold turkey. And let me tell you, life is far too precious to throw it away for something like that."

Rich paused, letting the gravity of his words sink in before continuing:

"In the same way chewing betel nuts was harming me, spending hours playing video games will have a similar effect. Sitting for hours in front of your window - or screen, or whatever you call it - takes its toll on your body. It messes with your eyes, weakens your muscles, increases your risk of injury, and slowly chips away at your health.

Can you imagine me sitting in front of a plant, just staring at it for hours, day after day?"

Joe blinked, shaking his head.

"Exactly," Rich said. "But it's not just physical, Joe. Mentally, it wrecks you. The longer you spend in that virtual world, the less you care about the real one. You stop wanting to hang out with your friends, you start isolating yourself. And before you know it, the only humans you interact with are other addicts – the ones who are just as lost as you are."

Joe's fingers fidgeted, his gaze glued to the floor.

"And when you get to that point," Rich continued, "nothing in the real world will make you happy. You'll chase that same high, that feeling of control you get from the games, but nothing will compare. You'll be frustrated, depressed, and struggling just to hold down a job, let alone keep your life together."

Rich leaned forward, his eyes locking onto Joe's.

"Is that the future you want, Joe? To lose everything - your health, your relationships, your potential - all for the sake of playing games?"

"No," Joe murmured.

"In that case, you need to break free from your addiction and find constructive ways to fill your time. Forge solid relationships with those who can help you grow, hone your skills, and expand your knowledge beyond video games. I've heard you're good with numbers, so channel that gift wisely - for your own benefit and those you care about.

I know, you can't play video games in the Jungle, but trust me, if you ever make it back to the City, you'll look back and thank me for my advice."

Rich paused, giving Joe space to absorb his words. Joe shifted, his knees and feet now facing Rich, his posture straightening. He avoided eye contact but wore a faint smirk, a flicker of understanding breaking through.

It's never easy to spark a deep conversation with someone as introverted as Joe, but Rich had succeeded in opening him up, delivering guidance Joe hadn't even realised he needed.

When Manu and Roger spoke of Rich, Joe had hoped he would help them find a way out of the Jungle, but instead, he received something even more profound – a moment of clarity that revealed the trap he was caught in.

As dusk crept closer, Joe glanced at the fading light and realised he needed to join his peers at the restaurant before the doors closed.

He thanked Rich for the conversation, his voice carrying a newfound sense of purpose, and made his way to the exit.

At the restaurant, the kids were buzzing with excitement, celebrating their success. Their energy peaked when Sina shared the news that Rich had bailed Asim out. All eyes turned to Manu and Roger, eager to uncover what had transpired between them and Rich. But the boys stayed tight-lipped, deflecting questions with practiced ease. They understood how quickly rumours could spread, and revealing too much could jeopardize everything they had worked for, even risking a dreaded trip to the Kilisi - a fate no one wanted to face.

"Can you at least talk about Asim?" Leila pressed, leaning forward with curiosity. "Did you convince Rich to set him free?"

"He's not free," Manu replied evenly. "There's no such thing as a free dinner."

"What do you mean?" Leila asked, her brow furrowing.

"Do you think Rich would waste his wealth bailing out someone he doesn't know?" Manu said. "We just told him we wouldn't leave without Asim. That's all. I didn't know he was going to bail him out."

Joe, arriving just in time, joined the conversation.

"He sees Asim as an investment," he said.

"What does that mean?" Leila asked, confusion deepening.

"He's betting Asim will become a loyal worker for him," Joe explained, though even he wasn't entirely sure of Rich's intentions.

Roger took a deep breath, wrestling with conflicting emotions. Relief that Asim had been bailed out mingled with unease at Rich's motives. Was Rich genuinely helping them, or was he exploiting their desperation? Could this be another trap, swapping one form of captivity for another? Suppressing his doubts, he forced a reassuring smile and said:

"Don't worry. He's with us now."

The next morning, as the kids gathered for breakfast, the atmosphere shifted abruptly. Bill appeared, his sharp gaze locking onto Manu and Roger like a predator sizing up its prey. The air grew thick with tension as the kids watched, bracing for his next move.

Despite their success the previous day, they knew they weren't free yet. They had to wait and see if Rich was truly on their side. Before leaving their hammocks that morning, the boys had devised a backup plan: use their earnings to free as many of them as possible. But the traders' demands and Rich's steep twenty-thousand Lape consultancy fee hung over them like a storm cloud.

Though they held a considerable sum of Lapes in their hands but weren't sure how much was truly theirs to keep. As Bill's fiery gaze shifted between Manu and Roger, the boys sat trembling, ready for whatever confrontation awaited, knowing their futures hung in the balance.

CHAPTER 11

It was another pristine morning at Bill's village, but Susan and Olivia barely noticed. The vibrant hues of dawn went unappreciated as they rose early, quietly discussing the previous day and their peers' peculiar behaviour, particularly Manu and Roger.

"They're definitely up to something," Olivia said, her brow creased in suspicion. "Have you noticed how secretive they've been?"

Susan shrugged, her tone dismissive. "Let them have their fun. I don't care. When my dad's helicopter shows up, they'll be begging to come with me."

"You mean us?" Olivia asked, a trace of doubt in her voice.

"Yeah, us," Susan said with a nod. "But seriously, I'm not losing sleep over their little schemes."

"It's not the first time they've hatched some secret plan," Olivia pointed out. "And once Bill finds out, you know they'll be in serious trouble. Just like last time."

"Guaranteed," Susan said. "I just hope it doesn't blow up in their faces. If it does, we'll probably get dragged into it too."

"True," Olivia said, her gaze drifting towards the horizon. "Still, part of me is curious. What could they possibly be planning this time?"

"Something that involves sneaking around, obviously," Susan replied. "And knowing those two, they'll probably end up needing a rescue."

Just then, the sound of laughter echoed from outside, pulling their attention away from their conversation. It was

Manu and Roger, animatedly discussing something that seemed to delight them both.

"See what I mean?" Olivia said, rolling her eyes. "They're up to no good."

"Come on, let's just get breakfast," Susan suggested, shaking her head. "We can worry about them later. Right now, I'm starving."

As the two girls prepared to head to the dining area, the laughter suddenly ceased.

Curiosity getting the better of her, Olivia rushed to the entrance of their hut and poked her head outside.

"Psst!" she signalled urgently to Susan, beckoning her to join.

Bill stood beside the table where Manu, Roger, and a few of the other kids were waiting for their breakfasts. His intense gaze was fixed on Manu and Roger, a simmering tension radiating from him.

"I told you," Olivia whispered, her eyes wide. "Look out for the guards. They're probably going to take them, just like they did with Asim. It'll help cool their heads."

The girls strained to catch Bill's words, but no sounds reached them. Suddenly, Bill spun on his heel, frustration evident in his posture, and stormed off towards the Guest House.

"Whoa," Olivia breathed, her heart racing. "He's definitely not in a good mood."

Susan nodded, her stomach knotting with anxiety.

"This could turn messy. We should keep our heads down," Susan murmured, her voice barely above a whisper.

The girls exchanged worried glances, their minds racing with the potential fallout from Bill's anger and the uncertain fate of their friends.

At the restaurant, Bill's infuriated demeanour left a dark shadow over the atmosphere. All eyes were on Manu, silently demanding answers.

"What was that all about?" Sina whispered, breaking the tension that hung in the air.

"I don't know," Manu admitted, his shoulders slumping under the weight of unease. "But he's definitely not happy with us."

Meanwhile, in the Guest House, Rich was already enjoying his breakfast when Asim, still frail and unsteady, wobbled out of his room. Rich looked up and smiled, gesturing for him to take a seat at the dining table.

"Come, join me for breakfast," he invited warmly, his voice smooth and welcoming.

Asim needed no further encouragement. He sank into a chair and grabbed a piece of yam, the familiar taste both comforting and foreign. Despite his painfully cracked lips and aching body, a flicker of renewed spirit shone within him, ready to face whatever lay ahead. Struggling to recall the details of the previous day, he asked:

"Where am I?" his voice was soft.

"You're with me," Rich replied, chuckling lightly. "I'm Rich. We're in Bill's Guest House."

"How did I get here?" Asim asked, his brow furrowed in puzzlement.

Rich took a deep breath, his expression turning serious.

"You see," he began, "everyone possesses some sort of talent, and it's up to the individual to discover what they excel at and seek ways to develop those skills. Your friends Manu and Roger are exceptionally talented in business. They devised a brilliant plan to break all of you free from Bill's trap and establish a manufacturing venture."

"Excuse me?!" Asim interrupted, his heart racing in disbelief. "Are you telling me those two orchestrated my release?"

After being locked up and feeling abandoned, Asim had never dared to imagine that anyone besides his family cared about him. As Rich revealed the intricacies of Manu and Roger's plan, a whirlwind of emotions surged through him - a blend of shame for doubting his peers and profound gratitude.

"They could have easily left you to rot in the Kilisi," Rich explained, his voice steady and reassuring. "But not even your twenty thousand Lapes bail deterred them from fighting for you as their valued friend."

Asim felt tears welling in his eyes.

"So... all this time they cared about me?" he asked, struggling to comprehend the weight of Rich's words. "Twenty thousand Lapes? How... how did they come up with that much money?"

Just then, the gate swung open, and Bill stepped inside, cutting the moment short.

Asim's disbelief morphed into fear. Was he being tricked? Were they going to beat him and lock him up again, or worse, send him to the Kilisi? Tremors shook his body as panic set in.

"Asim," Rich said, his voice calm and steady. "It's okay. You're safe. Go to the restaurant and eat whatever you'd like. And make sure you thank your friends for saving your life."

Asim's mind was reeling from the revelations he had just absorbed. Focusing hard on keeping his balance, he slowly made his way towards the restaurant, uncertain but determined to face whatever awaited him.

Bill took a seat at the dining table, positioning himself directly across from Rich. He initiated a round of polite small talk about Rich's stay at the Guest House, but it was clear the niceties were merely a prelude to the real reason for his visit.

"Listen, Rich, it was incredibly unethical of you to steal my manufacturing business…"

Before he could finish his sentence, Rich interjected:

"I think what's truly unethical is your reliance on free labour."

"What are you talking about?" Bill's voice escalated, his irritation bubbling to the surface. "I'm paying them market rates."

"Stop the sugar-coating, Bill! What about the exorbitant training fees you're charging them on credit? You know it's just a cheap trick to deepen their debt to you."

"They need training, don't they?" Bill defended his position, crossing his arms defensively.

"Really? Four weeks of training for something that can be learned in a couple of days?" Rich shot back, his tone incredulous. "Your business strategies are your concern, but don't call me unethical when I'm mentoring talented kids you're trying to exploit! How much do you want for all the kids?"

"Why on earth would I want to give you my trained workers?" Bill replied, anger flaring in his eyes.

"Come on, Bill! We both know you can't afford to keep them. You don't have a choice."

"Yes, I do!" Bill insisted, his voice rising further. "I have plenty of other work for them."

Rich nodded, unfazed.

"I'm offering you 10% of the credit from each of the kids, if you take my offer right now."

"You're insulting me, Rich! They owe me an average of over 2,000 Lapes, and you want to give me 200 for each?"

His anger surged, and he struggled to catch his breath.

"Get lost, Rich!" he added and sprang up from the table, fury radiating from him as he stormed out of the Guest House.

Rich maintained his serene composure, a smirk playing on his lips as he continued to savour his breakfast. He had anticipated Bill's explosive reaction to his lowball offer. For him, this was just part of a calculated game - one he was more than willing to play, knowing he held the upper hand. To him, it was simply another move in a strategy that was unfolding exactly as he had planned.

Meanwhile, at the restaurant, the atmosphere erupted with joy as Asim appeared in the distance, slowly making his way towards their tables. His legs were weak, his body still aching from confinement, but none of that could dim the radiant smile that broke across his face. Tears filled his eyes as he watched his friends rise in unison to greet him, their excitement infectious. Each step felt like a lifetime, every breath filled with the weight of his past and the promise of his future. Asim had doubted if he would ever feel this kind of warmth again, and now, seeing the pure joy in their eyes, it was as if a heavy chain had been cut from his soul.

He remembered the story that had drifted in and out of his mind during his darkest moments - a tale of a boy who, after years of despair, found salvation in the love he had forgotten both in himself and in others. Asim thought to himself,

"Maybe this is my chance... my new beginning."

Sina was the first to reach him, pulling him into a gentle hug.

"Easy, easy," she teased. "We didn't save you just to break you in half, you know!"

Her playful words sparked laughter that rippled through the group, but beneath the humour was the tenderness of friends relieved to have him back.

One by one, they embraced him, each hug a silent affirmation that he was wanted, that he belonged. But it was Josh, the last in line, whose quiet presence spoke the loudest. Their eyes met, and for a moment, the noise of the world disappeared. It was just the two of them - two boys who had walked through different fires but shared the same scars.

Josh broke the silence with a deep, sincere nod.

"I'm sorry, mate. Truly. It's good to have you back, and... I regret the trouble I've caused you all these years."

His voice trembled slightly, carrying the weight of all the unspoken words between them.

"It's all good," Asim replied, his voice thick with emotion. "I'm just glad you're here. We thought we lost you."

Josh's eyes softened.

"We both got a second chance."

"Indeed," Asim whispered, tears now freely spilling down his cheeks.

They hugged, their bond deeper than words could express. Both had come from fractured families, both had known the sting of abandonment and the relentless grip of poverty. But in that moment, they understood that the greatest gift they could offer each other was not pity, but love - the kind that asks for nothing in return, the kind that saves.

Leila, sensing the raw, emotional energy, started clapping. Slowly, the others joined in, their applause filling the air with the sound of shared triumph. Asim turned to face his friends, struggling to find the words that could capture the depth of his gratitude.

"Thank you," he said, his voice breaking. "Thank you for not giving up on me."

Manu stepped forward, his eyes locking with Asim's.

"We never would have left you behind," he said firmly. It was more than a statement; it was a promise, one that had been kept against all odds.

They clasped hands before pulling each other into another tight embrace. For Asim, the warmth of their touch felt like a homecoming. Only a day ago, he had been ready to surrender to despair, believing no one cared. But now, he stood surrounded by friends who had fought to save his life, who had reminded him of his own worth when he had forgotten it.

The intensity of the moment eventually gave way to lighter conversations, laughter replacing the tears of joy.

"What are you two up to today?" Sina asked, her tone light but curious.

Josh glanced at Asim, a smile tugging at the corner of his mouth.

"How about we head to the forest? We could gather some food, help knock down a bit of the group's collective debt to Bill."

Asim chuckled softly, wiping away the last of his tears. Just like that, life moved forward. But for him, this wasn't just another day – it was the beginning of something new.

"That sounds good," he said, his spirit as joyful as ever. "I wouldn't mind catching some fish while we're at it."

But Manu had a different idea.

"How about replicating Josh's bow and arrow instead?" he suggested. "We can still get food from the restaurant for now, but we need to be ready when we finally get the chance to leave."

Despite the enormous success they had the previous day, leaving Bill's village felt like a distant dream for most of the kids. While they heard Rich explain what to do with their earnings, they weren't aware of the deal Roger and Manu had struck with him.

"What about me?" asked Imogen. "Manu, should I make more drawings?"

"Absolutely!" Manu replied with enthusiasm. "I'm certain we'll have more chances to sell your artwork."

As the kids began to scatter, Roger pulled Manu aside, lowering his voice.

"Did you see Bill storming into his office? What's going on?"

"I don't know," Manu answered, his brow furrowed. "Rich probably tried to close our deal with him. But if he had succeeded, he would have left the Guest House by now, giving us the green light to leave. The way Bill stormed off... It doesn't look promising."

"We should talk to Rich, don't you think?" Roger asked, anxious.

Manu paused, thinking it through.

"Not yet. Let's wait until lunch."

Roger, trusting Manu's judgment, gave a nod. He knew Manu wasn't one to procrastinate without reason. They parted ways with their usual thumb grab and shoulder bump, a gesture they'd adopted from watching athletes. Both walked off with thoughtful expressions and a heavy sense of uncertainty.

At the factory, the morning flew by. The workers buzzed with conversation, most of it about Asim and his surprising transformation he went through. His joy was contagious, spreading warmth to everyone. He took every moment to offer a kind word, the stark contrast of his past making his fresh light even more remarkable.

As the sun climbed to its peak, Manu and Roger, though separated, were united by the same gnawing worry. Their unease grew harder to conceal with each passing moment. They had expected Rich to finalise their deal with Bill by now, but the silence stretched endlessly, amplifying their anxiety. Every minute without an update felt like a countdown, each second bringing darker thoughts. Had something gone wrong? Was Rich still in the village, or had he vanished, leaving them at Bill's mercy? They knew all too well how easily Bill could fabricate a reason to imprison them or send them to the Kilisi.

Relief came only when Joe arrived at the restaurant with news.

"Rich is still at the Guest House," he said, dropping into a chair. "He's been inspecting the clothes and shoes from the factory countless times."

It wasn't the resolution the boys were waiting for, but at least Rich hadn't disappeared, taking their fragile hope with him.

"Imogen, what did you draw this morning?" Leila asked, oblivious to the storm brewing in the boys' minds.

"A flower," Imogen said casually.

"A flower?" Leila repeated, surprised. "I haven't seen a single flower in this entire valley. Can we see it?"

"They're everywhere," Imogen chuckled, flipping open her notepad. She revealed her latest sketch, a breathtaking flower that dominated the page. Its petals flowed gracefully, layered in exquisite detail. Every curve, every delicate vein was etched with precision. The heart of the flower, with its finely shaded stamens, radiated a lifelike vibrancy, as if the drawing could breathe. It was a masterpiece, a tribute to nature's intricate beauty.

The kids were astonished. How had she managed to create something so detailed and mesmerising in just a few hours? And more importantly, where had she even seen such a beautiful flower?

"It's right there," Imogen laughed, pointing towards a small patch of grass by the restaurant.

"Where?" The kids craned their necks, seeing nothing but weeds.

With a smile, Imogen strolled over to the patch and plucked a tiny flower, no bigger than the tip of her pinkie finger. She placed it on the table, and the group erupted into laughter.

"You've got to be kidding me!" Josh exclaimed, shaking his head in disbelief. "How on earth do you notice stuff like this when the rest of us are blind as bats?"

Imogen just shrugged, a smile playing on her lips.

"You've got to look closely," she said softly. "Beauty's all around - you just have to know how to see it."

Shortly after, their lunchbreak ended, and it was time to head back to work. Roger, once again, pulled Manu aside, leaning in to whisper:

"Now?"

"No, let's wait until the evening."

Roger smirked, teasing:

"Look who's procrastinating now."

But the sun hadn't made much progress across the sky when Joe burst into the factory, grinning from ear to ear.

"We're free!" he announced.

The kids exchanged uncertain glances, struggling to process Joe's words. The idea that Manu and Roger's secretive efforts might be tied to their freedom felt too unbelievable - especially for Maria and the former Guest House keepers, who had long learned to temper hope with caution.

"What are you talking about?" Leila asked, her brows knitting together in confusion.

Joe's grin only widened.

"Ask Manu," he said.

All eyes turned to Manu. His expression, equal parts bewildered and guarded, mirrored the confusion of the group. He had spent the entire day on edge, anxiously awaiting news from Rich. Even for him, Joe's bold statement felt like wishful thinking - an impossible dream spoken aloud too soon.

"What's going on, Manu?" one of the factory workers asked, their voice a mix of hope and hesitation. Others quickly echoed the question, a ripple of anticipation spreading through the room.

Manu hesitated, his mind racing.

"Roger and I have been trying to set up a manufacturing deal with Rich," he finally explained. "If what Joe's saying is true, it means Rich might've sorted out the last missing piece of the puzzle. That's my guess, at least. I need to find out for sure."

Without another word, Manu jumped to his feet and hurried out with Joe, leaving behind a flurry of whispered questions and mounting anticipation.

Maria's heart swelled with joy as she observed the confused expressions on the kids' faces. She had seen this moment coming long before any of them. When she first met Manu, many things about him reminded her of her old friend, Rica - a spark, an unshakeable determination to escape the grip of Bill's village. Rica had once declared, just like Manu, that she wouldn't remain a paid slave for long, and Maria had no doubt that Manu would follow the same path. She believed in him more than he knew. Since the kids' entrapment, she quietly nurtured the belief that Manu would figure out a way to break free, and now, seeing the look in his eyes, she knew that time had finally come.

What filled her with even more quiet satisfaction was the certainty that Manu wouldn't leave his friends behind. It was in his nature to pull others with him, to share whatever freedom he could carve out. She took pleasure in the mix of bewilderment and hope flickering across the kids' faces - each of them sensing that something monumental was unfolding, but unsure of the details.

Meanwhile, Manu and Joe sprinted up the hill, their breaths sharp and hearts pounding as they raced to find Roger. As soon as Roger saw them, he knew they were free.

The distance to the gate of the Guest House seemed to be shorter that afternoon as in a blink of an eye the trio found themselves ready to barge in.

"Wait here," Manu told Joe.

Joe's face fell, a flicker of disappointment crossing his features. He had been the one to deliver the great news to Manu, and now being asked to stay behind left him feeling pushed aside. In his mind, he deserved to be part of whatever was about to unfold.

Manu placed a hand on his shoulder.

"We'll fill you in when the time is right," he said, his tone firm but not unkind.

Reluctantly, Joe nodded, and Manu and Roger pushed open the gate.

Inside, they found Rich lounging comfortably on a straw couch, surrounded by an assortment of clothes and a pair of shoes. He looked up as they entered, a mischievous grin spreading across his face.

"You're free, my friends," Rich greeted, the corners of his mouth curling into a smirk. "Or should I say, my partners?"

Manu blinked, struggling to absorb the words.

"What happened?"

Rich leaned back, exuding satisfaction.

"We finalised the deal with the traders yesterday. They'll supply the raw materials and buy your finished products. Today, I cleared your debts with Bill. You're free to leave with me. We'll kick off your manufacturing operation as soon as we can."

"How much debt did we actually have to pay?" Roger asked, cutting straight to the point.

Rich's eyes gleamed.

"This morning, I offered Bill 10% of each person's debt. He told me to get lost and stormed off. But I knew he'd come around eventually. Bill's not stupid. As an entrepreneur, he understands the mess he's in - he can't keep piling on debt for workers who are relying on him for their wages. If his workers can't earn, they can't pay off their debts, and he can't keep up with the payroll. The more employees he holds hostage, the deeper he digs himself into a hole. Letting some of them go and forgiving their debts is his only smart move."

Manu and Roger were hanging onto every word. Rich paused for effect, a smile playing at his lips.

"And were you right?" Manu asked, dying to find out the answer.

Rich chuckled, drawing out the suspense.

"Of course. After lunch, he came back, ready to accept my original offer."

The boys erupted with joy, high-fiving each other, their grins stretching ear to ear.

"Hold on," Rich said, laughing at their reaction. "That's not the whole story."

The boys paused, their excitement turning into tense curiosity.

"I told him the offer was no longer valid," Rich added, a sly smile playing on his lips.

The boys' expressions froze, caught between disbelief and suspense.

"I let him squirm for a bit," Rich continued, clearly savouring the memory. "But in the end, we settled on 5%. He had no choice - he needed this deal more than we did."

Manu and Roger exchanged glances, their faces frozen between disbelief and astonishment, unsure if they had truly heard what Rich just said. A brief pause, a couple of blinks - and then it hit them. The realisation washed over them, and they erupted into uncontrollable laughter, the kind that left their sides aching. For nearly two weeks, they had been dying to escape Bill's clutches, willing to face the brutal realities of survival in the unforgiving Jungle just for a taste of freedom. And now, it was finally here. Not even the looming responsibilities they had to Rich could dull the sheer joy coursing through them.

"The thing is," Rich began, leaning in with a smirk, "I could've gotten him to agree to zero Lapes per head, but Bill owes me a decent sum. If I pushed him too hard and bankrupted him, I'd never see a single Lape of that money."

The boys' laughter died down as they absorbed his words, their eyes locked on him, hanging on his every syllable.

"So, I left him some crumbs," Rich continued, his tone matter-of-fact but his eyes sharp, reading the boys' rapt expressions. "Enough for him to regain his footing. Remember this lesson for the rest of your lives: when you truly understand the situation of the other party, you hold all the cards. It enables you to get what you want."

Manu and Roger nodded, the weight of Rich's words sinking in. This was more than a deal - it was a master class in strategy. They knew they'd carry this lesson with them long after their laughter faded.

"There are all sorts of great opportunities around us," Rich continued, his voice steady and deliberate. "But they don't just fall into our laps because we feel entitled to them. You have to fight for them. In business the fight happens through negotiations. The better you are at it, the more abundant your life will be. Think of negotiations as a form of art - one you must master if you want to thrive.

You also need to accept that compromise is part of the process. If you try to take everything, you'll often end up empty-handed. Today, I gave up 5%, but that's nothing compared to the 95% we gained. Now, listen, we have six days before the Totoli Group comes back for the rest of their money. Go gather the team. Make a list of everyone joining us, along with their debts, so we can pay the agreed amount. I'll meet you all at the restaurant shortly."

As soon as the boys were out of sight, Roger, unable to contain his excitement, shoved Manu with both hands, almost sending him toppling over.

"Do you even realise how much he just saved us?" Roger asked, laughing breathlessly.

"Of course!" Manu grinned. "We went from needing 14,000 for raw materials to 1,400. And instead of paying Bill 2,000 Lapes per person, it's down to 100."

"Yeah, our debts alone would've cost us 26,000, and he got us all out for just 800," Roger added, shaking his head in disbelief.

Joe, amused by their excitement, was eager to catch up.

"What's going on?" he asked.

"What's going on is that we're about to get out of here," Manu said, his voice full of excitement. "We just need to pack up."

"Who do you think is coming with us?" Roger asked.

"There's only one way to find out," Manu replied and dashed off to the factory.

Inside, the workers were buzzing with anticipation, eagerly chatting and waiting for updates, the air thick with the hope of freedom and the unknown adventures ahead.

Manu stepped forward, addressing the group with a mix of excitement and urgency in his voice.

"Roger and I, with Rich's backing, have started a new manufacturing venture. If any of you want to join us, get ready to leave."

The workers erupted into cheers, springing to their feet in a wave of celebration. Joyful hugs were exchanged, their excitement palpable. But amidst the jubilation, three figures remained seated - Susan, Olivia, and Maria. Detached, the two girls were quietly watching the others, while Maria shared their enthusiasm in her way.

Leila, noticing Maria hadn't moved, gently sat beside her.

"Maria, will you come with us?" she asked softly.

Maria turned to her with a melancholic smile, her eyes carrying the weight of 46 long years spent in Bill's village. She looked around at the young faces, full of life and hope, a stark contrast to her own worn-out spirit.

"No, my dear," she replied, her voice tinged with quiet resignation. "Most of my days here have been clouded by sorrow. But you kids - just in these last two weeks - you've brought light into my life. Still, I'm too old for change now."

She paused, her gaze lingering on the group's bright faces, filled with vitality and ambition.

"You, though - you're young, full of energy, determination, and the fire of motivation. You must go on! But promise me one thing: never let anyone trap you like this again."

Her words hung in the air, a solemn reminder to never lose the freedom they had fought so hard to regain.

Unfortunately, Maria's perspective was not unique. It echoed a sentiment shared by many around the world who, out of fear or habit, use age as an excuse to resist change, even when that change could lead to a better life. Mai, for example, immediately thought of her own grandmother, who, like Maria, stubbornly clung to her old, crumbling house despite its desperate need for renovation.

Maria's decision, though it saddened Mai, also fuelled her determination to return to the City. She saw Maria's life as a cautionary tale, a source of inspiration to help her grandmother confront her own fear of change.

The threat of being swallowed up by the Jungle felt small compared to the excitement of leaving Bill's village. But she wasn't alone in her conflicted feelings. While Bill's village had imposed a heavy financial burden on the kids, it also provided a safety they couldn't find beyond its protective walls. Their time there had softened the memories of the hardships and life-threatening challenges they faced before their arrival.

"We've got to go!" Manu urged, his voice brimming with excitement.

As Maria tearfully bid them farewell, her heart was torn. She was genuinely happy for the kids, knowing they finally had the chance to embark on a new journey. Yet she also understood that their departure marked the end of the lively atmosphere they had brought to the village - the laughter, the deep conversations, the excitement that had once filled their days would now fade, leaving a quiet emptiness in its wake.

The group moved swiftly, gathering their belongings and assembling at the restaurant. But as Manu scanned the crowd, he noticed Olivia and Susan were missing. Frowning, he turned to Roger.

"Summarise everyone's expenses. I'll check on the girls."

He slung his backpack onto a bench and dashed towards the factory. Inside, to his surprise, Olivia and Susan were casually chatting, half-finished clothes draped over their laps, raw materials scattered around them.

"Aren't you two coming?" Manu asked, his voice a mix of confusion and frustration.

They were moments away from leaving, and the girls didn't seem the least bit ready. What were they thinking? Olivia and Susan exchanged a glance, lost in their own world.

"Nope," Olivia replied, her tone carrying a hint of defiance. "Why would we want to work for you?"

Manu's eyes widened. He hadn't expected that. After risking his life to free them all from Bill's grasp, this was their response? The opportunity for freedom was right there, yet their pride was blinding them to reality.

"We're not in a rush to trade one job for another," Olivia added, folding her arms.

Manu shifted his gaze to Susan.

"And you?"

Susan shook her head.

"I don't want you as my boss either."

Manu swallowed the sting of rejection, nodding slowly as his father's words echoed in his mind:

"You'll never be liked by everyone. Don't fight it. Stay true to yourself."

"Alright then," he said evenly. "Good luck."

He wasn't angry - more disappointed. He had wanted the best for all of them, but now it seemed like they were choosing a different path, one that likely meant they'd never cross paths again. Turning towards the exit, he was about to leave when Olivia's voice pierced the air.

"We'll think of you from the seats of our helicopter."

Manu paused mid-step, a flicker of doubt creeping into his mind. Had he miscalculated? Was he leading the others into a dead-end? The girls' logic was compelling - staying in the village increased their chances of being found by a rescue team. The dense Jungle canopy would make it impossible for anyone to spot them from the sky. However, there was no guarantee that a rescue team hadn't already given up after nearly three weeks of searching, assuming the worst.

Noticing Manu approaching the restaurant by himself, Roger asked:

"Aren't they coming?"

"No, they have their reasons," Manu shrugged, pushing away the lingering doubt. "How did you go with summarising everyone's debt?"

"Only you, Joe, Imogen, and myself have records," Roger replied.

Manu shook his head, frowning.

"Rich isn't going to be happy about that. Where is he?"

"Talking to the guard at the Guest House," Roger said.

"Let's go get him," Manu suggested, his confidence slowly returning.

They made their way to the Guest House to let Rich know they were ready to leave. Rich quickly instructed one of his assistants to gather his belongings and follow them to the restaurant.

"Did you get the list I asked for?" he asked.

"Yes, but most of them don't have a clue how much debt they've racked up," Manu admitted, bracing himself for Rich's reaction.

Rich's silence was telling - he wasn't pleased. When they regrouped, he addressed everyone with a firm but composed tone.

"How can you not know where you stand financially? If you're unaware of your financial health, you're always at risk - either of making bad decisions or being exploited. Bill can claim whatever he wants now, and we have no way to dispute it."

He motioned Manu and Roger aside, and with a slight smirk, offered them another lesson, this time with a reassuring tone.

"Don't stress too much. That 5% we secured earlier gives us plenty of cushion. Even if Bill inflates the numbers, we'll still come out ahead. Let's get this over with and move forward."

Manu felt the weight lift as Rich's calm confidence melted away the tension. They were ready to face Bill's tricks with a sense of preparedness that had once felt impossible. Entering Bill's office one last time, the trio settled their accounts, while the rest of the group eagerly awaited the moment they'd dreamed of since arriving.

One person, however, wasn't joining in the celebration. Sina sat quietly, gazing into the distance, her brow knit with worry. Mai, perceptive as ever, joined her, draping a comforting arm around her shoulders.

"What's wrong?" Mai asked gently.

Sina's eyes welled up, and she took a deep breath.

"I don't know what to do. If I leave, Sika and Broko will be left alone, with no one to look out for them. I can't just abandon them."

"Remember your talk with Vaipor?" Mai asked. "He said: use your creativity to regain your freedom and build something sustainable for your friends."

Sina nodded slowly, her gaze dropping.

"I know, but… I need more time. I now have my freedom, but it's only half of it. I don't have anything to offer them to leave them secure. They're like family to me, and leaving them… it feels like a betrayal."

Just then, Leila and Imogen joined, sensing the weight of Sina's conflict. Sina had formed a deep bond with Sika and Broko, and the idea of leaving them behind felt like tearing a piece of her own heart.

Meanwhile, Rich and the two boys emerged from Bill's office, their faces lit with wide grins that mirrored their shared sense of accomplishment.

"It's time to say goodbye to this 'luxurious village of slaves!'" Manu shouted, his laughter contagious as the group erupted with cheers. All except Sina, who sat with her head in her hands.

Imogen's voice cut through the excitement, her tone serious.

"Sina, listen - you can't look after the whole world. Sometimes, you have to be a bit more selfish and think about your own future. If you stay, you won't be safe, and you might never see your family again. Don't you deserve to look after yourself, too?"

Sina looked up, her red eyes meeting Imogen's. She gave a small, grateful smile and rose, embracing her friends.

"You're right. I needed a bit of courage, but… I think I'm ready."

"Let's go!" Leila exclaimed, already eager to move.

But Sina hesitated, one last thought tugging at her.

"Imogen, could you lend me a few Lapes?"

Imogen's eyes lit up with understanding. Without a moment's hesitation, she handed over 200 Lapes, her expression filled with quiet pride.

"Thank you," Sina said sincerely, her voice tinged with emotion. "I know it's not much, but it'll mean something to them - to know I gave more than I had."

Bolstered by her friends' unwavering support, Sina made a quick stop to see Sika and Broko. She handed each of them 100 Lapes, her parting gift simple yet heartfelt.

The farewell was swift but heavy with unspoken sentiment. The group had already started up the hill, and Sina, fighting the lump in her throat, turned away before the moment could linger too long.

With a final glance back, Sina and the girls dashed to catch up, their steps quickening with each stride as they hurried to join their friends on the path towards freedom from Bill's village.

As the group departed, the village took on a quieter, almost unfamiliar atmosphere for those who remained. When Bill entered the factory, his usual brisk stride was tempered by a rare calm. Like every seasoned entrepreneur, he had endured countless setbacks over the years, and while losing his weaving business was a blow, he knew that resilience was measured not by the number of defeats but by the speed of recovery.

After wrapping up his negotiations with Rich, Manu, and Roger, Bill returned to his office to plot his next steps. The popularity of his products at the market offered him a glimmer of hope; if he could secure new traders, he could rebuild his business. Manu's ideas from earlier drifted back into his mind - he had recognised their merit even then but let his pride get in the way. Accepting his oversight, Bill understood that an immediate shift in his business practices was essential.

Bill addressed the remaining three workers with a new-found energy, a faint smile playing on his lips.

"It's a lean team today, isn't it?" he remarked, pausing as the trio looked up at him, intrigued. "Starting now, we're rolling out some important changes. Each morning, you'll be responsible for preparing the Guest House, ensuring it's always ready for guests. Once that's done, the rest of your work hours will be flexible - you can set your own schedules. You'll receive a base salary for managing the Guest House, and beyond that, your earnings will be performance-based. The more clothes and shoes you produce, the more you'll make."

He let his words sink in before continuing:

"Additionally, every twenty working days, you'll earn a paid day off. You can use it right away or save up for several consecutive days off when you need them."

Then, Bill turned specifically to Susan and Olivia, his gaze more focused.

"As for you two, your training is officially complete. I've been watching your work closely, and I'm confident you can produce goods of the quality we need."

The workers stood momentarily stunned by Bill's unexpected shift in his mood. His new approach to business now carried a sense of mutual respect - something even he hadn't foreseen but now found invigorating.

He left the factory with renewed determination, understanding that the future of his businesses depended not only on his ability to adapt, but also on a team that demanded - and deserved - respect.

✿ ✿ ✿

Four weeks passed, and every moment Susan and Olivia had spent together in the Jungle, away from family, friends, and the other kids, began to weigh on them. Confined within the boundaries of Bill's village, they found themselves increasingly irritated by the other's habits. They missed not only their loved ones but also the variety that came with being part of a larger group - a mix of personalities that kept things fresh and entertaining.

In Bill's village, the days blurred together without distinction. Weekends were irrelevant; doing nothing all day was somehow more exhausting than working and getting paid for it. With Bill focused on rebuilding his manufacturing business, the usual diversions - parties, market days - disappeared. Besides Bill's restaurant, there was nothing the girls could spend their money on. As a result, their savings grew steadily, and by the end of four weeks, they had each accumulated over 300 Lapes — a small fortune compared to what they'd expected.

Each night, they counted their growing stash of Lapes, finding brief comfort in its reassuring clink. But the more they saved, the more their doubts grew. They both knew that no amount of Lapes could buy a fool proof way out of the Jungle. Their earnings might signify wealth amongst the Voivokis, but out in the wild, they would be worth nothing against the raw threats of nature and the uncertainty of survival.

On one such uneventful day the monotony was finally disrupted when two Voivokis arrived at the Guest House, planning to stay the night.

"They're traders," Maria whispered, unaware that this seemingly ordinary encounter would ignite a chain of events beyond anything Susan and Olivia could imagine - pulling them into a darkness that would make even their worst nightmares pale in comparison.

CHAPTER 12

The evening was unusually cool and windy in Bill's village, a sure sign of another torrential storm rolling in. A chorus of colourful frogs croaked louder than ever, their celebratory calls drowning out even the distant chatter of macaques, eagerly awaiting the next downpour. But the workers paid them no heed. As soon as their shift ended, they rushed to the restaurant, eager for a meal before taking shelter from the storm.

In the queue, Olivia leaned closer to Susan, casting a furtive glance towards the traders, seated at a table brimming with vibrant dishes. Their animated laughter drew her attention like a magnet.

"Did you notice the feast they're having?" Olivia murmured, her eyes lingering on the colourful, unfamiliar dishes.

"Yeah, they must be hungry," Susan replied, shrugging it off. She didn't think much of the traders' meal - it was just food to her, nothing more. But Olivia? She saw something different. She saw wealth - real wealth. The kind of abundance that made her stomach tighten with longing. To Olivia, their meal wasn't just food; it was a display of privilege, a hint of connections, and maybe even power.

"But look," Olivia pressed, her voice dropping lower. "They're eating things that aren't even on Bill's menu. They must be pretty important for Bill to treat them like that. Maybe they know Rich too."

Susan frowned slightly.

"Why would that matter?"

"Think about it," Olivia replied. "We've been stuck here for so long, waiting for something - anything - to change. If they know Rich, they might be able to help us find Manu and the others. With them, we have a greater chance of getting back to the City."

Susan's didn't respond. Her gaze remained distant, burdened by thoughts she couldn't shake. Unlike Olivia, she clung to a fragile belief: that a rescue team would come, that her parents had never stopped searching for her after the accident. That belief was all she had, and she held onto it like a lifeline. The possibility of her parents giving up on her was too painful to consider.

Olivia, however, had let go of that hope a long time ago. She often regretted staying behind in Bill's village instead of leaving with the others. Every day in the village felt like a slow, suffocating spiral into monotony. The traders' presence stirred something dormant in her - a fragile spark of optimism, a chance to escape the village's isolation and reunite with their peers.

As the line moved forward, Olivia grabbed her dinner and glanced back at the traders' table. Her resolve hardened.

"Come on," she said, her voice firm.

Susan hesitated, anxiety prickling at the edges of her expression. The thought of Olivia leaving - leaving her alone in Bill's village - was terrifying. Reluctantly, she followed, torn between fear and intrigue.

When Olivia stopped beside the traders' table, she met their curious gazes with a hesitant smile.

"Can we join you?" she asked, her voice steady despite the nervous energy coursing through her.

The traders exchanged quick glances before grinning warmly. They shifted to make room, gesturing for the girls to sit.

Susan settled into the seat beside Olivia, her tension easing slightly under the traders' welcoming smiles. It didn't take long for the conversation to drift towards the girls' origins. The traders, fascinated by the rare opportunity to meet people from the City - a mysterious world they'd only heard whispers about - hung on every word.

"We can't wait to get home," Olivia said with a wistful sigh. "Our friends are waiting for us at Rich's place. Do you know him?"

One of the traders nodding knowingly.

"Of course, many of us know Rich," he replied.

The girls exchanged a brief smile, a flicker of relief passing between them.

Emboldened by their response, Olivia pressed on.

"We've been saving up for ages, and now we're ready to leave. Do you know where his place is? Could you help us get there?"

The traders' smiles deepened, an almost conspiratorial glint flickering in their eyes. Their reaction caught the girls off guard, and they exchanged puzzled glances, unsure what to make of it.

Finally, one of the traders spoke, his voice calm and inviting.

"We're actually heading to Rich's place ourselves. If you're ready to leave, you're welcome to come with us."

The offer landed like a dream come true, so perfectly timed that it felt surreal. Olivia's eyes lit up, and she turned to Susan, who met her gaze with a look of shared excitement. Though initially Susan didn't want to leave the safety of the village, she came around, her nod sealing their unspoken agreement.

"We'll leave at first light," came the instruction from one of the traders.

The promise of departure filled the girls' spirits with a newfound sense of freedom. For the first time in weeks, the monotonous cycle was breaking, replaced by the hope of finally reuniting with their peers and continue their search of the way to the City.

That evening, they approached Maria to share the news. Maria listened in silence, her expression darkening with every word. When Olivia finished, Maria closed her eyes and shook her head, her brows furrowing deeply. A tremor underpinned her voice as she spoke, her words heavy with the weight of past regrets.

"My friends and I once trusted strangers," she began, her tone measured yet sombre. "We thought they were our ticket to freedom. Instead, we found ourselves fleeing for our lives… and later, trapped here by Bill's father. Trust is a luxury in this place - one that can cost you dearly."

"Maria, we've heard your story a dozen times," Olivia replied. "I understand why you're worried, but our situation is different. These Vois are traders, not thugs. We've talked to them. We know them."

Maria's gaze softened with sadness, but her worry didn't fade.

"My dear, no amount of talk can truly tell you who someone is," she replied. "I can't stop you, but this all feels eerily familiar. It's… déjà vu."

Susan tilted her head, her confusion evident.

"Déjà vu?"

Maria gave a weary nod.

"It's that strange, unsettling feeling that what's happening now has already happened before. In this case, it's not your past, but mine you're echoing. And it didn't end well."

Her voice wavered, and tears welled in her eyes. She had already lost so much - her friends, her freedom, and the hope she'd once clung to. The arrival of the kids weeks ago had brought a fleeting sense of joy, but now that joy was fading, replaced by the fear of losing the last two companions who tethered her to the present.

Maria's warnings grew more urgent. She reminded the girls that a friendly conversation didn't mean they truly knew the traders. Trust, she argued, had to be earned over time, not exchanged in mere hours. But Olivia's stubborn resolve held firm.

"We've waited over six weeks for help, Maria," Olivia argued. "If no one's come for us by now, it's because they don't know we're here. Even Jane and Jess haven't come back. How much longer should we wait?"

Maria hesitated, but Olivia pressed on, her tone firm.

"The traders told us that Bill's village isn't on any of the Voivokis' main routes. If even the Voivokis don't know about this place, how can we expect anyone from the City to find us? Just as businesses fail when they remain unseen, so will we. Staying here might be safe, but it's like hiding in a shadow. If we want to be found, we need to step into the light."

Susan glanced at Maria, her expression conflicted.

"They're right, Maria," she said softly. "The longer we stay, the less likely anyone will find us. We can't keep waiting."

Maria's shoulders sagged under the weight of their words. She understood their logic, but her intuition screamed against their decision. She wanted to beg them to reconsider, to wait just a little longer, but she could see the resolve in their eyes. Her warnings fell on deaf ears.

The following morning, despite the steady downpour outside, Olivia and Susan packed their few belongings. The traders waited for them at the village's edge, their faces bright with a promise only they knew. As the girls prepared to leave, Maria stood at the entrance of her hut, watching them with a heavy heart.

"Be careful," she called out, her voice cracking. "And remember - you can't always go back once you leave."

The girls turned to her, their faces a mix of gratitude and determination.

"We'll be okay," Susan assured her, though the tremble in her voice betrayed her own doubts.

With that, they stepped into the rain, filled with hope and anticipation. Every step away from Bill's village felt like a step closer to freedom - and yet, a shadow of uncertainty loomed over them.

They clung to one fervent wish as they walked: never to return.

The rain was unrelenting, soaking them to the bone as they trudged through the Jungle. Thick underbrush clawed at them, and sharp thorns snagged their clothes as they climbed the first muddy incline. Memories of their initial harrowing days in the Jungle resurfaced, reminding them of the exhaustion and danger they had once barely escaped before reaching Bill's village. Yet, their resolve held firm, bolstered by the excitement of finally on the go. But that thrill began to wane as the traders grew impatient, complaining about their progress.

Hardened by years of navigating the Jungle's depths, the traders set a pace that would have daunted even the fittest City dwellers. Olivia and Susan, unaccustomed to such an arduous trek, quickly found themselves struggling.

By the time they descended to a rocky riverbank, the sun had already crept past its peak, unnoticed, obscured by a blanket of rainclouds. The scene before them was serene yet formidable

- the Jungle opened up to reveal a broad, wild river, its banks framed by the intricate interplay of plant and stone. Towering trees vibrated with the pulse of nature, their roots entwining like thick ropes around twisted lianas, all stretching desperately skyward, hungry for the rare shafts of sunlight.

On the opposite bank, erosion had carved a precarious cliff face, forcing trees to sink their gnarled roots deep into the rocks, anchoring themselves to the mountain's edge. These roots stretched and twisted over the stones, a testament to the resilience and adaptability of life in the Jungle.

The traders stopped, waiting for the girls to catch up.

"Rich's place is in the valley behind that mountain," one of the traders said, pointing across the river with a casual gesture. "From here, you're on your own."

The words hit the girls like a blow. Susan's heart sank as she stared at the surging river between them and their supposed destination.

"But… it's impossible to cross this river," she said, her voice trembling.

"Head upstream," the trader replied, his tone flat and unsympathetic. "You'll find a place to cross eventually. But before we part ways, there's one last thing - our payment."

"Payment?" Olivia's voice was sharp, a mix of confusion and outrage. "You never said anything about payment!"

The trader's expression hardened.

"Who works for free in this world?" he shot back coldly. "Time is money. You owe us a thousand Lapes."

"A thousand?" Olivia's voice cracked as panic began to creep in. "We don't have that kind of money!"

"Hand over your bags," he said, stepping closer, his voice low and menacing.

Susan's breath caught in her throat as the second trader moved behind them, effectively cutting off any chance of escape. Olivia looked at her, wide-eyed and desperate, but they both knew there was no way out.

Trembling, the girls surrendered their bags, their hands reluctantly letting go.

The traders rifled through their belongings with brutal efficiency. Shiny Lapes were extracted with greedy hands, leaving their savings gutted - over 800 Lapes gone in seconds. Susan flinched as they yanked out her cracked tablet and their phones, inspecting the battered devices with disdain.

"Junk," one of them sneered, tossing the items into the mud at their feet. The tablet landed face-down, its cracked screen splintering further. The Voivokis discarded their remaining possessions with the same indifference, scattering them as if they were worthless.

Satisfied, the traders turned and disappeared into the foliage without a backward glance, their departure as abrupt as their betrayal.

The roar of the river filled the silence they left behind, underscored by the steady drum of rain on leaves. Olivia and Susan stood motionless, drenched and shaking, their eyes fixed on the muddy remains of their belongings.

It felt as though the Jungle had stripped them bare. The safety of Bill's village, their savings, even the illusion of control - they had lost it all.

Having nothing but the unforgiving Jungle ahead, the bitter weight of their choices pressed down like the storm around them, unrelenting and suffocating.

Olivia was the first to shake off the shock. Despite their harrowing circumstances, she clung to a fragile thread of determination.

"Come on, Susan. We have to find a way across the river," she urged, scanning the rugged landscape for any sign of hope.

"This is all your fault, Olivia!" Susan's voice cracked through the rain, sharp and trembling with fury. Her cheeks flushed as she clenched her fists, her body trembling with the heat of anger. "You came up with this stupid idea! Maria warned us, but you just had to drag me into this mess! Look where it's gotten us!"

The frustration bubbled over, unchecked, and for a moment Susan teetered on the edge of violence. She had never hit anyone but now, in the suffocating grip of desperation, the urge felt almost unbearable.

"Really? My stupid idea?" Olivia snapped back, her voice rising. "At least I had an idea! What did you bring to the table? Nothing but complaints!"

Susan's anger flared, her words laced with venom.

"Maybe if you'd listened instead of acting like you know everything, we wouldn't be stuck in this nightmare!"

Olivia's eyes narrowed with frustration.

"You think you're so much better, don't you? You're so spoiled that you don't even know what it's like to fight for anything!"

The accusation lingered between them, raw and cutting. Susan felt her mother's voice echo in her mind, urging her to never back down from an argument. She spat the words before she could stop herself:

"Spoiled? At least I'm not pretending to be someone I'm not! You and your mother are nothing but liars - just a pair of beggars pretending to belong!"

The insult landed like a slap. Olivia froze, her face crumbling for a split second before she turned away. Susan saw the pain flash in her eyes, a wound laid bare, and for a fleeting moment, guilt threatened to override her anger.

But Olivia didn't give her the chance. She grabbed her scattered belongings with trembling hands and stormed off into the rain, her shoulders set with furious determination.

"Olivia, wait!" Susan shouted, her anger dissolving into panic. Scrambling to gather her things, she stumbled after her friend. "Please don't leave me!"

Olivia didn't stop. She moved quickly, her figure a blur through the rain. But though she refused to look back, she couldn't bring herself to truly abandon Susan. She slowed her pace just enough, pausing occasionally to glance over her shoulder, ensuring Susan wasn't far behind.

Unaware of Olivia's silent mercy, Susan pushed herself to the limit, every step fuelled by terror at the prospect of being left alone. She clawed at thorny plants, her palms stinging as she hauled herself up the steep, muddy incline. Her lungs burned, her muscles screamed, but the thought of being stranded in the Jungle kept her moving.

As Olivia neared the mountain's peak, a sudden, chilling scream tore through the air. It echoed against the relentless roar of rain, sharp and gut-wrenching, before fading into an eerie silence.

Olivia froze, her heart pounding in her chest. The oppressive quiet that followed made her stomach churn. She knew, with grim certainty, that Susan was in serious trouble.

Turning back, she scanned the treacherous path below, her pulse hammering in her ears. Gritting her teeth, she began her descent, gripping the same thorny plants that had once guided her climb. The rain blurred her vision, but she pressed on, determined to reach Susan before the Jungle claimed her for good.

At last, she found her friend crumpled on a jagged rock jutting over the river. Relief and dread warred within her as she took in the scene. The rock had broken Susan's fall, sparing her life, but her ankle was twisted, the injury vivid and unmistakable.

Tears streaked Susan's mud-smeared face as their eyes met, her expression a mixture of agony and regret.

"I'm sorry," Susan gasped, her voice thin and broken.

"Apology accepted," Olivia replied softly, managing a faint, shaky smile. Relief coursed through her, tempered by the gravity of the situation.

Crouching beside her, Olivia assessed the damage. The sight of Susan's swollen ankle and her trembling hands clutching it filled her with a pang of guilt.

"How bad is it?" Olivia asked.

"Really bad," Susan admitted.

"I'll get help," Olivia said quickly, already scanning the landscape for the fastest route.

"No!" Susan cried, her fingers clamping around Olivia's wrist. "Don't leave me here! It'll be dark soon - go in the morning!"

Olivia hesitated, her eyes flicking to the mountains looming above and the churning river below. Beyond the peak she'd just climbed, she was sure there was a safe crossing - Rich's place was close. One more mountain, and she could reach safety before nightfall.

"I'll be back before dark," Olivia promised, though the words felt hollow. She pried Susan's fingers from her wrist and stood.

"What if you don't make it back in time?" Susan's voice wavered, panic tightening its grip.

"I will," Olivia said firmly, locking eyes with her. Then, without another word, she turned and began to climb.

Susan's desperate pleas trailed after her, mingling with the relentless patter of rain. Olivia didn't look back. Each step felt heavier, guilt clawing at her resolve.

Alone on the rock, Susan hugged her knees to her chest, her sobs muffled against her arms. The Jungle around her was vast, cruel, and indifferent. With darkness closing in, every shadow seemed to bristle with danger. Immobilised and alone, she felt the crushing weight of her vulnerability.

Olivia, too, felt fear gnawing at her edges, but she refused to let it dictate her actions. She rationalised her choice as the only viable one: staying with Susan wouldn't protect either of them. They were defenceless against the predators - or the Voivokis - that often stalked the Jungle at night. Finding Rich's place and returning with help was the best course of action, even if it meant abandoning Susan until morning. At least one of them would be safe. At least one of them had a chance.

As Olivia pressed deeper into the Jungle, suppressing the lingering guilt, reality hit hard. The pampered girl, lacking experience in navigating treacherous terrain, struggled to find a suitable place to cross the river. Darkness enveloped her faster than anticipated, and despite her basic survival instincts, there was no time to construct a shelter. She sought refuge beneath a large tree, clutching a broad leaf over her head in a futile attempt to shield herself from the relentless downpour.

Perched in exhaustion, Olivia awaited the night's veil to lift, her gaze catching a gentle glow seeping through the dense foliage. At first, elation sparked in her eyes, but the bitter memory of heartless traders who had ruthlessly stripped away everything valuable from her and Susan earlier that day quickly cast a shadow of doubt. Hesitation gripped her as she pondered whether to approach the source of light.

"Can I truly trust anyone here?" she wondered to herself, the weight of desperation bearing down. Yet, with nothing left to lose, she pushed through the wet thicket, drawn to the faint promise of hope.

As she neared, Olivia saw a Voivoki seated in a carefully crafted shelter, his legs propped on a log serving as a makeshift bed. The structure was spacious enough for two, shielding him and his crackling fire from the rain – his fire casting a warm, inviting glow.

Driven by both exhaustion and a creeping sense of entitlement, Olivia quickened her steps. Her focus shifted to a piece of paper in the Voivoki's hands, his face lit with a fleeting joy as he studied it. Her heart leapt - was it something from her classmates? Could he know where they were? Dropping her improvised leaf umbrella, Olivia stepped beneath the shelter's roof without hesitation.

But the Voivoki's expression hardened instantly.

"This shelter is taken," he said sharply.

"There's room for both of us," Olivia countered, forcing a smile, hoping he was joking.

"My friend is on the way," he replied.

"At least let me stand under the roof until they arrive," Olivia pleaded.

"This shelter is taken," he repeated, unflinching, his focus returning to the paper in his hands.

The weight of his words settled on Olivia like the rain soaking through her clothes. Reluctantly, she stepped back into the downpour. For a moment, she stood frozen, staring at the fire, its warmth a cruel reminder of her own vulnerability. The cold soon jolted her back, and she fumbled for her leaf umbrella, resigning herself to a long, wet night.

But as she turned to leave, the Voivoki spoke again.

"Because kindness touches even the most wicked, I'll let you take cover here," he said, his voice calm but firm.

Stunned, Olivia stepped back under the shelter, a mix of relief and disbelief washing over her. Then she froze. A jolt of recognition shot through her as her eyes adjusted to the firelight. It wasn't just any Voivoki - it was Vaipor.

Memories of her earlier cruelty resurfaced: the day she had refused him a seat at Bill's restaurant, forcing him to eat standing while she and Susan laughed. Her cheeks burned with shame. Yet here he was, offering her refuge, holding no trace of resentment. The gesture struck her harder than any scolding could have.

Humbled, she sank down beside the fire, avoiding his gaze.

"What brings you here alone?" Vaipor asked, his tone even, though his eyes held a quiet intensity.

"We were at Bill's village, but a few weeks ago our friends left without telling Susan and me. Yesterday, two traders promised to help us find them, but they robbed us instead." Olivia's voice wavered with frustration and regret.

"And Susan?" Vaipor pressed.

"She sprained her ankle. We agreed it was best for me to get help," Olivia replied. "Can you please help?"

"I'll help you," he nodded, though he made no move to leave his shelter. The rain drummed steadily on the roof as Olivia basked in the fire's warmth, torn between the guilt pricking at her and the comfort she craved.

"How could you leave your best friend alone in the Jungle with a sprained ankle?" Vaipor's voice cut through the quiet, sharp as the crackle of the fire.

"I was trying to help her," Olivia said defensively.

"Help her? By leaving her alone for the night?"

"I thought I'd find the others before dark," she muttered, her confidence slipping.

"And then what? You expected them to rush through the Jungle at night, risking their own lives to carry her to safety?"

Shame surged through Olivia, cracking her defences. Deep down, she had always known how precarious Susan's situation was when she left her friend behind - immobilized and terrified in the Jungle's merciless depths. Yet her own fear and longing for comfort had outweighed her responsibility to stay. Now, Vaipor's words stripped away the justifications she had clung to, exposing the selfishness of her choices.

Though humiliation burned within her, Olivia's resilience began to surface, steadying her expression despite her unease. That flicker of resolve faltered when Vaipor held up a drawing, Imogen's signature unmistakable in the corner. Her eyes widened in recognition, embarrassment giving way to relief. If Vaipor had this, he knew where her friends were.

"Where are they?" she asked, her voice trembling with excitement.

Vaipor's gaze sharpened, his calm tone cutting deeper than she expected.

"I'll be frank - you're a tangle of lies."

Olivia flinched, her confidence unravelling once more.

"Not long ago, you wouldn't let me sit at your table. You claimed the seats were 'reserved for friends,' but you were alone, eager to find favour with the wealthier Voivokis. Because I looked like a poor Voi, you dismissed me without a second thought. And when I offered you your favourite dessert, you couldn't even meet my eyes, much less thank me."

Her stomach churned as the memory resurfaced.

"I'd hoped that small act of kindness might make you reflect," he continued, his voice unyielding. "But here we are, and you're still weaving stories to save face, to make yourself the victim without a shred of remorse. You left Susan, not out of concern for her, but because you wanted to reach Rich and the others before dark - to share their safety and comfort, leaving her to fend for herself."

Olivia's breath hitched. The truth she had tried to ignore pierced through her like a blade.

"It's hard to believe Susan asked you to abandon her," Vaipor went on, his tone sharp. "Especially since you misled me about how the others left Bill's village. I know the truth - they told me you and Susan had the choice to leave with them, but you both stayed behind. All this time, you've clung to her, hoping her father would somehow rescue you. But when your patience wore thin, you convinced her to join the traders. And when she couldn't go on, you dropped her without hesitation."

He paused, letting the silence drive his point deeper.

"And now, here you are, alone in this Jungle, where survival is bleak without allies. Suddenly, you need someone else to latch onto. I'm convenient - a stepping stone with fire, food, shelter, and knowledge of your friends' whereabouts. If I had none of these, you wouldn't look at me twice. I'd be as invisible as I was at Bill's village."

Olivia's face burned, her head spinning under the weight of his words.

"Look around you," Vaipor said, his voice softer but no less severe. "This darkness isn't like anything you've known - it consumes the unprepared. I could've sent you away, left you to face it alone. Perhaps you'd never see daylight again. But because kindness touches the heart of even the most wicked, I'm giving you a gift tonight - a mirror, to show you who you've become. Only you can decide what to do with it."

The silence that followed was heavy, suffocating. Olivia felt the enormity of her actions press down on her, the emptiness of her self-preservation laid bare. The fire crackled, but she felt no warmth - only the cold reality of the choices she'd made. Overwhelmed, she buried her head between her knees, tears streaming down her face as her body shook.

"I'm sorry…" she whispered, her voice trembling. "I'm so sorry."

Vaipor remained silent, watching her. He knew this moment was crucial. Olivia had been adrift for years, ever since her parents' separation left her without guidance. Her loneliness had hardened into mistrust, manipulation, and deceit, a fortress that kept others out and left her isolated.

He waited until her sobs quieted, letting her sit with the weight of her apology. Then, in a low, steady voice, he spoke.

"Trust is fragile. Once broken, it's never the same. That's why it's precious - why it must be protected. Tell me, Olivia… do you trust many around you?"

Still hiding her face, she shook her head.

"No," she whispered. "Not really."

"Who do you trust most?" Vaipor asked.

A long pause, and then a quiet response.

"My mum."

"Tell me about her," he encouraged gently.

Olivia lifted her head, taking a deep breath as her thoughts drifted back to her life in the City. For a moment, her weary expression softened, and Vaipor could see a glimmer of the girl she might have been. She began to recount the places she and her mother would visit - the boutiques, the theatres, the busy cafés. Each memory seemed to lift a weight from her, and her voice grew more animated, her hands moving expressively as she described the friends she once had, the parties, the comforts of her life.

Vaipor listened with patient attentiveness, his eyes never leaving hers. As she spoke, he noted how her stories revolved around wealth and social status, each friendship a transaction tied to privilege and convenience.

When she paused, he asked gently:

"Do you choose your friends based on what they have?"

His question caught her off-guard, and she looked at him, startled. The flicker of understanding in her eyes was brief but telling. She opened her mouth to respond but found herself at a loss for words. She sensed a discomfort from the unsettling truth she was beginning to confront, one she had rarely acknowledged even to herself.

Staring into the dancing flames, Olivia silently replayed her memories, sifting through the names and faces of the kids she called "friends." Most of them were children of her mother's friends, kids she had grown up with by default, their friendships rooted in the social connections of their parents. She hadn't exactly chosen these friends; they'd fallen into her life as easily as the luxuries surrounding her. But even among those familiar faces, some were fading from memory, as if they'd drifted away when they no longer served a purpose.

"Many of my friends I've known since I was little," she finally said. "I didn't choose them. Our mums are friends."

Vaipor nodded, his gaze calm but attentive.

"And what about friends you made on your own, those who aren't connected to your mum's circle?"

Olivia thought of the kids from school. In her younger years, when play was simple, she'd been content building sandcastles or playing tag without a thought of her friends' backgrounds. She remembered the fleeting friendships that blossomed for an afternoon, when a fancy toy might catch her interest, but that had been natural curiosity, not calculation. Yet as she considered her more recent friendships, the truth began to crystallise - she had, without fully realising it, distanced herself from kids who didn't fit her social expectations. Her heart sank with the weight of this revelation.

"I… I do have friends who don't come from wealthy families," she admitted slowly. "But… it's awkward sometimes. They can't go to the places I like. Their clothes don't look nice, they can't afford things, and… their houses feel small and cramped. I end up feeling… uncomfortable, I guess."

Vaipor tilted his head, a faint smile playing at his lips.

"Sounds like you're fortunate to have a wealthy mum."

Olivia shrugged, brushing off his remark.

"She works hard. And the banks keep sending her credit cards, so it's easier for her to pay for things."

Vaipor raised an eyebrow, intrigued.

"Credit cards? How does that work?"

Olivia's face brightened, eager to explain.

"It's kind of like 'buy now, pay later.' You don't need all the money up front. Say I want a thousand-dollar phone, but I only have a hundred bucks. I can still get it and pay the rest in instalments. Sure, there's some interest, but at least I don't have to wait forever."

Vaipor nodded thoughtfully.

"And how much extra do you pay with the interest?"

"Not much," Olivia said with a shrug. "Maybe three or four hundred dollars, or something like that. Honestly, I don't really know. It doesn't matter. The main thing is I can still get what I want."

Vaipor frowned slightly, leaning forward.

"But if you don't have the thousand dollars and need a phone, why not buy a less expensive one?"

Olivia hesitated, her gaze dropping.

"Because… it would be embarrassing," she muttered.

A quiet sadness crossed Vaipor's face, but he said nothing, letting the moment sink in. He recognised the trap she was caught in - a relentless chase for appearances, sacrificing stability for fleeting validation.

Breaking the silence, Olivia asked hesitantly:

"Did I say something wrong again?"

"No," Vaipor replied, his voice calm but firm. "You didn't say anything wrong - unless, of course, you weren't being honest. But after our last conversation, I trust you wouldn't lie to me again. What saddens me isn't what you said - it's the mindset behind it.

"You see, you and your mother aren't better off than the friends you find embarrassing. Yet you look down on them, pretending to be above them by borrowing against your future.

You're spending money you don't have, sinking into debt just to keep up the illusion of wealth."

Olivia stiffened, instinctively defensive, but Vaipor's words struck a chord, undeniable in their truth.

"You're embarrassed to go without the things wealthy people have," he continued, "but instead of finding ways to earn that wealth, you're digging yourself deeper into debt with every purchase. And the deeper you go, the harder it is to climb back out.

Imagine standing waist-deep in a muddy pit. Would you be able to climb out easily?"

Olivia nodded slowly.

"I think so."

"Now imagine I hand you a shovel. Would you keep digging?"

A faint smile tugged at Olivia's lips.

"That'd be like digging my own grave."

Vaipor smiled back, his expression tinged with both warmth and sadness.

"Exactly," he said softly. "The deeper you dig, the harder it is to climb out. So, next time you're tempted to buy something beyond your means, remember this: a loan - whether it's a credit card, a store card, or any other kind of easy credit - is like that shovel. It feels useful, even empowering at first, but with every swipe, every signature, you're digging deeper into a hole that may one day become inescapable."

For the first time, Olivia felt the full weight of her and her mother's choices. The ease of those swipes, the thrill of 'buy now, pay later', suddenly seemed less like freedom and more like a trap. A dull ache settled in her chest as she realised how their lives had been slowly sinking under the guise of convenience.

Vaipor rose to his feet, the firelight casting flickering shadows across his face. He added a fresh piece of timber to the flames and spoke again, his voice quieter now but no less piercing.

"Of course, that's assuming you even make it out of this Jungle alive."

The ominous words sent a shiver through Olivia, her stomach tightening. Her eyes darted to him, searching for reassurance, but his expression remained unreadable. Was he planning to leave her here? The thought clawed at her, filling her with panic. She had assumed he would stay with her through the night, guiding her back to safety in the morning.

"Material things might bring fleeting happiness," Vaipor continued, "but they'll never bring true fulfilment. That comes from the bonds we form with others. In the end, people won't remember the clothes you wore or the gadgets you owned. They'll remember how you treated them. Shallow connections masked by appearances will only leave you more lonely."

He turned, lifting his backpack.

"If you ever meet another human, enrich your life with genuine friendships. That's worth far more than anything you can buy."

"Are you leaving?" Olivia asked, her voice trembling. "You said you wouldn't leave at night!"

"I said I'd help you," Vaipor replied. "And I have. Now it's time for you to learn to see beyond the surface."

Before she could respond, he stepped into the darkness, unfazed by the rain and the shadows that swallowed him whole.

"Vaipor!" she called, her voice breaking as it echoed through the Jungle. Only silence answered her.

Tears streamed down her face as she stumbled back to the makeshift shelter, feeling as vulnerable as the day she first found herself in this unforgiving land. She cried herself to sleep, clutching her knees, every rustle of leaves a reminder of how exposed she was.

The dawn broke with pale light filtering through the canopy, but Olivia felt no relief. Her muscles were stiff from her restless night, her spirit weighed down by the stark reality of her situation. Still, a fragile thread of determination pushed her to her feet.

Retracing her path to the river, she trudged upstream, scanning for a safe place to cross. Hours passed, and her legs ached, her body crying out for food and rest. But as the sun climbed higher, she crested a ridge and froze.

Below her, nestled in the valley, a village came into view. Wisps of smoke curled into the air, promising warmth and human connection.

Hope surged through her, lending her weary body new strength. She scrambled down the slope, the smell of smoke and the hum of life urging her forward. Reaching the outskirts of the village, she stopped, her breath catching in her throat as a joyful voice rang out.

She turned towards the sound, her eyes widening in disbelief.

CHAPTER 13

After enduring a sleepless night, Susan couldn't be more appreciative of the first rays of the morning sun delicately touching her shivering body. An attempt to rise was met with the persistent ache in her sprained ankle, compelling her to confront the reality: waiting for Olivia's return with the others was her only option.

However, uncertainty clouded her hopes as she pondered Olivia's possible return. Looking up at the clear blue sky, Susan's attention shifted to the beautiful birds engaged in their daily rituals. Their melodious tunes harmonised perfectly with the rhythmic burbling of the river beneath the rock that both sprained her ankle and saved her life. The peaceful ambiance served as a comforting embrace, lulling her into a much-needed slumber.

How long she slept for, no one knew, but something deep in her subconscious stirred her awake at the perfect time. She blinked blearily, eyes adjusting to the brightness of the sky, and glanced down at the river. There, gliding gracefully through the shimmering waters in a dugout canoe, was a figure - silent, purposeful, and moving with the ease of someone intimately familiar with the Jungle.

Her heart quickened. Summoning all the courage she could, Susan fought against the pulsing pain in her swollen ankle and the icy grip of her fear of heights. She sat up, her body trembling with the effort, and began screaming for help, her voice ragged but loud as it cut through the sounds of the river.

Moments later she found herself lying on the soft earth beside the riverbank. The gentle hands of a stranger - a Voivoki

- were massaging her injured ankle with a fragrant blend of oils. The scent of frangipani mingled with the cool relief of peppermint, easing her muscles and dulling the pain. The Voivoki then carefully selected broad, sturdy leaves from nearby plants, weaving them together with vines into a makeshift cast. With practiced hands, she wrapped the leaves around Susan's ankle, binding them snugly with the vines to create a brace as firm as plaster.

"Maria, one of the women at Bill's village, often spoke about her old friend Rica," Susan said, her voice still shaky from both the pain and the surreal turn of events. "Wouldn't it be strange if she was talking about you?"

The hands that had been so gentle paused. Rica's eyes, wide with surprise, locked onto Susan's. She tilted her head, a flicker of disbelief crossing her face.

"You came from Bill's village?" she asked, brimming with a mix of excitement and disbelief.

"Yes," Susan nodded. "Do you know about it?"

"Know about it? I lived there!" Rica's voice quickened, the words spilling out as though a dam had burst. "I'm heading that way now, actually.

Maria and I - we were close. Grew up together, shared countless adventures. But one day, we ended up at Bill's village. That day changed everything."

Susan blinked, processing this revelation. Rica's energy buzzed around her like an electric current.

"That deceitful Bill tricked us - lured us into a trap with his deceitful generosity. We thought we could escape, but the debt was too much." Rica's tone hardened, her memories clearly still raw. "At first, I tried selling things at the market. Maria and the others joined in, but they couldn't handle it. Slowly, one by one, they all gave up, leaving me to struggle on my own.

But I didn't quit. After many moons of relentless work, I earned enough Lapes to break free from that cursed place and build a life with my business."

She paused, just long enough to ask:

"How is she, though? Maria, I mean. Crikey, I miss her. Bill must be rotting in the spirit world by now, eh?"

Susan tried to answer, but Rica's thoughts raced ahead of her once again.

"Wait - don't tell me it's that spoiled son of his, running things now. I couldn't stand that kid."

Rica's hand gave Susan's leg a light, almost affectionate tap as she leaned in closer, her voice softening with genuine concern.

"So, tell me, how is Maria? Is she well? I've wondered about her all these years."

Finally, Rica fell silent, giving Susan the chance to speak, her eyes wide and expectant.

Susan shared her story, a mirror of Rica's past struggles, and recounted Maria's decades of hopelessness - trapped in a cycle of relentless labour, her life reduced to nothing more than a cog in the monotony of Bill's village.

"I'm sure Maria will be thrilled to see you," Susan added, gesturing towards the steep thicket she had painstakingly climbed just the day before. "You're about a day's journey from here, in that direction."

Rica glanced towards the dense brush but shook her head gently.

"I'm afraid that's not quite right," she said. "Bill's village isn't there. It's actually behind the mountain, across this river."

The blood drained from Susan's face, her heart dropping like a stone. She stared at Rica, wide-eyed, barely able to comprehend what she was hearing.

"That can't be true!" Susan gasped, her voice trembling. "The traders - those heartless thieves who left us stranded - swore that Rich and the others live there!"

Rica sighed, her expression softening with sympathy.

"I'm sorry, dear," she said, her voice filled with understanding. "But it seems they've tricked you. They likely exploited your lack of knowledge about these lands, leading you around the village to throw you off course."

Tears welled in Susan's eyes.

"How could they do this to us?"

Rica placed a gentle hand on Susan's arm, her tone now a delicate balance of empathy and practicality.

"I know this is hard to hear, but in a twisted way, they've spared you from a worse fate. By bringing you close to Bill's village again, they've left you with a chance - an opportunity to survive. Yes, they've taken your Lapes and valuables, but they haven't cut off your path to life. Believe me, money is the least of your worries right now. Bill, as ruthless as he is, would be more than happy to have you back under his control."

Susan felt like the ground had fallen out from under her. The thought of returning to Bill's village was suffocating. She had escaped once, full of hope and determination, only to find herself deceived and led back to the very place she had so desperately tried to leave behind. The humiliation stung just as much as the betrayal.

Rica noticed the turmoil in Susan's eyes and quickly shifted her tone, offering a kind distraction.

"Here," she said, pulling a small bundle from her pack. "Eat something, you must be starving."

Susan accepted the food with a nod, her gratitude masking the overwhelming weight of the situation. Rica's gesture, though simple, was a lifeline - a small moment of kindness in the midst of a crushing realisation.

As they savoured their breakfast, Rica offered a piece of advice that resonated with the wisdom of someone who had faced her own share of struggles.

"There's no point beating yourself up over what's already happened," she said gently. "You can't change the past. What you can do is decide how to move forward. Focus your energy on what comes next, not on what went wrong."

Susan nodded, though the weight of recent events still lingered in her chest.

Rica briefly scanned the horizon before shifting the conversation.

"But hey, tell me about your life in the City."

A genuine entrepreneur at heart, Rica had always been hungry for knowledge, and though she'd heard rumours about the mysterious City, she had never encountered anyone who knew where it was, let alone lived there. This was a rare chance to learn about a world outside the Jungle's grasp.

"Well," Susan began, now perked up, "my family is quite wealthy, and I'm something of a social media celebrity."

Her tone was unmistakably proud as she launched into a detailed account of her life.

"I have hundreds of thousands of friends who follow me online, always watching my posts, liking my pictures, leaving comments... so many that I can't even remember the names of most of them."

Rica tilted her head, intrigued but slightly puzzled.

"What exactly is social media?"

Susan's eyes sparkled as she began to explain, eager to show off this slice of the world Rica had never known. With a patient tone, she described social media as an expansive digital network - a place where people from all over the globe connect, share their lives, and communicate through electronic devices. She reached into her bag and pulled out her phone, handing it over to Rica.

Rica took the small device, her weathered hands tracing its smooth surface, her brow furrowing in concentration. The phone - cracked and lifeless - was like an artefact from another world, something completely alien to her existence in the Jungle. She turned it over, examining it as though it held some hidden secret, her curiosity evident in her eyes.

"That's my phone," Susan said with a grin. "Well, it was my phone. Unfortunately, phones and rain don't get along too well." She chuckled lightly, though there was a hint of frustration in her voice. "Anyway, we use these to take photos and videos, and then we share them with the world."

Rica, still holding the broken phone, looked up, bemused.

"So, people watch your life through this... box?"

"No, they have their own boxes," Susan replied, her enthusiasm bubbling over. "Everyone has one. They get to see what I'm doing - whether I'm on vacation, at a party, or just taking a selfie at home. It's how we all stay connected."

As she spoke, Susan noticed Rica's growing perplexity, realising that the idea of photos, videos, and even the concept of "staying connected" in this way was likely foreign to her. She adjusted her tone, trying to explain more simply.

"See this part here?" Susan pointed to the cracked screen of her phone and the small camera lenses on the back. "We press this part - it's called the screen - and it's like the phone has its own eyes. It remembers what it sees, and then with another press, anyone around the world can see what the phone's eyes recorded."

Rica, who had lived her whole life in the Jungle, accustomed to the natural rhythms of the Voivokis' world, listened intently. This strange technology Susan described seemed to stretch far beyond anything Rica had ever imagined. She blinked, trying to make sense of it all.

"I'll be honest, it's hard to wrap my head around this," Rica admitted with a wry smile. "But these 'friends' you're talking about - they don't sound like real friends to me." Her gaze softened as she handed the phone back. "Tell me more about your real friends. The ones you actually spend time with."

Susan paused, caught off guard by the question.

"You mean the people I meet up with sometimes?"

Rica nodded.

"Yes, the ones who are actually in your life, your true connections."

Susan hesitated, then shrugged.

"Well, they're... different. Most of them only want to be around me because I'm rich. They always want something - money, gifts, attention. And then there are others who keep trying to be my friends, but... they can't even afford decent clothes or shoes. I'm not going to embarrass myself by hanging out with saggy friends."

Rica's expression shifted from curiosity to quiet compassion.

"I actually feel sad for you," she said softly, surprising Susan with the remark.

Susan blinked, taken aback. "Sad? Why?"

Rica smiled gently, her eyes reflecting a lifetime of wisdom earned through hardship and true connection.

"Let me tell you a story about a friend of mine, Bosta. We grew up in the same village, but her life was worlds apart from ours. Her father was filthy rich, owning vast plantations, markets, fisheries, holiday homes - you name it. From the moment she was born, she was surrounded by maids and servants, all watching over her, ready to fulfil her every wish.

If she wanted to travel to other parts of the Jungle, strong Voivokis would carry her, ensuring she remained clean and well-rested. There was even someone who'd go ahead, clearing the path of vegetation and spider webs, while another would burn plants around her to repel insects. In short, she was completely shielded from the Jungle's harsher realities.

As kids, none of this mattered. We played together without thinking much about our different circumstances. But as we got older, the differences became harder to ignore. Bosta was kind in many ways, but her luxurious lifestyle often made us feel insignificant. What finally drove a wedge between us was her tendency to boss us around as if we were her servants.

Some kids put up with it because being close to her came with perks. For instance, she had a leopard cub as a pet. But only a select few were allowed near it, while the rest of us just admired the cub from afar. And when her family hosted visits from other wealthy families, we'd watch as she formed friendships with kids as rich as she was.

For us, it was amusing to see those rich kids compete over who had more extravagant possessions or who'd been on the most exciting adventures. Their bragging always led to arguments over the most trivial things.

Years later, after I escaped Bill's village and built several successful businesses of my own, I returned to reconnect with old friends. That's when I learned about Bosta's downfall. Her father had suddenly fallen gravely ill, leaving no time to prepare her to take over the family empire. Her mother didn't understand business, so, as the only child, she had no choice but to step up.

The problem was, Bosta had spent her entire life in a bubble. She knew nothing about running a business and couldn't even handle basic calculations. Worse, she was so used to giving orders that she alienated everyone around her. Her arrogant attitude drove away the people who could have helped her, and soon even their business partners abandoned her.

One by one, everything her father had built fell apart. The empire crumbled, and with it, Bosta's life. When I asked about her, my old friends told me she had spiralled into a deep depression, refusing to speak to anyone and barely eating. Then, one day, she simply shuffled out of the village... and was never seen again."

Rica finished her story with a heavy sigh, her gaze drifting towards the distant mountains down the river. Though she had worked her way from the Jungle's simplicity to a life of prosperity through hard work and determination, recalling Bosta's tragic downfall stirred a deep sadness within her. It was a sobering reminder that wealth alone did not shield one from hardship. Rica, now well-acquainted with the complexities of success, felt both grateful for her own journey and a deep empathy for Bosta's untold struggles. The story highlighted the fragile balance between achievement and loss, and Rica couldn't help but reflect on the weight of responsibility that came with success.

"Why did you tell me about Bosta?" Susan asked, her curiosity piqued.

Rica turned to face her, her expression thoughtful.

"Because we all have something to learn from others' mistakes," she said gently. "You reminded me of Bosta, and if you're clever enough, you can make sure you don't repeat her mistakes."

Susan shifted her position but said nothing.

"By the time Bosta was about ten," Rica continued, "she had no real friends left. Her arrogance had pushed everyone away. Back then, she didn't think it mattered - why would she, when she had an army of maids to cater to her every whim? But when everything fell apart, there was no one by her side. When she finally asked for help, all she got was the Voivokis' revenge. One of her maids, who had served her for 26 years, stole a huge sum of money from her and disappeared. That's what happens when you treat people like tools, not as equals."

"I'm not like that," Susan protested. "I'm not arrogant or stupid."

Rica's smile was soft, but her eyes were serious.

"Oh, my dear, I've known many Voivokis - hundreds, in fact - through my businesses. And while I don't know you well yet, from this short conversation, I can tell you share more similarities with Bosta than you think. It might be wise to reflect on that before it's too late."

Susan fell silent, unsure of how to respond.

Rica leaned closer, her tone growing more serious.

"Even if your family's fate remains fortunate and your wealth intact, one day you might feel an emptiness inside that money can't fill. Then, you'll realise that genuine connections - real friendships - are more valuable than anything material. Think about it. If you were to fall seriously ill, who would you reach out to for help?"

"My mom," Susan answered confidently.

Rica nodded.

"And if your parents weren't around?"

Susan hesitated, her bravado fading. She searched for an answer but found none.

"You might consider asking your wealthy friends for help," Rica continued, her voice steady, "but just like you, they'll likely reject anything that doesn't benefit them. The same way you turn away those less fortunate, they'll do the same to you. And if you turn to your less wealthy friends, well, they won't be inclined to help either - because you've pushed them away."

Susan shifted uncomfortably, sensing the truth in Rica's words, but Rica wasn't done.

"This leaves you with paid help. But paid help is exactly that - driven by money, not loyalty. They're only interested in taking what you can offer, and when the money dries up, so will their support. You'll end up surrounded by people who leech off you, pretending to care as long as you can pay them. The moment your resources are gone, they'll abandon you without a second thought, leaving you alone and miserable."

As Rica's candid words settled in, Susan felt a ripple of discomfort spread through her. The raw honesty forced her to confront uncomfortable truths about her behaviour and the potential consequences. The thought of facing loneliness during times of need, as Rica described, made her feel vulnerable. A sense of unease stirred within her, hinting at a realisation that her current path might lead to isolation and shallow, transactional relationships.

Rica pressed on:

"It's in our nature to judge others constantly. Just as the strongest male macaque captures the attention of females, the wealthy naturally attract attention from others. But there's a difference: in the wild, the strongest macaque has to fight, often fiercely, to earn his position at the top. In human society, some of us are simply born into wealth, inheriting power and privilege without lifting a finger."

Susan furrowed her brow, confused by the comparison to macaques, but curious about where Rica was going with this.

"If a macaque could inherit his position without any effort," Rica continued, "do you think he'd earn the same admiration as a leader who fought tooth and claw for it?"

"Probably not," Susan responded, still unsure but following along.

"Exactly," Rica nodded. "You're fortunate to be born into a wealthy family, and with that comes a kind of admiration from those who envy the things you can afford - the luxuries and experiences most can only dream of. But don't be fooled. With that admiration comes an equal amount, if not more, resentment. You didn't create your wealth; it was handed to you by your parents or grandparents. And that's why it's so important to be wise with your words and actions. You must be respectful, kind, and considerate to everyone, regardless of their status."

Rica paused briefly for emphasis, letting her words sink in before continuing.

"It's different for those who build their wealth from scratch. They may still face envy, but they earn something more powerful - respect. Respect like the macaque who fought his way to the top. People admire them not just for what they have, but for the struggle and determination it took to get there. If you want to avoid the pitfalls that Bosta fell into, you need to understand that difference.

Do you understand what I'm saying?"

Susan nodded, though her throat tightened with the weight of realization. Gratitude for Rica swelled in her chest, too deep for words. Rica's insight had cut through her defences, revealing the trap that had been slowly consuming her - a trap she hadn't even recognised.

Her mother's fierce protectiveness loomed large in her memory. Perfection was the standard her mother demanded, especially in how Susan was treated. A slight against her, no matter how trivial, ignited her mother's wrath, leaving shame and discomfort in its wake for anyone who dared fall short. Susan admired and imitated that behaviour, believing it was strength. But it wasn't strength - it was isolation.

It had cost her so much. Friends, connections, trust - all lost to her mother's standards and her own reflection of them. For the first time, Susan saw herself clearly. She didn't like the person she had been, but she also saw a chance to change.

"It's time to go, Susan," Rica's voice pulled her back to the present.

Susan glanced down at the makeshift cast Rica had carefully tied around her swollen ankle. Despite its crude appearance, it held firm, giving her just enough stability to limp alongside Rica as they resumed their journey. Each step was a test of endurance, but Rica's steady encouragement kept her moving.

The river crossing was effortless with Rica's canoe gliding smoothly across the water, but the climb up the muddy, rain-slick hillside was a different story. The slope was unforgiving, and Susan's injured ankle required her to crawl. Yet, as they battled upward, Rica's stories lightened the weight of their struggle, weaving a sense of camaraderie into the challenging trek.

By late afternoon, the sprawling plantations surrounding Bill's village came into view. A familiar voice called out from ahead.

"Welcome back, Susan!" one of the guards greeted.

Susan forced a smile, recalling Rica's advice about treating others with kindness and respect, irrespective of their social status. She returned the guard's greeting with warmth, even managing a polite exchange before he wandered off. But the moment he was out of sight, the weight of it all came crashing down.

Her composure broke, and tears spilled freely. It was raw and uncontainable - an outpouring of frustration, disappointment, and the crushing reality of being back in Bill's village just a day after leaving. The fragile hope of reuniting with her family felt farther away than ever.

"Susan!" a voice rang out, familiar yet distant.

Susan looked up sharply, her breath catching.

"Oli?"

Her heart leapt at the sight of Olivia rushing towards her. If not for her injured ankle, Susan would have run to meet her. Instead, she waited for her to get to her. They embraced tightly, their words tumbling over one another in a rush - apologies, relief, and joy spilling out like a dam breaking. For a moment, it was as if they were sisters reunited after a long separation, the weight of their struggles temporarily forgotten.

They made their way to the small restaurant, where Maria and Rica were locked in their own emotional reunion.

As the afternoon wore on, their joy of listening to Maria and Rica's reminiscing was cut short by other familiar voices approaching the village. Manu and Roger walked towards them, their faces lit with unmistakable excitement.

"We found a path!" Manu declared, his voice carrying the thrill of discovery.

For a moment, hope surged in the air, electrifying both Susan and Olivia. They exchanged wide-eyed glances, their hearts pounding. Could it really be true? Could they finally be one giant step closer to the City?

But as Manu and Roger explained, the details of the so-called "path" began to dim their excitement. With every word, the path seemed less like an escape and more like another barrier, twisting their hopes into bitter disappointment.

The City felt further away than ever.

ACKNOWLEDGEMENT

To my loving wife and my two beautiful girls - thank you from the bottom of my heart. I couldn't have reached this milestone without your love, patience, and encouragement. Writing this book has been one of the most colossal tasks I've ever undertaken, and your unwavering support kept me going through every challenge.

To my daughters, you are the spark behind this project. Your curiosity and hunger for learning inspired me to create something that's not only entertaining but educational, too. I wanted this story to reflect the lessons and values I hope to pass on to you, and I couldn't be prouder to dedicate this to the two of you.

To my wife, thank you for being my pillar of strength. You believed in me, even when I doubted myself. Your faith and guidance have been my anchor throughout this journey, and for that, I am endlessly grateful.

This book is as much yours as it is mine. It is a reflection of our shared dreams and the belief that we can all inspire, grow, and overcome.

Thank you for everything.

ABOUT THE AUTHOR

Lacking financial literacy and guidance, Peter faced financial challenges throughout his late teens and early adult years. These constraints led to setbacks and hardships, but through perseverance, determination, and hard work, he found a way out of poverty.

He created the *Teeth of the Jungle* series to provide the education and guidance he wish he'd had while growing up. His goal is for this series to empower readers with the tools and insights to overcome their own challenges, achieve success, and create lasting opportunities - not just for themselves, but for their loved ones as well.

THIRST REMAINS
THE SEARCH CONTINUES…

The kids have endured unimaginable trials - from wild animals and relentless hunger to the suffocating grip of the Voivokis' society. Survival has tested their strength and unity, pushing them to their limits. Yet the Jungle's Teeth are far from finished with them.

Will they escape the web of control and debt that binds them? Can they ever return to the City and the lives they once knew? Or will the Jungle claim them forever? Discover the answers in the next instalments of the *Teeth of the Jungle* series. To continue the journey,

visit: **tycoonitos.com**

www.ingramcontent.com/pod-product-compliance
Lightning Source LLC
Chambersburg PA
CBHW030805210726
48290CB00002B/438